Jared laid the tips of his fingers under her chin, gently raised her face to his. His heart clenched, for her eyes brimmed with tears. He longed to declare himself. To say, "Stay with me, Abby. Marry me, bear my children," but the timing was impossibly wrong. Jonathan Blaisdell, long years dead, loomed between them as solid as the granite on which they were sitting.

When planning this drive, Jared had thought to snatch a kiss. Truthfully . . . a bit more than a kiss. Not that he had intended a seduction in this sheltered glen, but surely he could not be faulted for dreaming of something more than a few short seconds of a chaste embrace. Could he? After all, his Abby was no longer the young girl Blaisdell had known. She was a woman with all a woman could offer. All a woman could want. Somehow, some way she would be his. Yet for the moment he must hold his peace. Only for a moment . . .

The Indifferent Earl

Blair Bancroft

A SIGNET BOOK

SIGNET
Published by New American Library, a division of
Penguin Putnam Inc., 375 Hudson Street,
New York, New York 10014, U.S.A.
Penguin Books Ltd, 80 Strand,
London WC2R 0RL, England
Penguin Books Australia Ltd, 250 Camberwell Road,
Camberwell, Victoria 3124, Australia
Penguin Books Canada Ltd, 10 Alcorn Avenue,
Toronto, Ontario, Canada M4V 3B2
Penguin Books (N.Z.) Ltd, Cnr Rosedale and Airborne Roads,
Albany, Auckland 1310, New Zealand

Penguin Books Ltd, Registered Offices:
Harmondsworth, Middlesex, England

First published by Signet, an imprint of New American Library,
a division of Penguin Putnam Inc.

First Printing, March 2003
10 9 8 7 6 5 4 3 2 1

Chapter One

*M*iss Abigail Todd, far from the scrutiny of her pupils in Miss Todd's Academy for Young Ladies in Boston, peered out the window of the post chaise with unabashed curiosity. Now that the city of London had been left behind, the countryside was remarkably familiar. New England had been aptly named, she decided. Although the fields here were smaller and laid out in a fantasy maze of uneven shapes framed in hedgerows, the overall feel of the land was so similar she might well have been traveling the post road from Boston to Providence. There were fewer acres of towering trees in this much older country, she conceded, but that was a boon, surely, for highwaymen could shelter in heavy woods, lying in wait for two lone women traveling the road to Bath.

Enough! A woman of eight and twenty, owner and head-mistress of her own school, had long since learned not to ask for trouble. She would leave the conjuring of bogeymen to her wide-eyed thirteen-year-olds.

"I cannot like it," declared a voice beside Abby for perhaps the twentieth time in the past two days. Mrs. Hannah Greaves, a lady of imposing angular shape that belied a heart as soft as butter, had been pressed into service as Miss Abigail Todd's companion for the long journey to England. "That man was surely hiding something," Mrs. Greaves continued her complaint. "And I fear to know what. Here we are, off to some unknown spot in the English countryside, just the two of us—"

"But it's an adventure," Abby teased, her usually solemn features dancing into a grin. "With Mr. Smallwood making the arrangements, for all we know we could be headed for Gretna Green or some Gothic castle with dark dungeons—"

"Abigail Todd!" Forgetting her own doubts, the older woman was shocked. "You cannot truly suspect Mr. Smallwood of such ah—*treachery*."

Abby laughed. "No, no, Hannah, indeed not. Though I cannot help but feel we are wandering among the enemy. The shipping lanes between our countries are barely open again, and here we are, plunging into the unknown like rats after the Pied Piper."

"I have never had much faith in men of the law," Mrs. Greaves declared. "That man knew more than he was telling."

"Poor Mr. Smallwood. I fear you wrong him, Hannah. Taking over his father's clients as he did . . . it's no wonder he can make neither head nor tail of Miss Bivens's estate."

"And your father just as bad—"

"Indeed," Miss Todd agreed. "I particularly dislike it when a gentleman prevaricates because he believes the truth unfit for a lady's ears."

"My dear, do you truly think?—"

"Oh, yes. I'm almost certain Papa knew the whole. But would he tell me why a Miss Clarissa Bivens left me her cottage in Somerset, England? Would he tell me who she was? Not a bit of it. Nothing more than a few mumbled words about Miss Bivens being a distant relative, he thought. One of those odd sort of kin no one speaks of. And perhaps it was best my duties in Boston kept me from fulfilling the terms of the will."

"So you immediately decided you must go to England," said Mrs. Greaves, who knew Abigail and her father, the distinguished Dr. Lucian Todd, all too well.

Abby darted a look of mirthful reproach at the older woman. Despite the number of years that proclaimed her a spinster firmly on the shelf, Miss Abigail Todd had a youthful face and figure which she had long been forced to disguise behind the severity of her appearance. Only a modest white piping decorated her dark blue poplin traveling costume. Her hair was confined in a ruthlessly plain coif, further concealed by a bonnet that in all charity, could only have been described as Puritan in design. And to exaggerate the austere image she wished to present as mentor for a bevy of young females, Abigail had spent considerable time in front of a mirror, years earlier, practicing the calm, almost severe, expression that had become the accustomed mask of the headmistress of Miss Todd's Academy for Young Ladies.

For nearly ten years now, ever since her father had allowed her to use her dowry to establish a place of education for young women without access to Boston's more exclusive halls of learning, Abby had managed to repress her venturesome spirit. The one physical attribute she had been unable to hide was her truly lovely green eyes, which, on occasion, were allowed to betray her eager interest in the world around her. Insatiable curiosity had tempted her from her professed life's work and brought her on what might well be a wild-goose chase deep into the heart of that enemy country, England.

Miss Abigail Todd, wrote Mr. Hector Smallwood of Selkirk, Dean & Smallwood, Lincoln's Inn Fields, London, had been bequeathed a cottage in the shire of Somerset, England. The bequest was dependent on Miss Todd residing at Arbor Cottage for at least two months and carrying out some small commissions specified by Miss Clarissa Bivens, whose final will and testament it was his duty to administer. The estate would pay for her passage and that of a companion.

Abby's first reaction had been astonishment, followed by intense curiosity, then disappointment. She longed to go, longed to discover why Miss Clarissa Bivens of Arbor Cottage in Somerset had bequeathed her a house. Why Miss Bivens had trusted someone she had never met to carry out a series of perhaps delicate personal commissions.

But what of her school, her pupils? Adding the weeks at sea, the journey would take a month more than the school's summer vacation. How could she possibly? . . .

In the end, all Abby had needed was her father's opposition to coalesce her repressed sense of adventure into action. A journey to the land where her father was born—the ancestors of most of her pupils as well—would be vastly educational. Ample excuse for returning to Boston well after the opening of the Academy's fall session. She would go to England, a country that had been considered the Monstrous Enemy for all of her life. The powerful island nation that had burned her country's capital and gotten its tail whopped by Andrew Jackson in New Orleans, all within the past two years.

Now here she was on the last leg of her journey to the home of a woman who remained a mystery not even Miss Clarissa Bivens's solicitor seemed able, or willing, to reveal. It was delicious, Abby thought. Her excitement mounted with each bumpy mile.

"I can't help but wonder about those commissions," Hannah Greaves declared, as if she hadn't repeated the same foreboding for each of the days of their long trek from Boston.

"I admit I am not best pleased to receive instructions about the commissions I must perform from the butler and the housekeeper," Abby mused. "With my inheritance dependent upon my carrying out these commissions, I certainly expected Mr. Smallwood to be aware of what is expected of me."

"He assured you the tasks would not be arduous and that there would be some local gentleman to assist you," Mrs. Greaves pointed out.

"A local gentleman!" Abigail huffed. "That's all I need, Hannah! I am quite capable of executing any commissions Miss Bivens wished me to do without the aid of some country bumpkin."

"But, my dear Abby, this is a foreign country. You cannot expect—"

"Indeed I do expect, Hannah! Mr. Smallwood said he *believed* most of the commissions were bequests that Miss Bivens wished to have delivered personally by her heir. A bit eccentric, granted, but not astonishing. And I cannot imagine needing help with such a simple—"

"We're turning!" Abby exclaimed, pressing her nose to the glass. "Can it be we've actually arrived?" For the many miles they had traveled from Plymouth to London, and now from London into Somerset, they had seen little but fields and charming villages, with an occasional glimpse of tall chimneys hidden behind trees and, once or twice, a distant castle-like structure that had caused both ladies to *oo* and *ah*, heedless of their dignity. But now, at last, they had left the main road and were venturing down a lane so narrow Abby could only wonder what would happen if they met another vehicle. Alas, tall hedgerows soon obscured the view on either side. With mutual resigned sighs, the ladies sat back on the brown-velvet squabs and cautioned themselves to patience. Not an emotion familiar or welcome to either one of the dynamic pair from the state of Massachusetts in the newly fledged nation of the United States of America.

Jared Reignald Fitzroy Verney, Earl of Langley, tousled his hands through overlong strands of chestnut-brown hair. His jacket of blue superfine was draped over the back of his chair, his cravat a white puddle on an Axminster carpet so well worn it had been relegated to the estate office. As he scowled at the account books on his desk, a sharp sound broke his reverie. His quill pen snapped under the tension of his long aristocratic fingers, spattering ink and the tip of the quill over his latest calculations. With a disgusted grimace, he dropped the broken piece still in his hand onto the ink-stained page, crumpled the paper around the sorry-looking feathers, and shied the balled-up wreck of his hopes across the room into the empty fireplace. The wrinkled remains of previous futile calculations littered the floor around him, his cravat lost among the many pockmarks of white. No matter how he juggled the figures, there was no doubt he was short of the money needed to purchase Arbor Cottage.

If the Boston spinster would sell, and not insist on maintaining an errant foothold in the Langley estate, as Clarissa Beaupré, née Bivens, had done before her.

Not that he hadn't liked the old girl. Of an age to be his grandmother, she had frequently been more of a mother than his own. But the scandal of her owning a cottage on ground that had once been part of the Verney family estate was a sore point which needed to be remedied. One would think La Grande Clarisse would have had the decency to return the property to its original owners instead of leave it to some female no one had ever heard of. Queer doings. But Clarissa Beaupré had been a woman of secrets. And the earl very much feared the key to this particular mystery was rooted on his own family tree.

Impossible! There was no way anyone related to Clarissa Beaupré could be headmistress of a school for young ladies . . . unless, of course, they were being trained in something other than the usual girlish graces. A grim smile crossed the earl's aquiline face. The Verneys were made of strong stuff. And the battle lines had been drawn.

To even the most casual observer, an inspection of the portrait gallery at Langley Park would quickly reveal that the female ancestors of the Verneys—Angle, Saxon, Celt, and Norman—had had intimate contact with Caesar's legions over the centuries of the Roman occupation. The arrogant sculptured features, the strong hawkish nose, dominated nearly every generation of Verneys, most recently the present earl and his younger brother Myles. There was also a reckless streak of devil-may-care in the Verneys that Jared, ninth Earl Langley, worked long and hard to suppress in himself while indulging his brother in a great deal more leeway of conduct.

Old Jared Verney, the present earl's grandfather, had spent money as if there were no tomorrow. And when tomorrow came, his son George had had no head for figures or interest in recouping the family losses before breaking his neck one chill morning while riding to hounds. It had been left to the next in a long line of Jared Verneys to bring the estate back into some semblance of order. This he had done over the past eight years, managing to find funds for his younger brother's schooling, then purchasing for him an officer's rank in a division of the Light Horse well-known for its young scions of the aristocracy. He had seen to the repair of his tenants' cottages and still had money left over for sponsoring his brother Myles's debut in the *ton,* an event long delayed by the aggression of the Corsican monster, Napoleon Bonaparte. And, naturally, he'd had to go to town himself to keep an eye on baby brother, who, at some eight years younger than himself, sometimes seemed more of a son than a sibling.

And now . . . Now Jared knew he had made a mistake. They should have waited a year. Put the money just spent on a Season in London toward buying back Arbor Cottage. But he could not have asked Myles to wait. Not after surviving five years on the Peninsula, then being sent to fight the up-start Americans, coming home with his tail between his legs too late to get in on the great battle at Waterloo. Not that Jared wasn't grateful Myles had missed that bit of carnage. But he knew, to the captain's way of thinking, he had missed the finish of the long fight against the Little Emperor, had failed to stand shoulder to shoulder with his comrades in the greatest battle in the history of mankind. Myles plunged into the Season of 1816 with frenetic joie de vivre, burning the candle at both ends and, as it happened, failing in his effort to wipe out the haunting memories of years of war. Return-ing to the country had been a relief for both brothers.

Until, that is, Hector Smallwood sent word that Miss Abi-gail Todd was on her way, and Jared realized he would now have to fulfill the promise made to Clarissa Beaupré, La Grande Clarisse, *courtisane extraordinaire.*

Hell and damnation! He was back where he started. No way out.

Brisk steps sounded in the hall outside. Without cere-mony, the door swung open, revealing a younger version of the present Earl of Langley. Though his hair was lighter, his nose less hawkish, Captain Myles Verney's years in the cav-alry had etched lines in his face that left him looking closer to his older brother's five and thirty than the actual years be-tween them dictated. The younger Verney, glancing at the debris encircling Jared's desk, grinned. "The dibs not in tune, brother mine? The witch's by-blow gets the cottage after all?"

Jared shook his head, managed a thin smile. He supposed Myles's insouciance had gotten him through the war. A soldier took his blows, made bad, even macabre, jokes about it and moved on. He wished he could learn to do the same. "I certainly agree that Clarissa Beaupré was *be*witching," he said evenly, "but she was also regal and elegant to the end. An old crone she certainly wasn't."

"I'll take your word for it," Myles said with a genial shrug of his broad shoulders, "but I don't remember her as anything but an old woman. I could never understand what Grandfather saw in her."

"Good God!" Jared was astonished. "Don't tell me you've never seen the portrait."

"What portrait?"

The Earl of Langley leaned back in his sturdy burgundy-leather chair, steepled his fingers in front of his mouth. A wicked gleam shone from his pewter-gray eyes. "We'll go now," he declared, "before the light fades. And before our dear cousin arrives. I've had a note from Smallwood saying to expect her tomorrow."

"Cousin?" Myles questioned. "Do you truly think so?"

"Why else would the old lady grant her the cottage?"

"Do you think she knows?"

"That she's a cousin? I have no idea. She could be anything, Myles. After all, a headmistress isn't likely to be a young woman. Perhaps she's an aunt instead of a cousin."

A look of revulsion crossed Captain Verney's angular features. "How fortunate it's you who must deal with the harpy, Jared. I wish you joy of her."

"Your gracious support is much appreciated."

Ignoring his brother's sarcasm, Myles flashed a quick smile, gave Jared a sharp slap on the back. "I've done my share of fighting the Americans, brother. Now it's your turn."

As they walked through the spinney that kept Arbor Cottage from intruding on the splendid view which distinguished Langley Park—not to mention out of sight of the simmering resentment of the dowager countess—Myles realized there was a question he had failed to ask his brother. "I say, Jared, what are these commissions the spinster has to carry out?"

"Haven't the foggiest," Jared grumbled, striding down the path at something close to quick-march tempo.

Captain Verney grabbed his brother's arm, hauling them both to a standstill. "Well, if you don't know," he demanded, "who does?"

"As far as I know, only Clarissa."

A short bark of laughter escaped the veteran of the Peninsula and the Battle of New Orleans. "Jared, be serious. *Someone* must know."

"I doubt it." Taking pity on his younger brother's outrage, Jared deigned to explain. "Deering and his wife are keepers of a series of letters, each to be given to Miss Todd in turn. Only when she opens each letter will she discover what she is expected to do."

Myles frowned. In precise military fashion he leaped straight to the heart of the problem. "What happens if she fails to fulfill the commissions? Do we get Arbor Cottage by default?"

"No." The earl fixed his gaze on the hand still clutching his arm.

Myles let go with suitable rapidity but did not still his tongue. "What, or should I say, who?" he demanded.

"What," his brother replied, with unflustered equanimity. "The cottage and its contents are to be sold to benefit the Beaupré's favorite charities."

"Bloody hell! But Grandfather gave her the whole—" Captain Verney bit off his words as a new thought struck him. "Better charities than the American spinster," he snapped. "And you are actually supposed to *help* her? It's beyond belief!" Myles Verney looked ready to grind Miss Todd's bones for breakfast.

"That was the promise I made." The Earl of Langley resumed his long strides toward Arbor Cottage.

Lunging forward, Captain Verney planted himself in his brother's path. "But *why*?" he demanded.

Around them the woods shimmered in the late afternoon of one of summer's longest days. Birds still twittered. Small creatures scurried through the underbrush, their passage marked only by a soft rustling of leaves and twigs. Jared Verney raised his pewter eyes to another set so like his own. "I've walked this path countless times," he said. "I liked her. She was kind, generous, always willing to listen. Even after I was grown, I continued to visit. She was the one person who would listen—"

"*Listen?* Is that what an old tart is reduced to? Listening?"

"It's not a bad attribute," Jared chided softly. "Looking back, I could have wished more of my *chère amies* had been so gifted."

"Are your bones so ancient, then, brother, that you've given up the muslin company?"

"Perhaps." Jared took time to consider his reply. "I confess I found a certain ennui when looking over the fresh crop at Hetty Jamison's establishment. As much, I daresay, as you found in the new bevy of maidens at Almack's. And even if I could afford to stay in town, I could scarce sport the blunt to set up an opera dancer or even a ripe widow. So you may have the right of it. I am getting old." Jared turned his back and strode off toward Arbor Cottage, leaving Myles to stare after him, wondering how his brotherly teasing had gone awry.

Chapter Two

"*T*his lane is even narrower," Hannah Greaves declared with some trepidation. "Do you suppose the postboy knows where he's going?"

Abby murmured reassurances, wishing she could believe her own words. For several miles now, a high stuccoed fence had replaced the hedgerows on the left side of the road. When they came to what was obviously the gatehouse for a vast estate, the postboy had paused to ask directions. She could only hope he had understood the reply, for it did indeed seem as if they were in danger of being lost in the wilds of Somerset.

Nonsense, of course. Soon she and Mrs. Greaves would be settled at Arbor Cottage, safe and secure, with none but a few minor errands or bequests to be seen to. Then she could entrust the sale of Arbor Cottage to an estate agent, and she and Hannah would be on the first ship back to Boston. There was nothing, absolutely nothing, to cause her anxiety.

"Oo-h!" Hannah Greaves, catching the first glimpse of Arbor Cottage, was betrayed into an uncharacteristic schoolgirl squeal that belied her status as the mother of six grown children.

"What . . . where?" Shamelessly, Abby slid across the seat, pressing the older woman into the corner, so she could look out her companion's window. "Merciful heavens! That can't be it," Abby choked out. "That has to be the house that belongs to the fence. We must have taken a wrong turn." But before she could lower the window to shout at the postboy, the chaise slowed and stopped directly in front of an arched portico that was obviously the main entrance to the startling edifice before them.

"A thatched roof," Mrs. Greaves murmured. "Perhaps that's why they call it a cottage."

"A cottage with at least eight bedrooms," Abby responded dryly. "With floor-length mullioned windows and at least a dozen dormers above." The least Hector Smallwood could have done was prepare her for this magnificence. Then again, perhaps he expected her to understand the way of things in England. He could have no idea of the modest expectations aroused in an American by the word *cottage*.

An elderly butler came out of the house, dressed with all the formality of his counterparts in Mayfair. A wave of his hand, and two footmen ran forward to help the ladies down. Since the butler seemed to have lost his tongue, Abby strode forward, offering her hand. "You must be Mr. Deering," she said. "I am Abigail Todd. This lady is my neighbor and companion, Mrs. Hannah Greaves."

"Just Deering, miss," the butler responded, still looking so dazed Abby wondered if he might be suffering from senility. After what appeared to be a brief struggle with his dignity, however, he accepted her hand. "Welcome to Arbor Cottage, Miss Todd. We trust you will enjoy your stay with us."

"I am sure I will, Mr. . . . ah—Deering. Arbor Cottage is far larger and more beautiful than I had anticipated."

A fleeting smile drifted across the old man's face. "Miss Clarissa hoped you would like it, miss. She was most particular that you should see it. And now if you'll come this way, Mrs. Deering has all the servants ready to meet you." The butler threw open the front door and ushered Abigail and Mrs. Greaves inside.

Oh, the school she could run in this place! Abby thought. *It was magnificent.* She could swear the entry hall alone was as big as the brownstone she and her father shared on Charles Street on Beacon Hill. She extended her hand to the plump gray-haired woman, dressed in severe charcoal-gray, who was hovering in front of a stiffly starched array of servants. Good heavens, Abby thought, once the estate is settled, I will be responsible for all these people. A sobering prospect. She would have to find places for them before she returned home. Or make their jobs contingent upon the sale of the cottage. In her mind Arbor Cottage had been an inanimate object. Now it had come alive . . . a living, breathing entity with all the obligations of *noblesse oblige* attached.

With smiles and nods Abby went down the line, knowing she would never remember the names rolling off Mrs. Deering's tongue. Shock had her in its grip. For the first time, it all seemed too much. She wondered what she was doing here. Why had she come?

For adventure, whispered a voice beneath her bonnet. Because Arbor Cottage was there. Because a stranger named Clarissa Bivens had asked, in her last will and testament, for Miss Abigail Todd of Boston, Massachusetts, to come to England and deal with her final requests. And because beneath the facade of a New England spinster beat a heart that longed for some spice in her life.

She was wicked. Quite, quite wicked, Abby freely admitted. Although accustomed to having employees, they were all at her school. Her father and she got along with a cook and a maid. She was mortified to discover her staunch New England soul *liked* having a butler, a housekeeper, a cook, three footmen, five housemaids, and a gardener. Mr. . . . no, *Deering* was apologizing because Miss Clarissa no longer kept a coachman, having been confined to the house for several years before her death. But there was a gig, which was used for trips to town. If miss would not mind using such a lowly conveyance? . . . Miss assured him she did not. She was, in fact, quite capable of driving it herself.

"We've put you in Miss Clarissa's room, miss. Those were the instructions she gave us. And your companion in the very next room."

Abby assured the housekeeper that this arrangement would suit them nicely, adding in an effort to be gracious, "I confess I was not expecting anything so elegant. Arbor Cottage is more like a mansion than the country cottage I had imagined."

The housekeeper chuckled. "Why, miss, wait 'til you see Langley Park. Now, there's as fine an English country home as you'll clap eyes on this side of Blenheim or Petworth."

"Langley Park?" Abby inquired.

"Seat of the Earl of Langley, miss. Closest neighbor to Arbor Cottage. Indeed, the land once belonged to the estate until the old earl—" Mrs. Deering, flustered, broke off. "Indeed, that's neither here nor there, miss. The earl will be calling on you tomorrow, and no doubt will tell you the whole himself."

"Did you say an earl?" Mrs. Greaves gasped. "A real live earl?"

Abby's lips twitched, though she was pleased her companion had deflected Mrs. Deering's attention from her own surprise. "And may I ask why we are to receive such an eminent visitor, Mrs. Deering? I assure you I am astounded to find myself on calling terms with an earl."

"The present earl's an old friend of Miss Clarissa's. Why, she used to stuff him with milk and biscuits any time he escaped his tutor and came running over here."

"Biscuits?" Mrs. Greaves muttered, looking to Abby.

"Cookies, I believe, Hannah. She means milk and cookies," Abby whispered.

"If you'll come this way, miss. Mrs. Greaves?" The housekeeper turned and led them, not toward the sweeping staircase, but into a long corridor extending off the right side of the entry hall. Abby, swallowing this further surprise, hurried after her.

Open doors revealed a series of light, well-appointed rooms. Abby, eyes lingering on a charming sunny room with furnishings of white wicker and colorful chintz, nearly stumbled over Mrs. Greaves's plump figure as the housekeeper paused in front of a door at the end of the corridor. "Here we are, miss," she pronounced in ringing tones.

Abby, accustomed to the no-nonsense tastes of Boston's Puritan ancestors, took three steps into Miss Clarissa Bivens's bedchamber and came to an abrupt halt, willing

herself to maintain the calm-in-the-midst-of-crisis facade
for which she was so well-known at Miss Todd's Academy
for Young Ladies.

"Lovely, isn't it?" the housekeeper said with a hitch in
her voice. "Miss Clarissa loved beautiful things, she surely
did."

"I—I'm overwhelmed," Abby murmured, desperately
wondering if there were any way she could ask for another
room without horrifying Mrs. Deering, who was looking at
her with eager expectancy.

"Goodness gracious!" declared Hannah Greaves, frozen
in the doorway as if afraid to set foot in the room.

"The furniture's French and Chinese," Mrs. Susan Deering informed them proudly. "Walls are hand-painted silk, the
carpet from Persia, or so Miss Clarissa said. Deering and me
'ave only been here twenty-six years while the cottage was
built nigh on fifty years ago. Got the old earl to buy her the
best of everything, she did."

Abby decided that was a remark best ignored. Perhaps
she had not heard it correctly. "Mrs. Deering, if you would
be good enough to show Mrs. Greaves to her room and then
send up a maid with some hot water, soap, and towels, we
would like to refresh ourselves. Then we can have a good sit
down, and you can tell me all about Miss Clarissa. She must
have been a most ah—remarkable woman."

"That she was, miss. That she was." Mrs. Deering
bobbed a curtsy, started toward the door, then abruptly
paused. "Ah, miss, I near forgot." She gestured toward a
pink silk curtain, some seven feet by four, hanging over a
section of the wall across from the foot of the massive bed.
"Miss Clarissa liked to have her picture where she could see
it all the time, remind herself of what she once was, she always said. But Deering and me, we thought you might
not . . . that is, we thought it best you get used to it gradual
like. So we had a curtain made for it. If you want to see it,
there's a pull-cord on the right." Another curtsy and Mrs.
Deering swept out, Hannah Greaves following in her wake.

Abby's feet seemed stuck to the shimmering pastels of
the Persian carpet. At least, now that she was alone, she

could openly gawk. The room was huge, with two pink-marble fireplaces. Floor-to-ceiling windows, arched at the top in Gothic style, lit the far end of the room on three sides where the bedchamber extended beyond the confines of the main structure. The windowed area was set up as a sitting room, with furniture upholstered in cream brocade and accented by throw cushions in rose and palest pink. The occasional tables and chests were decorated with the finest marquetry. The bed . . . Abby swallowed, felt a quiver of something quite strange flutter her insides. *Got the old earl to buy her the best of everything, she did.* Oh, my, yes. The bed was big enough to accommodate a dozen earls. The tester bed was walnut, at least seven feet long and six across, both canopy and posts elaborately carved. The scalloped valance skirting the wooden canopy was of heavy raw silk embroidered in a crewel design, as was the matching quilt. Rose silk hangings were tied back at each of the four corners by graceful ropes of metallic gold.

The room's remaining furnishings, the chests and wardrobes were *chinoiserie*. Museum pieces, Abby speculated, each elaborately painted in fantastic designs of a quality only Boston's most wealthy Brahmins could afford to purchase from the cargos of its world-traveling merchant fleet. She had come these thousands of miles, expecting little but the adventure of it. And because an unknown woman, now deceased, had wished her to. Now came the startling surprise. Obviously, Arbor Cottage was worth far more than she had expected.

The mystery deepened. Who was Miss Clarissa Bivens?

Curiosity unglued Abby's feet. She strode to the wall, pulled the cord on the silk curtain covering what Mrs. Deering had indicated was a painting of her former mistress.

Dear God in heaven! Abby closed the curtains faster than she had opened them. She stood, quivering, fighting the good fight with a long array of Puritan and Pilgrim ancestors. Her father might have been born in England, but her mother's forebears had stepped off the Mayflower itself.

Gingerly, she tugged on the cord, gradually reopening the

pink silk curtain. Perhaps on second view it wouldn't be so . . .

It was.

Abby lowered her eyes to the brass plaque set into the ornate gilt frame. *Clarissa Beaupré, La Grande Clarisse, 1767.* The last name might be different, but she knew this was Clarissa Bivens. And, with sinking heart, she also knew *La Grande Clarisse* was a relative. For only Abigail Todd, and possibly Hannah Greaves, who had shared the enforced intimacy of weeks at sea, knew that Abby's own naked flesh exactly matched the voluptuous curves on full display in the painting. Clarissa Beaupré lay stretched full length on a couch, clad only in her masses of shining cinnamon curls. The likeness to Abigail Todd extended from the fine lines of a startlingly beautiful face to the small brown blemish on her hip, a birthmark that Clarissa displayed as boldly as a beauty patch. A mark Abby also possessed. The only thing she did not recognize was the sultry, come-hither look in Clarissa Beaupré's green eyes. Never in her life had Abby allowed herself to look like that. Not even for Jonathan.

Or had she? Once upon a time when she was young and in love and thought she had a conventional life of husband, home, and children stretching out long years in front of her . . .

Ah, Papa, there's something you never told me. Not even when you knew I was coming here. How could you let me find out . . . like this?

"Oh, my!" Hannah Greaves's horrified tones rang through the room.

Abby jerked the curtains back over the painting. "My apologies, Hannah. I didn't realize you were there."

"But, Abby, what does it mean? She's the spit of you, I swear."

"Alas, yes," Abby sighed. "Obviously, I must speak with Mrs. Deering earlier than I had planned." She was about to ring the bellpull when a maid rapped on the open door. "Thank you," Abby said as the girl poured hot water into a porcelain basin, then laid out lavender-scented soap and linen towels from the chest of drawers below. "Will you be good enough to ask Mrs. Deering to attend me immediately?" she instructed.

Hearing the steel in her new employer's voice, the girl's eyes widened. She scurried off as fast as her legs could carry her.

When Susan Deering answered her mistress's summons, anxiety had replaced the pride in brown eyes deeply set into her plump cheeks. Her husband hovered behind her, in his hand a silver salver on which rested a folded sheet of parchment. With stately tread he moved past his wife, crossing to the sitting area where Miss Todd and her companion were waiting for Mrs. Deering. "This note was just delivered, miss," he declared, presenting the tray.

Abby eyed the missive with a strange mix of curiosity and foreboding. An impressive crest was stamped into the generous blob of red wax sealing the expensive heavy parchment. The writing inside was bold, decisive, even arrogant, Abby decided as she scanned the short missive.

> *Miss Todd,*
>   *As executor of Miss Clarissa Beaupré's estate, I have agreed to assist in the commissions which she has asked you to accomplish on her behalf. I shall call upon you at eleven o'clock tomorrow morning to discuss the matter.*
>   *Jared Verney, Earl of Langley*

Abby raised a haughty brow to her butler. "Must I reply?" she inquired sweetly, "or is it assumed I am so honored that I shall naturally make myself available for the momentous occasion of the earl's visit?"

Mrs. Greaves and Mrs. Deering gasped in unison, but Abby could swear the elderly butler was repressing a smile. "A verbal reply is sufficient, miss," he intoned. "Would you care to set a later time?"

Abby considered the matter. How very foolish to postpone the satisfaction of her curiosity just because the Earl of Langley had assumed a power over her that she did not wish to grant. What else could she expect of an enemy aristocracy so arrogant they had thrown away their American colonies without seeming to realize the extent of what was at stake? "You may inform the earl," she said, "that we await his visit with bated breath."

"Abigail!" Hannah Greaves groaned.

Abby opened her eyes wide. "But I do, Hannah, I assure you. My curiosity is rampant. Imagine, an earl no less. It must be quite as exciting as seeing the menagerie at the Tower."

Deering was forced to turn away, covering a bark of laughter with a cough. Amusement faded at the shocked look on his wife's face. Turning back to Miss Todd, he assured her he would see that one of the footmen delivered her message immediately.

"Sit down, Mrs. Deering." Abby indicated a chair across from her.

"Oh, miss," the housekeeper cried, nervous anxiety cracking her customary professional reticence, "you can't imagine how much you're like her. With your bonnet gone, your hair is just like the picture. Your face as fine. And your tongue as sharp as an adder. Kindhearted, generous she was but, oh, dearie me, could Miss Clarissa flay the skin off anyone with pretensions! Not that an earl can have pretensions. I mean . . ." Susan Deering, now floundering, paused. "Well, I'm sure an earl doesn't have to aspire to anything greater, miss. Yes, that's what I mean." The housekeeper frowned. "At least I believe that's so. Unless he wished to be a marquess, of course, or a duke or—"

"That's all right, Mrs. Deering, I understand," Abby said, taking pity on the poor woman. "I've committed a social solecism of the first magnitude, but you must understand that I am an American. I am not partial to titles or the arrogance that goes with them. Be grateful I am to be here for so short a time. I will not be disgracing your standards for more than a fleeting summer." Abby straightened her shoulders, folded her hands in her lap. "And now, Mrs. Deering, you will please tell me how it is that I so strongly resemble the woman in *that*." She nodded toward the expanse of pink silk curtains.

The housekeeper's double chins quivered as a series of strong emotions swept her face. Bowing her head, she dug deep into a pocket in her gown, producing another folded sheet of parchment, this one sealed in wax of a delicate shade of pink. "Miss, I was told to give this to you as soon as you arrived. I most sincerely hope that Miss Clarissa herself has explained all, for I'll admit it's not a job I relish. It's possible she's left the gist of it for Lord Langley to tell, for she kept her arrangements secret from us all—"

"Except for the commissions," Abby interrupted.

"Even that, miss. Deering and me, we've got the letters with her instructions, but we have no idea what's in them."

"I see," Abby mused. "Very well, Mrs. Deering, you may give me the letter and return to your duties. I will ring if I have further questions."

The housekeeper labored to her feet, executed a rather deeper curtsy than she had earlier that afternoon. "Supper will be at seven, miss. I'll send someone to guide you to the dining room." On wings of relief, Mrs. Deering fled.

Abby, not yet ready to deal with what might be a more fate-filled communication than she had imagined, allowed her gaze to wander from one tall Gothic-arched and mullioned window to the next. Through the two windows on her right she could see a heavy stand of trees behind low formal gardens and graveled pathways. To her left was a bricked courtyard with white wrought-iron furniture, and a fountain whose faint tinkling was soothing in this moment of agitation. To the left, flowers rioted in an informal abundance of colors, peacocks wandering among them, their long tails drooping onto the green grass and pebbled paths. In the distance . . . Abby narrowed her eyes, examining the odd structure next to the high fence at the rear of the garden. It was long, narrow. Green. A toolhouse covered in vines?

An *arbor,* that's what it was. Of course! *Arbor Cottage.* If it hadn't been for the letter burning her hand, Abby would have burst out the door tucked into the courtyard side of Clarissa Beaupré's bedchamber and investigated on the instant. Oh, what a glorious adventure this was turning out to be!

"Do you wish me to leave, Abby?" Hannah Greaves inquired softly.

"No, no," Abby murmured. "You must be as curious as I. And I doubt the actual scandal can be worse than what we already suspect." She broke the seal and began to read.

Chapter Three

My dear Abigail,
  Yes, I dare call you dear even though we have never met. Unfortunately, because of your father's insistence that Edmund and Miranda Todd are his true parents, it is quite possible you know nothing of me. Of Clarissa Bivens, who became Clarissa Beaupré, your father's true mother.

There it was, Abby thought. The truth that would explain her father's remarkably vague response to her inheritance, the polite evasions of Hector Smallwood. Her own burgeoning suspicions, which had been confirmed when she opened the pink silk curtains to reveal the naked beauty of Clarissa Beaupré.

During the years of your country's war of independence—when Lucian was of an age to be told of his origins—I was unable to continue my correspondence with Miranda, and Edmund persuaded her not to tell Lucian about me. By the time the war was over and I wrote to him directly, your father was set on his course in life, refusing to acknowledge me in any way. If you are reading this letter, my dear Abigail, then God has forgiven an unrepentant old woman and allowed you to come to Arbor Cottage, where I hope you will learn more of your heritage.

Abby leaned back against the cream-brocade couch, fighting a strong temptation to crumple Clarissa's letter and toss it into the pink-marble fireplace. Her grandparents— her beloved Todd grandparents—were not her own. No wonder her father had urged her to ignore her inheritance!

But curiosity was not easily put aside. Inevitably, her eyes were drawn back to the page.

> *Because my old friend Miranda finally took pity on me and has written to me about the particulars of your life, I know that Abigail Todd is very much like me in looks but, thanks be, not in character. I am told you are a good woman who lost her fiancé at sea and chose to establish a school rather than marry less than the love of her life. This saddens me, child, because your heritage is strong, your intelligence high. These gifts should not be lost to the world. Please do not be angry if I urge you to use your time in England to view our fine young men with something other than scorn. Particularly, my very dearest Jared's grandson, also a Jared, who is in as great a need of a soul mate as are you.*

Abby gaped. The outrageous old demirep was matchmaking? How dared she? And with the grandson of her lover, who . . . Abby frowned, attempting to fight her way through the maze of genealogical possibilities. If Jared Verney were the grandson of the old earl, then he was likely a cousin of some kind. Though, truthfully, such a close relationship mattered little compared to the yawning gulf between a belted earl and the granddaughter of a . . . a . . . woman who would pose naked for a portrait six feet long. Bitterly, Abby rejected all the other epithets that leaped to mind. And yet that incredible old woman dared speak of making a match . . .

Abby's anger grew. As if she would even consider an Englishman under any circumstances. A member of the hated aristocracy. A man who was not Jonathan Blaisdell, first mate of the *Louisa,* lost with all hands a decade ago to

a hurricane off the Bahamas. With eyes sparking green fire,
Abby returned to the letter.

> *Now to the commissions I ask of you. The*
> *Deerings are the caretakers of eight more letters. You*
> *will find most of the tasks remarkably easy. One or*
> *two may be more taxing. Since you can scarcely*
> *travel through England unescorted, I have asked*
> *Jared to assist you in each of the errands. Do not*
> *turn him away, I beg you! Not only will you need*
> *him, but it is my fondest wish you become better*
> *acquainted with the grandson of the man who*
> *brought such joy to my life.*

Joy? A demirep dared speak to her of joy? Of illicit lust?
Carnal delight? Abby struggled with a vision of her mother's
proper Bostonian parents discovering Dr. Lucian Todd's
mother was a courtesan. No wonder he had refused to acknowledge Clarissa Beaupré! The marvel of it was that he
had not tied his daughter to her bed rather than allow her to
take ship for England.

> *My dear Abigail, when all the commissions are*
> *completed—as I am certain you will manage to*
> *do—and Arbor Cottage is yours, I beg you will*
> *consider its disposition with care. I remind you it*
> *was once part of the Verney estate. If you had not*
> *existed, I would have given it back with a ready will.*
> *But you, my dearest grandchild, have chosen a*
> *solitary life. A particularly difficult road for a*
> *woman. You have an independent spirit. As have I. I*
> *must help you if I can.*
> *We have approached our independence in*
> *different ways, but I believe we may be kindred*
> *spirits. Do not, I beg of you, turn away from any of*
> *the requests I make of you. Not because you might*
> *lose an inheritance, but because I am almost certain*
> *your soul cries out for something more than the life*
> *you have chosen.*

*And pray do not judge me too harshly, nor scorn
what I made of myself. My choices were few, and
only extraordinary good fortune brought my darling
Jared into my life. You would be well advised to
accept my assurance that the Verney charm shines as
brightly in the younger Jared as in his grandfather.*

*And know, dearest child, that you have not heard
the last of me. This is only the beginning.*

> *Your loving grandmother,*
> *Clarissa Beaupré, née Bivens*

Abby thrust the letter at Hannah Greaves as if she could
no longer bear to touch it. Hands clasped tight in her lap, she
stared blankly at the toe of her half boot, which peeked out
beneath the hem of her dark blue skirt. Idly, she toed the intricate pastel flowers in Clarissa Beaupré's carpet.

Her grandmother's carpet.

The courtesan's carpet.

Dear God in heaven!

"Abby? Abigail," Hannah Greaves ventured after scan-
ning the letter. "It's not so bad, truly it's not. Your father's a
fine man. I'm sure sending him off with the Todds was the
hardest thing Miss Clarissa ever did, but look how well he
turned out. I'm that certain she was proud as punch of both
of you. Can't blame her for wanting you to know, for wanting you to have all her pretty things.' Hannah screwed up
her courage, plunged ahead. "You can tell your grandmother
Cabot that Miss Clarissa was what Dr. Todd had said, an eccentric connection of the family who was pleased to leave
you her estate."

Abby looked out at the arbor, its leafy covering dappled
by a sun slowly descending toward a brilliant summer sunset. "I fear deception is not one of my talents," she sighed.

"Nor should it be, child," Mrs. Greaves shot back, "but a
tiny tiny fib now and then—for a righteous cause—surely the
good Lord will forgive you."

"Perhaps. But nothing can forgive the matchmaking,
Hannah. It's absurd. Can you imagine an earl marrying a descendant of his grandfather's mistress? And, besides," Abby

added, perhaps a shade too vehemently, "I have no interest in marriage. I swore to be true to Jonathan for the rest of my life, and I *shall*."

After a resigned shake of her head, Mrs. Greaves glanced at Clarissa Beaupré's mantel clock where porcelain figures in elaborate costumes of the last century danced across the numbers on the lower face, cheerfully proclaiming the hour. Hannah bounded to her feet. "Goodness gracious, Abby, look at the time. We must dress for dinner. Now, not a single frown, my dear. Fallen on your feet, you have. Our cottage is a palace, and a genuine earl coming to visit tomorrow. Smile, my dear! Now aren't you glad you ordered all those fine gowns in London?"

Fine gowns, Abby mused. So much had happened in the past few hours, London seemed almost as remote as Boston. *Fine gowns.* A mischievous grin suddenly wiped away the anger and melancholy that had marred Miss Abigail Todd's classically beautiful face.

Naturally, Clarissa Beaupré's mirror was full-length, framed in gilt with a small marble shelf at its base. Abby experienced a momentary pang of covetousness. Could it be packed well enough to survive the rigorous voyage home? And, pray tell, what did a schoolmistress need with such a thing? her stern New England conscience mocked. *Vanity, vanity!* The very last sin she needed at the moment.

The incongruity of her image in the ornate mirror, which also reflected the bedchamber's sybaritic delights, brought a satisfied smile to Abby's lips. This was exactly how she wished to appear. A dull brown wren. Her gown of mud-colored galatea had once been good enough for the classroom but was now nearly ready for the poor box. She had packed it for walking on deck in rough weather and on the off chance she should be reduced to cleaning out Arbor Cottage with only Hannah Greaves to help. Her hair was confined into a severe coif on the nape of her neck, its glorious cinnamon red almost completely hidden under a voluminous white mobcap, borrowed from the underhousemaid.

To complete her ensemble, Abby slipped on a pair of mesh half gloves, which she hoped were sadly out of fashion.

There! It was five minutes before eleven o'clock and she was ready. Bring on the charming earl. Her cousin Langley.

"The Earl of Langley," Deering intoned.

Jared Verney paused in the doorway, assessing the two women waiting for him in Clarissa Beaupré's drawing room. The elder had jumped to her feet, dropping into a curtsy deep enough for the queen. The younger . . . *Good God!* It took all the *savoir faire* of Jared's aristocratic training to keep his jaw from gaping. The face . . . that exquisite face was almost a duplicate of the portrait, but the rest of her . . . Jared struggled with his sense of the ridiculous. For there the comparison stopped. The young American stood regally erect, spine unbending, her figure hidden beneath a hideous gown, hair lost beneath a cap a tavern wench would scorn. It never occurred to him her taste could be so execrable. No one so obviously related to Clarissa Beaupré, as she certainly must be, would ever dress that way except by design. Undoubtedly, Miss Todd was expressing her opinion of him, a scorned enemy. He was finding his promise to Clarissa more intriguing by the moment.

The Earl of Langley was, Abby had to admit, the epitome of an English aristocrat. She had hoped for a caricature and encountered an idealization. A *beau idéal*. His tall lithe body proclaimed both strength and energy; his clothing was so impeccably tailored it seemed molded to his body. As he approached, however, his sculptured features seemed to become more saturnine, his lips slipping into something close to a sneer, the pale eyes sparking a warning. Or so Abby thought until she finished the introductions and they were seated, face-to-face, with nothing more than a low table between them.

He was *amused,* she realized with considerable shock. Any annoyance over the deliberate disrespect of an American schoolmistress a mere flyspeck, a gesture totally beneath his notice. Abby feared a dull red was suffusing her face. This was the enemy, she reminded herself. The living symbol of everything that had driven the former British colonies to revolt.

Jared leaned back in the Louis Quinze chair, tapping one long finger on the arm while he examined Miss Abigail Todd of Boston. Was it possible she had an additional reason for hiding her beauty in such an appalling manner? Was her disguise more personal? What in the name of hell and the devil could Clarissa have done? . . . Had the old *demimondaine* been intent on matchmaking? *Impossible!*

Jared had felt himself fortunate to escape from the recent Season in London without a leg-shackle. It seemed every maiden and her widowed older sister, not to mention married sisters and even their mamas, had been casting out lures to the Earl of Langley. And yet this . . . this *American* was regarding him with her spine stiff as a board and scornful anger shooting from her remarkably fine green eyes. What did the chit think she was doing? If she insisted on sitting there glaring at him when good manners required her to initiate a conversation . . . Undoubtedly, the lady was a republican, raised on the mother's milk of revolution. Her drab disguise a deliberate insult to British nobility rather than an attempt to scorn Clarissa's matchmaking.

"Is it noblemen in general you dislike, Miss Todd, or myself in particular?" Miss Todd's companion, Jared noticed, had the grace to look chagrined.

Abby inclined her head thoughtfully, seemingly not at all put out by the earl's question. "It is true I am not in sympathy with the British aristocracy," she conceded, "but in your case I fear I dislike the implied connection to your family. I have been here just long enough to discover that it appears to have been—ah—highly irregular."

"But looks are deceiving, are they not, Miss Todd?" Jared purred. "I am no more my grandfather than you are Clarissa Beaupré."

A fair hit. Abby ducked her head, pursed her lips while her conscience struggled with her ingrained anti-British sentiments. "My lord," she murmured, granting him that mark of respect for the first time, "I cry pardon." She noted Hannah Greaves's sharp sigh of relief. "You are indeed correct.

The letter left to me by Claris—my grandmother—revealed only that she and a Jared Verney had been . . . close and that she had asked you to assist me in carrying out a series of commissions. I fear I endowed you with all my preconceptions of a titled nobleman, compounded by your family's association with what would constitute a supreme scandal in Boston. The fault is mine. If you could provide further enlightenment on this remarkable situation, I would be most grateful."

Though intrigued by Miss Todd's sudden *volte-face* and the graciousness of her apology, Jared could not help but wonder how much was genuine and how much an accommodation to the American's curiosity. Suspicious of Clarissa's schemes in that direction, he had been prepared to tolerate the courtesan's heir, but nothing more. Yet now he felt unaccountably drawn toward the American, repellent gown, mobcap, and all.

"You have seen the portrait?" he inquired delicately.

"I have," Abby replied faintly, red once again staining her cheeks.

"Then you have guessed the nature of her relationship with my grandfather?" Abby nodded. Jared heard his own words and marveled at them. Surely he could not be holding such a frank conversation with a spinster who, though far from tender years, broadcast virgin purity with every breath she took. "Very well," he conceded. "It was long before my time, of course, but I am told Clarissa Beaupré was the most renowned courtesan of her day. My grandfather was a widower with two half-grown children. His marriage had been the usual, a union of land and wealth. He was ripe for love. One glance at La Grande Clarisse and he never looked at another woman. He built this cottage on the family estate and visited her every day for nearly forty years."

A sniff sounded from Mrs. Greaves. "So romantic," she sighed. "A true love story."

"She was his mistress, Hannah," Abigail snapped.

"Just so," the earl agreed softly.

"You cannot be pleased by this blot on your family history, my lord." Abby declared. "How is it you have agreed to help me? Will you, too, gain an inheritance?"

"I have asked myself the exact same question," the earl replied, his full lips slipping into a wry grin. "Primarily, I believe I agreed to her request because I liked her and because I loved my grandfather. However, I freely admit I wished to ingratiate myself with you, so you would allow me the first offer on Arbor Cottage. It is time it was returned to the estate."

Oddly enough, Abby found his words made perfect sense. Jared Verney was a symbol of all she hated, including a class system that had never allowed her grandmother to rise above her position as a well-paid whore. And yet he was handsome, virile, exuding an aura of confidence and command without lifting so much as a finger. Clarissa had been right. Even while fencing with her, Jared Verney never lost his charm.

"Are we cousins then?" Abby asked.

"In truth, I do not know. Even your existence was unknown to me until several months before her death when Clarissa asked for my promise to assist you. She was determinedly vague about your antecedents. For all she would tell me, you might have been an aunt, half sister to my father. Until I walked into this room this morning, I knew only that you were headmistress of a school in Boston. It is not surprising I expected you to be older."

"I became an instructor at a very young age," Abby murmured without amplification.

A story there, Jared speculated, but they were still strangers, walking stiff-legged around each other, sniffing the air, wondering which would jump for the other's throat first. Time enough for revelations when—*if*—they became better acquainted.

"I wonder, Miss Todd, if you would care to drive out with me this afternoon? The countryside is quite lovely, and you would have a better feel for the life your grandmother led for the past fifty years."

"Surely we would be better employed beginning the tasks Miss Beaupré has set for us?" Abby responded coldly.

"A day to settle in is not out of line," the earl offered calmly. "I believe you will view Clarissa's commissions with greater equanimity if you acquire a feel for the country, as well as have time to rest after your long journey."

The man was maddening! Abby nearly ground her teeth. Accustomed to making her own decisions for far more years than she cared to count, she found the Earl of Langley's assumption of command infuriating. That he was absolutely right only increased her anger.

"I will drive out with you," Abby agreed stiffly, "if we may agree to meet here tomorrow morning to open the first of the eight letters Mrs. Deering tells me she is holding."

"Eight!" Jared didn't bother to hide his surprise.

"That, my lord, is why I am anxious to get started."

Ah . . . the wily old tart had hoodwinked him. Eight "errands" could encompass almost any number of strange possibilities, not to mention taking up most of his summer. *Clarissa, you old devil, Arbor Cottage had best be my reward!*

Or was it the lovely, if disguised, Miss Todd that was intended as his reward?

"Will three o'clock be convenient for our drive?" Jared inquired, rising nimbly to his feet. Even earls occasionally felt the need to escape.

When Miss Todd agreed, he began his farewells to the two Americans, pausing abruptly as a thought struck him. "There is—ah—something I should warn you about," the earl admitted. "My brother Myles fought at the Battle of New Orleans. He is, I fear, not as tolerant of Americans as I. If you should encounter him, I would hope that you will do nothing to inflame his temper—"

"Inflame his temper?" Abby cried. "What about mine? You stand there and tell me your brother was one of those who burned Washington and were defeated by our brave troops in New Orleans and dare ask I not inflame *his* temper? How can you be so absurd?"

She was magnificent with fire in her eye. It was all Jared could do to refrain from shouting, "Brava!" But no sign of it showed on a face whose handsome lines now seemed etched in granite. "If we are to endure this summer, Miss Todd, then you will control your temper, as I will instruct my brother to control his."

"Instruct! Do you dare give orders to a soldier as you do to me?"

"Oh, yes, Miss Todd. I was bred and trained to give orders. That is what earls do. And you would do well to remember it." Jared looked down his Roman nose at the little upstart from America. "I shall return at three o'clock. Until then." With a stiff bow to each of the ladies, he stalked from the room, every one of a long line of Verney ancestors marching with him.

"I won't go!" Abby declared as the Earl of Langley disappeared into the entry hall.

"Yes, you will," Hannah Greaves declared roundly. "That's a fine man, Abby. And you are bound to him whether you like it or not. You'll not be setting up his back with your quests not yet begun."

"I'll not have him telling me what to do."

"Your father granted you independence far beyond your years or your sex," Mrs. Greaves asserted. "Too much freedom, you've had, my girl. It's time you came to terms with the ways of the world. If you're to work with that man, then you must let him lord it over you. He's scarce to blame. He knows no other way."

"I won't."

"Abigail Todd, did you never hear that honey catches more flies than vinegar? You are a fool to get your back up over nothing."

"Nothing!" Abby mocked, though she could feel her fury beginning to abate.

"Yes, nothing. He is being a man, no more, no less. And he expects you to be a lady. Perhaps not an English lady, but a woman who does her own country proud."

Abby dropped her head into her hands. "Ah, Hannah, you shame me."

Her companion's voice softened. "My dear Abigail, I only remind you of what you already know. You are a stranger in a strange land. A female in a world controlled by men. You will accomplish what you set out to do only by accommodating yourself to the expectations of others. You cannot take on the whole world and win."

"I don't deserve you, Hannah," Abby murmured, "but I'm very glad I asked you to come along." She pinched a fold of the brown galatea between her fingers, shaking her head at her own folly. "You're a fine counselor and companion, Hannah my dear, but if you would be so kind, I would like to be alone for a few moments." With a sympathetic murmur and the soft swish of silk, Hannah Greaves left the room.

Abby tore off the mobcap, tossed it onto the floor. Only the stern strictures of her New England upbringing kept her from stomping it under her equally ugly half boots. Her adventure was off to a disastrous beginning. She had made a fool of herself in front of a man who must surely be one of the most elegant men in England. His reaction had been inevitable. She had overstepped the bounds of good manners and been brought up short by a nobleman who probably maintained his polite reserve when being threatened by highwaymen or . . . or being attacked by a wild boar or . . . posing stark naked for a male version of Clarissa Beaupré's infamous portrait.

Abby clapped her hands over her mouth, torn between laughter, horror at where her imagination had led, and shocking conjectures of just how such a painting might look. How could she possibly go driving with him? Every time she looked at him, she would think . . .

Frightful! She'd never be able to keep a straight face.

And yet, somehow her anger had dissipated. Jared Verney was no longer the enemy. This afternoon they would drive out together, and tomorrow . . . Tomorrow her obligations to her grandmother would begin.

Chapter Four

At fifteen minutes before three o'clock, Clarissa Beaupré's mirror reflected an image far different from the dull brown wren of that morning. Abby's earlier satisfied smile, however, had been replaced by a scowl. Was she bending her principles? Bowing to *force majeure*? Betraying her own hard-won independence, along with that of her country?

Nonsense! Compromise was not the same as rejection. She simply wished to accomplish her mission and go home. The sooner, the better. But had it truly been necessary to don her best carriage dress, whose deep azure-blue enhanced the green of her eyes and displayed the undisguised curvaceousness of her figure? Clarissa's mirror was remarkably revealing. Abby turned first one way, then the other, peering at the effect. Oh, my, she hadn't realized . . . The gown's high neck and long sleeves seemed to accent her assets rather than cover them up.

The high-and-mighty earl would be astonished. He would apologize for being a boor. He would grovel at her feet . . .

Idiot! The Earl of Langley was undoubtedly a connoisseur. He could have no interest in a schoolteacher from Boston ten years past the age of marriage.

As if she cared!

Abby grabbed up a bonnet of finely woven straw that boasted a small bouquet of silk flowers accented by the jaunty blue-green tip of a peacock feather. It had caught her eye in a milliner's window in Bond Street and was quite the most dashing bonnet she had worn since she was seventeen. After working gloves of cream pigskin onto her hands, she examined herself once again in the mirror, gave a decisive nod, then left her bedchamber. But not without insidious qualms of guilt over the possibility that, rather than taunt her cousin Langley, she had dressed to please him.

Truthfully, Abby was looking forward to a view of the countryside around Arbor Cottage, but when she caught a glimpse of the vehicle waiting at her door, she could only stop and stare. She was expected to ride in *that*?

"A curricle, cousin," Jared drawled. "Do they not have them in Boston?"

"Not that I have seen . . . my lord." The jaunty two-wheeled vehicle looked remarkably insubstantial.

"My high-perch phaeton is much more daunting," the earl assured her. "I thought the curricle quite unexceptional." Dark eyebrows raised a challenge above supposedly guileless eyes.

Dreadful man! Before the earl could assist her, Abby located the curricle's step, hiked up her skirts, and climbed aboard.

Jared restrained himself from a strong temptation to give her nicely rounded derriere a boost. Headstrong was his cousin Abigail. But a beauty who more than lived up to the promise he had glimpsed that morning. Clarissa's eight commissions were seeming less of a burden by the moment.

"I believe you will find the village of interest," Jared said with careful neutrality as he took the reins from his groom and allowed his matched bays to move off down the drive. All the clichés a gentleman used to compliment a lady chased through his mind, words which would have slipped easily from his tongue until his first sight of Abigail Todd. In London he was known as The Indifferent Earl, the most elusive nobleman in the *ton*. A man who offered all the expected compliments but remained heartwhole, untouched. Yet, to Miss Todd, he could offer only sincerity. She would scorn all else.

"You are looking very fine," Jared said at last, wondering if she would deny it just to be contrary.

"Thank you, my lord." A stiff murmur, the barest minimum response.

"It is some two miles to the village. Perhaps you might be willing to tell me something of your father as we go on. Since it seems likely he was my father's half brother, I confess to a certain curiosity."

"Very well." Briefly, Abby told him about Dr. Lucian Todd, whose skill was much sought after by Boston society, but who also offered his medical services free of charge one day a week in a ramshackle building down near the waterfront.

"A good man, then, your father?"

"An admirable man," Abby asserted stoutly.

"And your mother?"

Abby looked away, out over the green fields and hedgerows of Somerset. "She's been gone since I was fifteen, a victim of the wasting disease. I am blessed, however, by having two grandmothers . . ." She broke off, then continued in a determined tone. "Miranda Todd has been my grandmother all my life. I assure you I still consider her as such. Just as my father claims her as mother."

"No need to fly up into the boughs. I am quite certain Clarissa never expected you to reject the love of those you have known so long, although I suppose she hoped your father would acknowledge her. A perfectly natural human sentiment, I am sure you agree."

Abby's temper flared. How dare he chide her? Gripping her hands tightly in her lap, she continued to stare out over the landscape, her lips sealed against further conversation. Unfortunately for the success of her sulk, the village of Vernhampton was everything an English village should be. A small country church with sturdy bell tower, an inn whose courtyard boasted nothing more than a gig with one farm horse between the shafts, a small green with several sturdy oaks, a smithy, a half dozen shops and several row houses, each with crisp white curtains shining behind the glass. Solemnly, the earl pointed out the central market cross, which, like all others since the Cromwell era, was nothing more than a stub of granite.

"Wars, particularly religious wars, are so filled with hate," Abby murmured. "That people could destroy a cross when it is a symbol of their own beliefs . . ."

"Churches, convents, monasteries," Jared added. "The devastation was endless."

"I believe you are making a point."

"That war and hatred are senseless? I suppose I am. Yet I would be the first to admit that Napoleon had to be stopped. And that it was proper to fight to keep our colonies, even though our own stupidity brought the rebellion down upon us. But when it is over . . . then, my dear cousin, I think we must make accommodations."

"You wish to cry peace?"

"Most definitely. We must work together, you and I. There is no sense coming to cuffs over every imagined slight."

"I must tell you," Abby informed him, making a strong effort not to sound like an ill-tempered child, "I am more accustomed to giving lessons than to receiving them."

The earl had turned his horses at the ancient market cross and was now heading back through town. He pulled up near the village green. Wondering if he were taking his life into his hands, Jared touched the stiff edge of Abigail's straw bonnet, gently tugging her head around to face him. "Friends?" he inquired, his silver-gray eyes radiating surprising warmth.

Friends. Relief swept over her. This dynamic, powerful, handsome man was offering her friendship. *Accept my assurance that the Verney charm shines as brightly in the younger Jared as in his grandfather.* Abby's stiff-necked New England pride was not strong enough to resist.

She offered her hand. Jared lifted it to his lips and kissed it. Although the gesture was both old-fashioned and provocative, she could only regret the thickness of her pigskin glove. Snatching her hand back as if it had been burned, she ducked her head to hide the fire in her cheeks.

Once again, she found herself the gauche American unable to deal with a polished English gentleman.

"Abigail? May I call you Abigail?" The earl lowered his gaze to peer under the brim of her bonnet. "I meant it, you know. I have no idea if we are truly cousins, but I think the situation demands that we be friends. I am Jared, by the way. It would please me if you would call me so."

"Of course," Abby murmured, hoping the wide straw brim of the bonnet was shading her reddened cheeks. She had not blushed in years, she was certain of it, and now . . . now she seemed able to do little else.

"Of course?" The simple words hung between them, a challenge.

"Of course . . . Jared."

"Then, Abigail, let us be off to view the Verney acres. I have ordered tea at Langley Park in little over an hour, so we must be brisk about it."

As they drove past thatched farmhouses, numerous outbuildings, and a variety of livestock, past fields planted to wheat and barley, gardens filled with a multitude of green shoots, Abby suspected they were seeing only a small portion of the vast Langley estate. The earl's tenants appeared to be well fed, the men knuckling their foreheads as their earl passed by, the women bobbing curtsies, children smiling and waving. Certainly, she could not fault the earl as a landlord. But, then, wasn't that why she had succumbed to calling him friend? There was no way she could keep Jared Verney trapped in the niche labeled *Enemy*. Nor in the one labeled *Incompetent Aristocrats*. Alas, her cousin Langley was far more than she had expected. And far more dangerous to her peace of mind.

Another thing Abby had not expected, in spite of the earl's warning, was the presence of Captain Myles Verney at tea. Langley Park was intimidating enough. A Palladian structure of graceful lines and sweeping beauty, its vast walls and high ceilings were adorned with frescoes and plasterwork, its elegant furnishings quickly forcing her to see why Clarissa Beaupré's home was called a cottage. Awed by the grandeur around her, she was caught off guard when a second Verney male strode into the drawing room with all the vigor of a reserve troop called up to defend the citadel.

"So it's true," the captain declared, regarding her with legs spread, both hands on his hips. "The portrait could be of you!"

"Myles!" Jared roared, then, grim-lipped, made introductions in a tone that should have been a warning to both his listeners. As the earl seated his guest with care in front of the tea table, the unrepentant captain flung himself into a satinwood Sheraton chair, causing his older brother to raise his eyes to the cherubs on the ceiling.

If Abby had not been regarding the silver teapot with loathing, she might have enjoyed the earl's chagrin. As it was, she was uncomfortably aware that both men were watching her with avid interest. It was as if she were being tested on whether or not an American knew how to pour tea. She could feel a tremor building—anger, not fear—and was certain it would go straight to her right hand. The hot tea would splash into the Limoges saucer, onto the silver tray, ruining the undoubtedly priceless table beneath. Or perhaps it would fly onto the captain's stylish pantaloons . . . Now, *that* was a more intriguing thought—the captain prancing about the room, pain in his . . . well, ah . . . Humor saved her. Abby tightened her grip on the pot and poured each cup to the precise acceptable height. Sugar? Cream? The Verney men raised identical brows as she herself used nothing more than hot water to dilute the strength of the strong black tea.

There! They could not fault her performance. Swiftly, she reminded herself that only Myles Verney was the enemy. She and the earl were . . . *friends*. Astonishing!

Abby decided not to let sleeping dogs lie. "I understand you fought in the Battle of New Orleans, Captain?" she challenged. Was that a disapproving choke escaping from the earl?

Captain Verney's eyes, the gray only slightly more blue than his brother's, peered at her over his teacup. "Indeed, Miss Todd, but I failed to have the pleasure of visiting Washington."

The devil! Talk about taking up the gauntlet. Lurid tales of the British "visit" to her national capital rang in her ears. She could almost smell the smoke of the burning city.

Friends. The outrageous captain's brother was her friend. She was a guest in her *friend's* home.

While Abby was struggling with her temper, Jared intervened. "Miss Todd and I have come to an agreement," he declared. "Both wars with America are over, as is our long war with Napoleon. It is time to recall our common ancestry and forget our differences."

Abby could clearly see that Myles Verney did not appreciate his brother's peacemaking any more than she had earlier that afternoon. She found herself enjoying the captain's discomfiture. The incident also pointed out what Hannah Greaves seemed to have known instinctively: earls held a great deal of power, even over members of their own family.

"Have you found the arbor yet, Miss Todd?" the earl inquired smoothly.

Abby appreciated the not-so-subtle change of subject. "I have seen it out the window, my lord, but have not yet explored the gardens. Can you tell me about it? I am unfamiliar with anything more elaborate than a modest rose arbor."

While the Earl of Langley settled into a history of medieval arbors in general and the design of the latter-day imitation at Arbor Cottage in particular, Captain Verney accepted a second cup of tea and actually deigned to offer a small nod of thanks as Miss Todd returned his cup. Abby wasn't fooled. Jared Langley would make a match with the American schoolmistress over his younger brother's dead body.

Not, of course, that there was any chance of that happening. *A cold day in hell,* as the saying went. Even if cousin Langley was a . . . friend.

As the earl handed Abby down from his curricle, she thanked him, reiterating their agreement to meet the next morning to open the first of Clarissa's letters. But when she returned to her room, she did not bother to remove her bonnet. Ignoring the sound of Hannah Greaves's footsteps as the older woman hurried to discover news of her charge's afternoon with an earl, Abby stepped outside into the bricked courtyard.

Standing beside one of the marble benches surrounding the fountain, she gazed out over the precise lines of the rose garden, its pebbled walkways interspersed with white wooden trellises boasting a marvelous canopy of colorful blooms to augment the display in the rectangular beds below. Between the rose beds and the arbor at the rear of the property was a less formal garden, currently a riot of color. There was also something odd. Tucked between the rose garden and the masses of foxglove, delphinium, poppies, iris, lupins, and a variety of low-growing flowers Abby couldn't name, was something solid and green. Something that appeared to be made of grass, even though it was two or three feet above the ground. She moved forward to investigate.

Abby frowned down at the odd grass-covered rectangles, trying to remember something the earl had said when talking about the gardens at Arbor Cottage. *Medieval*. The arbor was an imitation of medieval design . . . and so were these benches. The grass-covered rectangles were places where people could sit to admire the gardens, roses to one side, flowering borders on the other. Spreading her skirt, she sat down on one of the turf benches. Her contemplation of the beauty the old Earl of Langley had created for Clarissa Beaupré did not, however, last for long, as the raucous cry of a peacock split the air. So far, she had been attempting to ignore the proud and strutting males who seemed to regard her with great disdain as she moved through their domain. Even in her new finery, which felt like false plumage, she experienced an empathy with the drab peahens. And the brilliant-colored prancing males? Oh, yes, they reminded her of her original resolve. These mincing foppish creatures were the perfect symbols of the British aristocracy.

Wrong. The peacocks might be representative of males of the last century with their colorful raiment so false even their heads were disguised beneath elaborate wigs of white.

But Jared Verney and his brother Myles? Arrogant, yes, but useless strutting peacocks they most certainly were not. Which was why she was escaping to the garden, where she might hide and think on this strange British world, which was not at all what she had expected. Hopefully, the peacocks would not follow her into the shade of the arbor. Abby left her comfortable turf seat and followed a maze of pebbled paths, which eventually brought her to the long mound of green, which took up a third of the width of the garden's rear wall.

Traditionally, her cousin Langley had said, medieval arbors were constructed of interlaced willow, white thorn, or hazel. Sometimes, until a more permanent covering of honeysuckle, roses, or grapes grew up to enclose the structure, fast-growing vines such as cucumber or melon were planted. This arbor, Abby noted as she approached, had had fifty years to complete its growth. The scent of roses and honeysuckle was almost overpowering. The buzz of insects, also delighting in the arbor, grew louder.

Abby paused at the entrance. The arbor was a tunnel thirty or forty feet long, perhaps ten feet wide, its roof a rounded arch, every inch covered by a mass of twisted vines. Along each side were wooden seats, designed for two, a small table between each set of seats. A *bower,* Abby thought. This was the private retreat mentioned in ancient tales. She ventured inside, wandering the length of the enclosure. The insect sounds grew louder, but the twittering of birds, the shrill call of the peacocks faded. She sank onto one of the benches, awed by the effectiveness of this shield from the world. In times of hardship and violence her ancestors had retreated to shelters like this, to fragrant, beautiful places of peace. And the elder Jared Verney, Earl of Langley, had re-created this exquisite shelter for his courtesan, Clarissa Beaupré. Her shield from the harsh judgmental world around her.

The romance of it cut straight to Abby's heart. She, Abigail Todd of Boston, Massachusetts, who prided herself on her pragmatic outlook on life, was sitting in the bower of an infamous courtesan and . . . *reveling* in it. Visions of Jared, her cousin Langley, hovered in the shadows around her. They called him The Indifferent Earl, Mrs. Greaves had told her. But the soubriquet did not fit. At least not today. When he looked at her, his pewter eyes had glowed with warmth. He was Jared Verney, her friend.

Abby suspected she was going to spend a good deal of time over the next two months calming her heated thoughts in the seclusion of the green bower that had given Arbor Cottage its name.

> *My dear Abigail,*
>   *Your first task is an easy one, for I do not wish you to be discouraged. But, of course, I would not expect a grandchild of mine to be fainthearted. I merely ask you to deliver a letter and this small trinket to Mr. Aldis Kirkby, whose direction is given below. Quite simple, is it not? But, remember, Jared must accompany you. You are not to venture out alone, Abigail, not even with a trusted female companion.*
>   *Your loving grandmother, Clarissa Beaupré*

"It's a gold locket," Abby said, digging into the small packet attached to the letter.

"Open it," Jared advised.

A small curl of cinnamon red gleamed up at them. "A lock of her hair," Abby mused.

"From when she was young," Jared agreed. "The question is, why did she not enclose it with Mr. Kirkby's letter. Why did she want you to see it before it was given away?"

"So I could compare it with my own?" Abby ventured. *For the romance of it? So I would know that fifty or more years later she still expected a Mr. Aldis Kirkby to appreciate the gift of a lock of a courtesan's hair?*

If Jared had any thoughts on the subject, he kept them to himself. Glancing at Mr. Kirby's direction, he said, "It is not far. If we leave by nine tomorrow morning, we can be back before dark."

"I did not care for that remark about not venturing out

with a trusted female companion," Hannah Greaves huffed
from her corner of the drawing room sofa. "She cannot have
meant that you were to go alone. Improper, most improper."

Abby snatched the letter back from Jared, who was about
to pocket it. She reread the passage. Before she could advance her own opinion, however, he spoke up in what Abby
thought of as his "earl voice." A lordly decree with which no
one was expected to argue. "I believe Clarissa only meant
that Abby was not to go on one of these quests without me.
I see nothing in her letter that prohibits a chaperon. And you
are quite right, Mrs. Greaves, Miss Todd cannot go jaunting
about the countryside with me on anything more than the
simple drive we took yesterday afternoon."

"Just so," Hannah approved. "Rest assured we shall be
ready at nine, my lord."

Abby opened her mouth to protest these high-handed
arrangements. This was *her* quest. *Her* grandmother. She
was an independent woman fast approaching thirty. There
had been no female to govern her movements since she was
fifteen . . .

Impossible man! Did he have any idea how much he annoyed her when he seized the reins right out of her hands?

Slowly, Abby clamped her teeth over her tongue. It was
going to be a most interesting summer.

Chapter Five

The manor house, not far from Wells, was modest but well kept, with a fine stand of copper beech trees adding color to the park. Mr. Aldis Kirkby might not boast a title, but he appeared to live the comfortable life of a country gentleman. He was also, the travelers soon discovered, exceedingly old, well beyond the expected span of years. But that was scarcely surprising, Abby realized. Her grandmother was thought to have been somewhere around five and seventy when she died, though none in her household had ever been made privy to her true age. The men she had known were presumably her age or older. It was remarkable there were eight left. Then, again, perhaps not all the commissions were bequests to Clarissa Beaupré's lovers.

"Forgive me for not rising." The voice that issued from the thin-faced figure bundled deep in shawls in the shadows of a wing chair was little more than a wisp of sound.

"Not at all," Abby murmured, dropping into a respectful curtsy.

"Sir," said Jared, bowing. "Forgive our intrusion but, as I told your housekeeper, we are fulfilling a last request of Miss Clarissa Beaupré. It is good of you to see us."

Which was exactly what Abby had been about to say when her words were stepped on by the abominable earl, who had now forged further ahead, introducing Miss Todd and Mrs. Greaves.

"Langley," Mr. Kirkby acknowledged, peering at Jared's card. "I am honored, my lord. Pray be seated." A wrinkled hand crept out from beneath the layers of shawls, waving them into nearby chairs. Silence reigned as the wizened old gentleman studied his youngest visitor. "You've the look of her," he told Abby, "though 'tis plain you're as respectable as a blancmange, so no need to fly up into the boughs. You'll forgive an old man for plain-speaking. It's the prerogative of my age."

Abby was not at all sure she cared to be compared to a dull white pudding. Since coming to Arbor Cottage, she had begun to suspect there was such a thing as too respectable. "I am an American, sir, and we too believe in plain-speaking. I had no idea Clarissa was my grandmother until she bequeathed me her home here in Somerset."

Mr. Kirkby's eyes gleamed. "And am I to discover you are a long-lost granddaughter?"

Abby's gasp was echoed by Hannah Greaves. "Oh, my goodness, I—I don't think so," Abby stammered. "Truly, I never thought of such a thing! I was under the impression that my father was the result of her long alliance with— Pray forgive me! My tongue runs on wheels."

"We are here," said the earl, coming to her rescue, "because Clarissa Beaupré asked Miss Todd to deliver letters to a small group of her former acquaintances. You, sir, are one of them. Truthfully, we have no idea what is in the letter, although we have both viewed the trinket which accompanies it."

Abby fumbled in her reticule, producing the letter and the locket. "Shall I light a brace of candles for you, sir," she inquired, "or would you prefer to read the letter in private?" If he did, she would be more disappointed than she had thought possible.

Abby hovered, wondering if she should offer to open the locket. Mr. Kirkby was staring as if at a ghost, dangling the gold heart and chain from white hands on which blue veins were clearly visible.

"Candles?" he murmured. "Yes, by all means." Jared leaped up to do the old man's bidding, waving Abby away. Standing behind the wing chair, he held the candelabra where it would shine directly onto the parchment. He was much too well brought up to read other people's mail, Jared told himself, but somehow his eyes refused to look away.

My dear Aldis,

I am writing to you for the sake of Sentiment. You may not remember me. Perhaps I was just another young thing, shy and inept and not worth the guineas demanded by the house. But you were my first professional acquaintance, and I have never forgotten. For the sake of your Gentleness and Kindness to a young woman who had no idea of the seriousness of the road she was taking, I wish you to have this locket. I have been told that you married and are blessed with children, grandchildren, and great-grandchildren. I am happy for you. I send you my own grandchild to deliver this letter and locket. You are a good man, Aldis Kirkby. Please forgive an old woman, who was not all she should have been, for saying so.

Clarissa Beaupré, who has not forgotten

Sentiment, Jared scoffed. His grandfather had allowed sentiment to rule his life, and look what that had done! His own father, succumbing to indulgence and inertia, had failed to repair the losses sentiment had incurred. Therefore he, the younger Jared Verney, had trained himself to eschew sentiment in all its forms. Oh, he was fond enough of Myles, and of his mother—as long as she stayed in her house in Bath—but sentiment was insidious, enticing a man away from his duties, from the serious responsibilities of noblesse oblige.

Abby snapped open the locket, showing it to the old man. The gnarled fingers reached out, touched the tiny cinnamon curl; thin brittle lips cracked into a smile. "Such a beauty she was," Mr. Kirkby sighed. "It wasn't just the one time. We had several nights together after that first, but my father died, and I was forced to leave London, find a wife, set up my nursery. By the time I went back to town, Clarissa Bivens had become Clarissa Beaupré and was being kept by a marquess." Aldis Kirkby shook his head, smiled. "Am I

wicked to speak of such things to you, Miss Todd? Please
forgive an old man his fond reminiscences."

"There is nothing to forgive," Abby murmured, repressing tears to match those brimming in the old man's eyes.
"We will leave you to your memories, sir. In my grandmother's name, I thank you for seeing us." Briefly, she
pressed the wrinkled white hand that was still gripping the
locket. The letter lay open in his lap. "Good day, Mr.
Kirkby." The earl bowed, Mrs. Greaves curtsied. The three
visitors left the drawing room and were escorted out by the
housekeeper who was almost as ancient as her master.

"Well, that was not so bad," Hannah Greaves declared
when they were settled in the earl's carriage. "I think we
may survive seven more without cutting up our peace."

"If that was easy," Abby said, "I am not at all sure I wish
to discover the ones which are more 'taxing.'"

Jared agreed. The cloying aura of sentimentality must
have drained Abigail as it had himself. To see a man of more
than eighty years with tears in his eyes for a woman he had
not seen in well over half a century . . . Jared could not think
of a single female who had ever touched his heart long
enough to be remembered past the next week. Oh, back in
his salad days he had allowed himself to pine over a few
sweet young things. But his grandfather's headstrong love
for a courtesan had cured him of ever being caught in *that*
trap. No, by God, not Jared Reignald Fitzroy Verney. *Never!*
Not that he wouldn't mind discovering if the old girl's passion had been handed down to her oh-so-prim-and-proper
granddaughter from Boston. He wasn't a monk, after all,
though he had been living like one for some time now.

A loud sniff from Mrs. Greaves, the vigorous blowing of
her nose, brought the earl out of his reverie. As sentimental
an old fool as Kirkby, Jared grumbled to himself. Hell and
damnation, he hoped the other seven letters weren't like this
one. Abigail, however . . . He regarded his American cousin
with interest. Stoic, that was Abigail Todd. He thought he'd
caught the shine of tears for a moment there, but now her
face was blank. She leaned back against the squabs, eyes
closed, devoid of any sign of emotion. An admirable

woman, Abigail Todd. But surely the fire that flared when she spoke of her country's wars with Britain indicated there was more beneath her bonnet than a mass of cinnamon curls?

Before she returned home, Jared vowed he was going to find out.

As they dined that evening in a private room in the Pike and Musket Inn, Abby decided, with apologies to her beloved Jonathan, that Jared Verney was quite the handsomest man she had ever met. If cynicism touched the planes and angles of his distinguished features, it was nothing more than she expected from an overindulged nobleman. He had endured today's journey with an equanimity with which she could find no fault. That he was revolted by the sentimentality he had witnessed was clear. He fairly bristled with it. And yet not a murmur, not a single complaint had passed his lips. But he had not been above reading Clarissa's letter, Abby was certain of it. Would he ever divulge its contents? She had no idea. She had known him for what? . . . all of three days. An unknown quantity was her cousin Jared. Yet today he had come through with flying colors.

"I would wish to reciprocate your hospitality," Abby told him. "Would you dine with us tomorrow? Your brother as well, of course. If he does not think we might offer him poison."

Jared nodded graciously while refilling her wineglass. "We have lived quietly since returning from town a fortnight since. I gladly accept for both of us." He turned to Hannah Greaves. "If you do not object to lively conversation, ma'am? I fear my brother and Miss Todd tend to come to cuffs at the slightest provocation."

Mrs. Greaves chuckled. "Indeed, my lord, I have been told of your brother. A fire-eater indeed. He and Miss Todd are well matched."

Well matched. The Earl of Langley discovered he did not care for the phrase. A decidedly unwelcome reaction. He might indulge in a few moments of flirtation with his reluctant cousin, more as a tease than anything else, but he was the last man on earth to succumb to the allure of a redheaded woman. His grandfather might have been a fool. The present Jared Verney was not.

"Indeed, I forgot to ask about your mother," Abigail exclaimed. "Does she live with you as well?"

"No, Miss Todd," the earl responded. "She enjoys the society of her friends in Bath, with occasional sojourns to Langley House in London. She is rarely seen at Langley Park. She—ah—never cared for the place." *Blast the chit! She was laughing.*

"I take it your mother was not bosom bows with my grandmother."

"Indeed not."

Jared's shock at the thought of contact between his mother and her father-in-law's mistress was palpable. "Then I shall not extend her an invitation to dine," Abby replied with perfect composure.

Hannah Greaves, her statuesque shoulders noticeably shaking, suggested the ladies refresh themselves before continuing the short remaining journey home. The earl was left to frown into his brandy snifter, wondering how years of milk and biscuits and a boy's fascination with an aging *demimondaine* could have brought him to what was looking more like a crossroads in his life with every succeeding minute.

The next evening, after a meal fine enough to prompt the Earl of Langley to send his compliments to the cook, in spite of the fact she was a local and a mere female, Jared and his brother Myles confined themselves to a single glass of port before joining the ladies. A matter of a few short steps as the drawing room of Arbor Cottage was on the ground floor, for only two guest apartments, servants' rooms and storage were above stairs.

"Do you play, Miss Todd?" Jared inquired. "I had the piano tuned so you might make use of it."

When Abby, once again annoyed by the earl's assumption of authority, failed to respond, Hannah murmured, "Very kind, I'm sure. Do give us a tune, my dear."

"I fear my duties as a headmistress do not allow me sufficient time for practice," Abby demurred, even as she emphasized that she was not one of the idle rich. "Your ears will be less assaulted if we confine ourselves to conversation."

"For shame, Miss Todd," Captain Verney taunted. "I had not thought you fainthearted."

"Perhaps you play, Captain?" Abby suggested sweetly. She turned limpid green eyes on Jared. "Or you, my lord?"

Accepting her challenge, the earl strode to the bench of the pianoforte, flipped up the tails of his black jacket, and seated himself. A chortle escaped Abby as he launched into a rollicking country tune, which she recognized as a song that had been parodied in the fledgling United States into a revolutionary ditty. She strongly suspected Jared Verney knew it. A glance at his brother revealed a dark scowl.

"Splendid!" Abby declared when the earl sat back with an ill-concealed twinkle of satisfaction. "Do give us another." Mrs. Greaves echoed her praise.

"I, too, am out of practice," Jared confessed. After a moment's thought, he added, "I fear Bach is better played on the harpsichord, but I shall make the attempt."

"I had no idea gentlemen played the piano," Hannah Greaves declared when the earl finished what could only be termed a highly creditable performance.

"You may be sure I shall not play after *that,* my lord!" Abby vowed. "I confess to being impressed."

"How about you, brother?" Jared challenged.

"My talent is with the saber," the captain hedged, "but I know ladies are required to learn such things. Miss Todd could scarcely become a schoolmistress without demonstrating talent on the pianoforte. It simply is not done."

"It is if you own the school," Abigail retorted, any semblance of company manners flown out through the open windows into the garden.

"Ah," said Myles Verney with a decided smirk, "then that is how a chit of a girl became a headmistress."

"A fact no different than buying an officer's rank!"

"In an army which would not have been needed if your

country had not spread revolution to France! A vicious canker we've had to fight twenty years to wipe out."

"Myles!" The earl jumped to his feet.

"Abigail!" cried Hannah Greaves.

The protests were too late. Miss Todd flounced to the piano and launched into a stirring rendition of "Yankee Doodle." Captain Verney leaped to his feet and stalked out of the room.

When the last defiant notes died away, the Earl of Langley turned to Hannah Greaves. "Would you be kind enough to leave us, ma'am?" he said in a voice of steel. Mrs. Greaves scurried out without a thought for her role as chaperon.

While Jared took time to compose his thoughts—as a man with power must if he did not wish to become a tyrant—he succumbed to the temptation of examining his hostess, who was still perched on the piano bench. Her color was high, which only enhanced the beauty that was so similar to her infamous ancestor. Her gown of soft green silk might not be in the latest mode, nor its décolletage as low as that favored by the London *ton*, but her shoulders were creamy, the glimpse of rounded flesh beneath her silver net fichu most intriguing. But appreciation of her beauty would not temper his scold.

"There is no excuse for my brother," the earl said. "I will see that he apologizes. But you, Miss Todd, amaze me. How can you possibly govern a school for young ladies when you cannot govern yourself?"

"How dare you?" Abby cried.

"I am an earl. I may dare anything I choose."

"You are no gentleman, sir!"

"My lord," Jared murmured, well aware of how she would take his correction.

Abby came to her feet, fists clenched at her sides. "You are abominable, Jared Verney. I cannot imagine how Clarissa put up with your grandfather for forty years."

"She was well paid, was she not?"

"Oo-oh!" Abby felt tears spurt into her eyes. This . . . *aristocrat* should not be able to hurt her. Yet in four days' time she had come to care about his opinion, wished to have his good will. And, yes, wished for his admiration. What woman would not?

"My apologies," Jared said stiffly. "My anger with Myles has spilled onto you. But it takes two to make a quarrel, I beg you to remember that. The summer is long, our tasks many. We cannot afford to be at daggers drawn over battles long since over."

"Yes, of course," Abby sniffed, searching in her reticule for a handkerchief.

"When do you wish to open the second letter?"

"After your brother's apology."

When hell freezes over. Jared rocked back on his heels, closed his eyes. "You will have it in the morning," he declared after a significant silence. "Shall we open the next letter the following day?" Glumly, Abby nodded. "Then I shall bid you good night."

Abby collapsed back onto the piano bench. As much as it rankled, the earl was entirely justified in his scold. She was not the stern pattern-card of propriety her position as a headmistress demanded. It was passion and pigheadedness that had launched Miss Todd's Academy for Young Ladies against every bit of common practice and advice. And she had made it a rousing success. The price she had paid was the repression of all personal passion and any further rebellion still lurking beneath her calm unruffled surface.

And now . . . five days at Arbor Cottage and her standards were eroding. She had battled Myles Verney like the lowest fishwife on the pier. And her thoughts of Jared Verney did not bear examination. They were shameful. She would not play the courtesan's grandchild. Absolutely not! Yet the temptation . . . ah, the temptation was there. How she was to survive seven more of Clarissa's commissions with Cousin Jared at her side, she could not imagine.

Torture, pure torture.

Attached to Abigail Todd's next letter from her grandmother were three more short missives, fastened together with a black ribbon, the topmost bearing the name of Mr.

James Wetherby of Southampton. There was no gold locket or trinket of any kind.

> *My dear Abigail,*
> *Your next assignment will not, I fear, be as easy as your first. James Wetherby is not a good man. Not even by the sometimes bizarre standards of the ton. Approach him with caution, with Jared at your side. Wetherby is not to be taken lightly. You are to return to him some letters. You are <u>not</u> to read them, my child! They are between Mr. Wetherby and myself. A bit of old business which I now must end. Do not—I repeat, do <u>not</u>—visit this man alone. He is a bounder. And, believe me, I have reason to know.*
> *Your loving grandmother, Clarissa*

"Good God!" Abby exclaimed. "She makes him sound like a monster."

"It is many years since I've heard much talk of him," Jared said. "Wetherby was a notorious gamester, as I recall. The kind even my father, who was exceedingly careless, warned me about. Wetherby clung to the fringes of society, fleecing young men on their first trip to town, making an occasional attempt on an heiress. I believe he moved in the Lade set at one time, forty or more years ago. Clarissa is correct. He is not a good man to know."

"But, like Mr. Kirkby, he must be quite old now. Scarcely a threat."

"Perhaps," Jared shrugged. "If we are fortunate, he will have passed on since Clarissa wrote this note, and we may burn the letters with no regrets."

"You are outrageous, my lord," Abby informed him roundly.

"Speaking of outrageous," Jared drawled, "I trust my brother paid you a visit?"

"Indeed," Abby grimaced. "Of five minutes' duration. The captain ground out his apology, and I reciprocated. Neither of us guarantees we shall mind our tongues in future."

"You discussed it?" Jared inquired with raised brows.

"It was mutually understood."

"Ah." The earl discovered he was repressing a smile. Ridiculous! The situation was not amusing. Far from it.

"Mr. Wetherby lives in Southampton, I see," Abby said. "Is that far?"

"Far enough to require a journey of two or three days overall. I trust this does not upset you?"

"I have come all the way from America, my lord. The prospect of further travel is scarcely daunting."

"And you, Mrs. Greaves?" the earl asked politely.

"I came on this trip for the adventure of it, my lord, as did my dear Abby. We will be ready whenever you say the word."

"The day after tomorrow then. I prefer time to make proper arrangements so I know we will have nothing but the best accommodations available."

"Very thoughtful, I'm sure," said Hannah Greaves. "Most kind, my lord."

"I shall have great expectations," Abby murmured. Provocatively.

"You, my dear Abigail, are a minx," Jared declared with certainty. He stood, raised her hand to his lips, turning it at the last moment to press a breath of a kiss on the inside of her wrist. "Until Friday then," he murmured, and was gone, leaving his American cousin quivering from head to toe.

Chapter Six

*S*oberly clad in the brown wren dress, which blended into the weathered wood of the arbor seat, Abigail Todd contemplated her life. Had she made a mull of the last ten years? Proud of her accomplishments in educating young women of modest means, she had thought herself content. After having her youthful starry-eyed dreams ripped from her at the age of barely eighteen, she had plunged into teaching with all the fervor of a drowning woman's grip on a piece of flotsam. Why, then, did she now feel as if a long miasma of pain was being lifted from her? Why did she feel herself blossoming like a flower raising its face to the sun? Could the serious, exceptionally proper woman who was a headmistress in Boston be the same person who had looked back at her this morning from Clarissa Beaupré's decadently elaborate mirror?

Abby doubted it. Even after she had donned the well-worn brown gown, the eager-eyed beauty in the mirror more closely resembled the voluptuous painting on the wall than the American spinster who had boarded the *Nancy Belle* in Boston harbor. It was as if she had taken one look at her grandmother's flagrant display of flesh and red hair and known she had been living a lie. Not that she admired her grandmother's occupation, Abby corrected hastily, nor wished to emulate her, but the freedom to be herself . . . to allow her spirit, even her temper, to show—ah, that was liberty indeed. She was like a long-starved green plant springing to life after a drought. How *could* she have allowed herself to grow so staid?

A bee droned by within a foot of Abby's nose. She merely smiled and watched it go. Why should a bee not enjoy the fragrant masses of honeysuckle blossoms? And his sting? Abby discounted the risk. The world she had grown up in was full of retributions, admonitions, stern rules of conduct. And now, though it sorely pained her to admit it, she was discovering the allure in what she had always thought of as British decadence. Jared Verney was not a decadent aristocrat. Arrogant and annoying, yes, but a surprisingly admirable human being. Even his disdainful hot-tempered brother, who had fought for what he believed to be right, was not to be scorned. And her grandmother, the courtesan, was now revealed as a woman capable of great love and strong sentiment.

So where did that leave Abigail Todd of Boston?

Confused. Depressed. Fearful.

She had thought herself strong. But did she have enough courage to seize this new world that was opening before her? If she allowed her broadened mind-set to add color to her life, would she be able to return to Boston and take up her duties as before? Or had this week in Arbor Cottage already, insidiously, changed her life forever?

"Abigail? Abigail! Where are you, my dear?" Hannah Greaves's voice penetrated Abby's fog. "Come at once. Your new clothes have arrived."

Trust Hannah to stick her head out the back door and shout, never thinking to send a maid. A smile suddenly lit Abby's face. She supposed the household staff, as well as the arrogant earl and his brother, had a thing or two to learn from the Americans as well. A bit of clear Yankee breeze wafting through stuffy British halls.

Abby hastened to the arbor entrance, breathing in the scent of damask roses, which had gone unnoticed a few minutes earlier. "Coming!" she called. Peacocks and peahens, alike, scuttled out of the way as she strode toward the house.

*   *   *

On the first night of their journey to Southampton, Abby requested that Mrs. Greaves go up to bed before her. "Five minutes," Hannah declared, "or I shall come down to get you." As the older woman departed, she carefully left the door to the inn's private dining room fully open.

Jared's eyes were twinkling as he shifted his gaze to his cousin Abigail. "A most proper woman, your Mrs. Greaves. I wonder what she thinks we can get up to in five minutes? She might have granted us ten at the very least."

"Your humor is wasting time," Abby declared. "For a full five days I have wished to know what was in Mr. Kirkby's letter. And do not say you did not read it, for I shall not believe you!"

"Sentimental claptrap," Jared tossed out. "You would not wish to know."

"Yes, I would. It is not at all fair for you to know and not tell me."

Jared retrieved a brandy snifter from the sideboard, poured out a glass for Abby, and set it down in front of her. "You are not averse to a glass, I trust? I find myself in need of a strong restorative when I recall that letter." He scowled at the amber liquid in his own glass.

"Come now, it could not have been that bad," Abby coaxed. She took a tentative sip, fell into a fit of coughing.

"I want you to know that is some of the finest brandy I have ever tasted," the earl informed her. "Undoubtedly smuggled. It's high time you developed an appreciation for such excellence."

Abby caught her breath, put her snifter firmly from her, shoving it across the table toward her abominable cousin. "Do not try to distract me," she choked out. "The letter, if you please."

Jared leaned back in his chair, closed his eyes. "Let me think a moment," he said, glad enough for an excuse to shut out the sight of Abigail in her obviously new Bond Street finery. Her figure-hugging gown of soft beige, smartly decorated with rows of gold buttons, was both eye-catching and daring. Not at all what he'd come to expect of his circumspect American cousin. And, having put her bonnet aside while dining, Abby's reddish-brown curls, though confined at the nape by a ribbon, had managed to froth about her porcelain face in enticing ringlets. A delectable vision. One he was determined to ignore.

"Clarissa said she was writing to him for the sake of sentiment," Jared told her. "She was not at all certain he would even remember her. But he had been gentle . . . kind, and she wished him to have the lock of her hair. She knew he had married, had children and grandchildren. She wanted him to know she was happy for him." Jared shrugged, tossed back his brandy in one swallow. Abigail blinked.

"And that made you angry," she mused.

"What makes you think so?"

"Perhaps scornful would be a better word," Abby said. "You glowered as you read, and for hours thereafter."

"I am not an advocate of sentimentality," the earl agreed, idly swirling fresh brandy in the snifter held in long aristocratic fingers.

"Why?" Abby challenged.

"Look what it did to my grandfather."

"Ah!" Abby pounced. "And, pray tell, what *did* it do to your grandfather?"

Silver eyes turned to charcoal in the flickering candlelight. "This is scarcely the time nor the place to discuss an affair which lasted forty years."

"Tell me," Abby insisted. "I need to know what was so terrible about your grandfather loving my grandmother." She bit her lip. "Other than the obvious, of course," she muttered beneath her breath.

Jared got up, stalked to the fireplace, bare of logs in this, the early days of July. "Your precious grandmother bankrupted the Verney family. He gave her everything she desired . . . and probably a good deal more he thought of on his own. Where it all went, we'll never know. The Verneys were once good for an income of twenty thousand a year. Now I struggle to put thatch on the tenants' cottages."

"But you live like King Midas himself," Abby protested.

Jared pushed off the mantel, sank back into his chair. "I confess to a modicum of exaggeration. We are not about to

be taken up by the bailiffs. My mother lives well. Myles and
I are comfortable, my tenants content with their lot. But a remarkable amount of money has disappeared from the estate.
And looking at what remains in Arbor Cottage, I can only
wonder at it. For all her fine things, Clarissa's furnishings
cannot account for a quarter of what has been lost."

"Did they travel?" Abby asked.

"To the best of my knowledge, they never left Somerset.
Oh, my grandfather made brief sojourns to London, an occasional shooting trip to Scotland, but that's all I know of."
Jared ran a hand through his heavy chestnut hair. "That's the
mystery of it. My grandfather lived simply enough. Clarissa
was surrounded by luxury, but never left the cottage. To the
best of my knowledge, neither gamed nor gave remarkable
sums to charity."

"Bad investments?"

Jared sighed. "Possibly. It's a mystery my father inherited
but never solved. He was content to live a comfortable life
without taxing himself over why the family circumstances
were reduced. He was fond of riding to hounds," the earl
reminisced softly. "Spent as much time in Melton country as
he could. Until he took a hedge with an unseen ditch beyond."

"Then he was not earl for long?"

"Five years only."

"I am sorry," Abby said softly, her earlier pique forgotten.
She reached a hand across the table, her fingers closing over
his.

A loud cough interrupted the moment. "Abigail," Hannah
declared, though not without a note of indulgence, "it is high
time you came upstairs to bed."

"Yes, ma'am," Abby murmured meekly, snatching her
hand back from Jared's. "Good night, my lord." She fled.

At close to two hundred years old, Boston was the New
World's grand old city. Only New Orleans could rival its
claim. But as the three travelers approached the vast waterfront in Southampton, Abby realized Boston was a raw infant compared to this English port city. Many of the

buildings clinging to the shoreline were so ancient they seemed to sag in place. The harbor itself was so covered in towering masts the water was scarcely visible. Abby experienced a pang for her country's honor. The fledgling states were so proud of their globe-circling merchant fleet, but England must surely be the hub of the shipping universe. Would the United States ever catch up?

"Impressed?" Jared inquired.

"Yes," Abby breathed. "Are we seeing the sights, my lord, or does Mr. Wetherby live along the harbor?"

"Both. His direction appears to be a place of business close by. We may presume, I believe, that he lives there as well." The earl opened a panel behind his head and directed Moorhead, the coachman, to make inquiries.

The Red Rover had pretensions, Abby could plainly see as the coach halted before the front entrance. The brick building took up a full third of the block. White lace curtains shone at the windows of the two upper floors. Colorful flowers drooped from window boxes extending the width of the front. An inn, a tavern, Mr. Wetherby's residence? Perhaps all three.

The barkeep's lip curled when Jared, entering the establishment alone, inquired after Mr. James Wetherby. "Goin' t'have a bit of trouble, m'lord," the burly man told him. "Less'n you want t' take a ride up t' ta boneyard."

"Mr. Wetherby is deceased?"

"Got that right, guv'nor. Dead as a doornail these five months past."

Greatly relieved, Jared thanked the man and turned toward the door. The sooner they were out of this neighborhood the better.

"One moment!"

Jared recognized the tone. The sharp authority of a man on his own turf. A man accustomed to giving orders. The earl turned.

The voice belonged to a man of perhaps fifty years. Tall, powerful, dressed in jacket, shirt, and breeches not markedly different from a country squire. His dark hair showed little sign of gray. Shrewd blue eyes gleamed from a face still lean and hard. Not a man Jared cared to meet in an alley on a dark night.

"It's not every day we get a toff in the Red Rover, my lord. May I ask what your business was with my father?"

Moving away from the bar, Jared lowered his voice so only the younger Mr. Wetherby could hear. Tersely, he explained his errand, begged Mr. Wetherby's pardon for troubling him, and declared that they would consign Clarissa Beaupré's three letters to the flames.

"Now, I don't know about that, m'lord," said Broderick Wetherby. "Seems like those letters are mine now. A great curiosity, my father getting letters from the queen of the tarts. Would have thought she'd have been well above his touch." Wetherby rubbed the side of his nose. "Seems like curiosity is a bad itch, m'lord. Needs to be scratched, it does."

Jared opened his mouth to tell the man to go to the devil, then snapped his jaws shut. He had not failed to note Abby's reaction each time he seized the authority to which he was so accustomed. An arbitrary decision here could cost him more than he was willing to lose.

"I shall consult with Miss Todd, who is outside in my carriage," he replied coolly. Mr. Wetherby, not a trusting soul, followed him out.

"Of course he may have the letters if he wishes them," Abby declared, thrusting them into Jared's hand. "There was no injunction against giving them to his heir."

"Abigail, I don't believe—"

"Give them to him," Abby insisted.

"I doubt they're full of sweet nothings."

"If he is his father's heir, then he is welcome to them," Abby insisted.

Broderick Wetherby's head appeared behind the earl. "Ladies." He nodded curtly. "I want to hear more of this. Will you come inside? We're not without a cup of tea above stairs."

For some reason, perhaps because the earl's eyes were flashing a warning, Abby accepted the invitation. She had journeyed to England for adventure. This was it. "Come,

Hannah," she declared, and was forced to push Jared aside as she descended from the coach.

True to his word, Broderick Wetherby led them up a narrow staircase and into a suite of rooms that reflected the colorful cheer of the flowers in the window boxes outside. Someone took pride in these rooms above a waterfront inn.

"Mary. Mary!" Wetherby shouted through the door into the hallway. "Tea for our guests. And be quick about it!" He waved his visitors to seats covered in brightly colored chintz. "My wife's off at the market. Good woman. But the maid's a bit slow, if you know what I mean." He remained on his feet, scowling. "I suppose you think I've come down in the world, my pa mixing with the *ton* as he did?"

"Not at all," Abby countered swiftly. "I am an American, sir, and firmly believe a man should work for his keep." *And you may take that any way you like, cousin Jared!*

"Well, now . . ." For a moment Broderick Wetherby's sharp eyes showed a suspicion of a smile. "I'm innkeeper here at the Red Rover. We've a good tavern, two gaming rooms as well. My father never lost his love of a good card game"—he shrugged—"though it's many a year since I thought him an honest man. 'Tis a good living. My family's wanted for naught. Glad enough I was to leave the fops and their follies behind."

He turned to Miss Todd. Abby had retrieved the letters from Jared and was currently clutching them in her lap. "So what is it that brings you here, my lady?"

"I'm a mere miss, Mr. Wetherby," Abby corrected gently. "I am here to settle one of several tasks my grandmother set for me. I assure you I have no idea what is in these letters. They are just as they were given to me. You are indeed Mr. James Wetherby's heir?"

"I am."

"Then these are yours to do with as you see fit." Abby rose gracefully, placing the letters in Broderick Wetherby's hands.

Without hesitation, the innkeeper ripped open the letter addressed to his father. His scowl deepened as he scanned what appeared to be a short missive. "What the devil?" he muttered as he tore open the second. Slowly, he sank into a chair near the window, where the bright sunlight revealed his ruddy face gone pale, a tremor strike his hand. "Bloody hell," he whispered softly, failing to beg the ladies' pardon.

Wetherby ripped open the third, and last, letter. His head fell forward. Mouth agape, he stared at the ornately feminine writing on the parchment. The black ribbon that had wrapped the letters dangled between his knees.

"Was it blackmail?" Abby asked softly. "Oh, pardon me," she cried, "I should not have asked." Neither Hannah Greaves nor the earl chided her.

Broderick Wetherby raised his head, still looking stunned. Abby had not thought he was a man who could ever appear anguished. He did so now.

"This answers an ancient mystery, my la—miss. Each year, at Michelmas, my father sent a single guinea to a Miss Clarissa Beaupré of Vernhampton. I never knew about it until his later years when I had to take care of it myself. I could not help but wonder at his connection with a woman whose name was still spoken with awe decades after she'd left London, but he refused to tell me of it." Broderick Wetherby tapped the third letter against his knee. "But it's no wonder I sometimes got the impression they had not been friends."

The innkeeper of the Red Rover closed his eyes, leaned his head back into his chair. At that point they were interrupted by the arrival of tea. When all had cups in their hands, Broderick Wetherby looked up into three expectant pairs of eyes.

"I'm a hard man," he said. "Takes a lot to surprise me." He turned to the earl. "You were right, my lord. 'Twould have been better to burn these letters. I would've had my illusions that my father once enjoyed the favor of one of the world's most beautiful women. Instead . . . instead, I discover he's a murderer. That he beat a women to death in a brothel these many years ago. And that Clarissa Beaupré, who knew of it, blackmailed him into marrying my mother."

A gasp from Hannah Greaves punctuated the innkeeper's

story. Abby's eyes went wide. The earl leaned forward, readying himself for a swift reaction to almost anything.

"It seems my mother was the daughter of the secretary of Clarissa's current lover. She was with child. Myself, I suppose. The Beaupré used her knowledge from years past to force my father to marry her. Evidently, the payment of the guinea was her way of reminding him he was never safe. Her revenge, y' might say. This first letter, the one to my father, absolves him of further payment. The other two are her sworn statement to Bow Street about the beating and a personal letter to my mother revealing all. Although she never sent them, it's plain she wanted my father to know the letters existed. That her threat was genuine."

"I am sorry, truly sorry," Abby said, shocked by what she had done in giving Broderick Wetherby the letters intended for his father. "You will not, of course, tell your mother?"

"My mother is long gone," Wetherby replied. "But, no, this is not a tale I will tell my wife or my children. It ends here."

Jared caught Abby's eye. She nodded. "Then we will take our leave," he said. Standing, he held out his hand to help her up, sensing his cousin's knees were far from steady.

"Thank you for your hospitality, Mr. Wetherby," Abby managed. "I truly regret we have cut up your peace."

Broderick Wetherby stood foursquare in front of the window, his solid bulk nearly blotting out the sunlight. "I run an inn on the waterfront in one of the greatest ports in the world, miss. I'm not easily upset by anything. 'Tis scarce pleasant to discover my father a murderer. Then again, I would not have cared to be born on the wrong side of the blanket. So it seems I owe your granny some thanks. And you, miss, you have her spirit. Coming here could not have been easy. I wish you better luck with your next bequest."

Silence reigned as the Verney coachman turned away from the teeming harbor. All three travelers were glad to leave Southampton behind.

Chapter Seven

*W*hen the gloom permeating the coach persisted past Salisbury, Jared deemed it time to break the silence. "There was nothing else we could have done, Abigail. No way to avoid what happened."

"We could have written ahead, ascertained that Mr. James Wetherby was dead, and destroyed the letters without ever going near Southampton," Abby shot back bitterly, the direction of her thoughts for the past few hours all too apparent.

"You have eight commissions to execute within as many weeks. Corresponding with each and every one in advance is quite impossible."

"You said we should burn the letters," Abby pointed out. "It was I who insisted on putting them in Mr. Broderick Wetherby's hands." Though her voice was calm, a visible shudder racked her body.

"Once he knew of the letters, Abigail, there was no going back. He *would* have them, and I did not deem the matter worth pistols at dawn. Not even worth a good mill."

Abby's gaze flew to his face, her lips twitching toward a smile. "I think you would have found yourself measuring your length on the floor if you had."

"I want you to know I am good with my fives; Gentleman Jackson himself has told me so." The earl's indignant words were belied by the twinkle in his eyes.

Abby began to feel a small lightening of her guilt. "He would have taken you," she countered flatly.

"I believe that is what I was trying to say, my dear girl. Mr. Broderick Wetherby would have had his letters whether we wished to give them to him or not. So you may cease suffering from guilt. There are a great many people, you know," Jared added, "who believe that truth is a great healer."

"How can it ever be good to discover your father a murderer?" Abby cried.

"Wetherby was already well aware his father was not an exemplary character. I believe Clarissa's blackmail was more of a surprise than the charge of murder. Fortunately, his mother is no longer alive to be hurt by it."

"Mere chance!"

The earl sighed. "Can you imagine a man like Wetherby running to his mama and telling her the whole?"

"Absurd!" Hannah Greaves declared from her seat next to Abby, where she had been taking in the whole of the argument with considerable interest. "An iron man, that one. I've no doubt he holds half the secrets of Southampton harbor under his hat, with nary a word to a soul."

"At least half," Jared agreed solemnly.

"You are in league!" Abby snapped. "Quite unfair."

"Abigail," said Hannah sternly, "you have just over six weeks left in England and as many tasks yet to fulfill. "You do not have time to quibble over niceties. In fact, we may only hope the other commissions do not take three days on the road to accomplish."

Abby, temper still high, turned her nose to the window. "This is not the same road we took before," she accused, once again glaring at her cousin.

"A slight detour," Jared admitted. "There is something I thought you might enjoy seeing. Since we are in the vicinity, it would be tragic for you to return home without seeing one of Britain's greatest treasures."

Without giving him the satisfaction of a reply, Abby pressed her nose to the glass. She strongly suspected Jared had improvised this jog in their journey to distract her from her melancholy. When, she wondered with a distinct clench around her heart, was the last time a man had made such an effort on her behalf? Abby blinked back a tear.

Dear God in heaven, what was that? "Jared?" she gasped, never taking her eyes from the window.

The earl's cheek brushed hers as he peered out. "Ah, yes, we are nearly there."

"But what is it?" Abby demanded.

"A pile of rocks, my dear. Just a pile of rocks."

"Rocks!" Hannah Greaves exclaimed. "You have taken us out of our way to view a pile of rocks? Then you may very well do it on your own. I shall sit right here while you caper about outside. Rocks, indeed!"

"But, Hannah, they are *enormous*," Abby said.

"Is it a castle?"

"I don't think so."

"No," the earl informed them, "our castles are mostly Norman, not more than eight centuries old. Some say these rocks were placed here before the pyramids were built in Egypt."

Hannah leaned across the seat to look out Abby's window. "Good gracious," she grumbled. "Most impressive, I'm sure, but how anyone can get excited about rocks, I cannot imagine. Go on, go on." She shooed them out as Moorhead slowed the coach to a stop. "If you wish to twist your ankles on that treacherous ground, far be it from me to stop you. I shall be cozy enough right here."

After Jared helped Abby down, they stood, side by side, regarding with awe the giant rocks that were scattered like jackstraws in a jumbled heap on the grassy plain. "It is called Stonehenge," the earl said. "You must watch your step, as there is a ditch and a mounded circle of earth built around it, with only two paths through. Not to mention the stones which have fallen through the aeons. Sadly, the locals have used the site as a quarry, and many of the stones are gone forever."

"Is it truly so ancient?"

"I am inclined to believe those who say so. You have only to feel the atmosphere here to know that it goes back to a time so old we know nothing of it. Come"—he offered his arm to Abby—"I have been here twice before, and I see Moorhead has put us down at the main path."

As they neared the huge mass of stones, some standing, many canted at crazy angles, others lying where they had fallen, Abby and the earl came to a single stone set directly into the path. "This marks the midsummer solstice," Jared told her. "It is one of the few things the so-called experts agree on at the moment. "This whole area must have been a religious site, for there are barrows surrounding it for miles."

"Barrows?"

"Grave mounds. There has been some excavation over the past decade. They've found daggers and tomahawks of bronze, stone battle-axes, bead jewelry."

"Tomahawks?" Abby questioned swiftly.

"I believe our academics adopted your Red Indian word as the best description of what has been found here," Jared replied smoothly. "After all, it has been two hundred years since Englishmen first encountered your aborigines."

Carefully stepping around a number of grounded stones, once man-high, they stopped before two towering gray stones three times Jared's height and capped by a stone lintel that must have weighed well over a ton. Abby placed her palm against one of the plinths, the wonder of such massive and enduring construction clearly shining on her countenance. Jared, entranced by her glowing beauty, was forced to shake his head, clear his throat, before he could continue his lecture.

"Think of it, Abby," he said, "these stones have stood, holding their burden, for as much as four thousand years. Does it not make you feel small and insignificant in the scheme of things? Here we are, mere ants, raising our hand to the knee of a giant."

"I am awed," she agreed. "I had no idea."

Hands on his hips, Jared looked around at the tons of megalithic stones. "I like to think that someone will one day restore what is left of it. Straighten the stones, reset the lintels, so we may have a better idea of how it once looked."

Impelled by emotions she could not name, Abby held out

both hands. The earl responded with alacrity, grasping her hands in his. "Thank you, Jared, for bringing me here. I shall remember this moment for all of my life."

A shiver shook him as he ruthlessly repressed the words that swept into his mind, the fervent assurance that he would forever treasure this hallowed ground as the place where he had become certain that no other woman would do for him. *No!* He would not succumb to the Verney curse. Would not be bewitched by this reincarnation of his grandfather's mistress.

"Shall we walk around the outer ring?" Jared suggested, pasting on his most innocuous smile. He dropped Abby's hands, tucked one arm through his. Slowly, pointing out the sights to each other as they went, the two friends circumnavigated the wonder that was Stonehenge.

"What I cannot understand," Abby said a few hours later as they dined in a modest inn in Amesbury, "is how they raised the lintels to the top of the stones."

Jared leaned forward, eager to impart knowledge to the schoolmistress. "It is believed they built a series of crisscrossed timbers, gradually moving the lintel stone—"

"I am sorry, my lord," Hannah Greaves declared, "but if I hear so much as one more word about that pile of rocks, I shall scream. What you find so fascinating, I cannot imagine. Particularly when we should be considering the possible hazards of six more commissions. Pray excuse me. Abigail, I shall expect you upstairs shortly." Mrs. Greaves shoved back her chair and left their minuscule private dining room.

"Shortly," Jared mused. "I believe she is mellowing."

Abby smiled. "She is a good, sensible woman and a dear friend. Yet she cannot see the splendor, the . . ."

"Romance?" Jared supplied.

"Exactly!" Abby agreed. "To us, the sight is thrilling. The wonder of how it was created, the people who could have managed such a thing—"

"The satisfaction of creating something that would last for thousands of years."

"Yes!" She looked up, straight into silver eyes that

gleamed with far more than reflected candlelight. Abby caught her breath. *No!* She could not, would not allow herself to be drawn in by this man. If he had any interest in her, it was the same as his grandfather for Clarissa Beaupré. An earl of the realm could not have honorable intentions toward an aging American schoolteacher of doubtful ancestry.

Clasping her hands tightly in her lap, Abby sat back in her chair, veiling her betraying green eyes under lowered lashes. "Thank you. You are a fount of knowledge," she stated coolly. "Perhaps Hannah is right, my lord. I cannot help but worry about the remaining tasks. My confidence in the ethics of our assignments has been shaken."

"I cannot deny I feel some guilt in this matter," Jared admitted, the warmth in his eyes fading into a frown. "I was so concerned about arranging a pleasant trip, decent accommodations and meals, that I never gave a thought to what we might find at the end of our journey. I was as naive as you yourself, and should not have been. I am years older"—he waved away Abby's protest, repeating—"*years older*. It is my grandfather who made this odd situation possible. It is my responsibility to see that all goes well with your quests. I extend my abject apologies, Miss Todd."

Abby did not fail to note the earl's deliberate reprisal for her addressing him as "my lord." "It is now plain to see why she insisted on your accompanying me," she confessed. "And, I assure you, I am grateful for it."

Jared nodded absently. "When must you go home?"

"We are scheduled for the *Rose of Sharon* on the third of September."

"Six weeks, six bequests." The earl steepled his fingers, his frown deepening to a scowl. "Do you suppose the Deerings would allow us to preview the letters so that we might write, apprising the other recipients of our visits?"

"Unlikely," Abby returned with scarcely a moment's thought. "The Deerings are intensely loyal to my grandmother. Whatever pattern she has set up must not be broken. I fear we must live with the uncertainty."

"And be more careful," Jared said, muttering what sounded suspiciously like, "Bloody hell!" behind his steepled fingers. "We will be home by mid-afternoon tomorrow. Will it be too soon if we open the next letter the following morning?"

"Not at all. If Hannah is not up to another trip so soon, I can always take one of the maids." Abby stood, the earl rising with her, topping her by at least six inches. His head was lost in the shadows above the candlelight, so it was impossible for her to tell what he was thinking. "Good night . . . Jared." Alas, her feet did not want to move. Forcing her body to turn, she glided toward the door, head up, shoulders straight. Miss Abigail Todd leaving the classroom after a lecture on the deportment expected from ladies of quality.

The Earl of Langley watched the delectable Miss Todd leave the room and wondered how it could all come right. Six weeks. Six possibly strange, even dangerous, situations. Anything could happen.

> *My dear Abigail,*
>   *After Mr. James Wetherby, I must grant you a simple task. Jeremy Tomkin, Viscount Granby, lives in Bath, an easy journey. He is a sweet, simple man from whom you have nothing to fear. (I trust James was not a problem, though you must now realize why I insist that Jared accompany you at all times.)*
>   *Lord Granby and I share a secret, and I wish him to know I will take it to my grave.*

"More blackmail!" Abby gasped, looking up at the earl. They were seated in the bright morning room with the white wicker furniture and chintz upholstery that had charmed Abby at first glimpse. Far less formal than the drawing room, the cheerful surroundings buoyed all their spirits as they tackled Clarissa Beaupré's third commission.

"Finish it," Jared said. "Perhaps it is not as bad as you think."

"That's all," Abby replied. "There's nothing more than her signature and Mr. Tomkin's direction."

"Let me see," Jared said. "Good God, he lives in the Circus!" Abby raised her brows. "One of the two finest locations in Bath," the earl explained. "Top of the trees. A man of means, Granby."

"That is good, is it not? No more waterfront taverns," Abby said with a smile.

"Mrs. Greaves," the earl said, not unaware of that lady's resigned face, "if you wish to have a longer rest after our journey to Southampton, I am certain one of the maids—"

"I came as Abigail's chaperon, and that's what I'll be," declared the redoubtable lady from Boston. "And, truthfully, I've wanted to see Bath all my life. My father's mother was born there."

"Then, by all means, you must come with us," Jared replied gracefully. "I believe I shall invite Myles to accompany us as well, if you ladies have no objection. Bath is always a fine treat, and I would like to see him become better acquainted with his American cousin."

Abby could think of nothing which could put a worse damper on a trip to Bath, but considering her gratitude for the earl's efforts on her behalf, there was no way she could say no. "By all means, invite Captain Verney," she responded. "He will be most welcome."

She was becoming more adept at prevarication, Abby noted, as the earl expressed his pleasure and took his leave. Only as she heard his matched bays trotting down the drive, did it occur to her that the Earl of Langley was hedging his bets. When going into the unknown, a veteran of two wars could be a distinct asset.

The much-vaunted family charm was working, Jared thought—a tad on the smug side—as he and a reluctant Captain Verney entered the coach early next morning to begin the short drive to Arbor Cottage. Somewhere on the three-day sojourn into Southampton, the cold and hostile Miss Abigail Todd had disappeared completely. The earl's satisfaction was suddenly marred by a frown. Bringing Abigail and Myles together for an entire day could well be a step back in turning his cousin up sweet. Then again . . . A smile played across Jared's aristocratic features. Abby could not possibly stay angry while enjoying the day he had planned in Bath. If all went well with Granby, that is.

"Penny for 'em, Jare," the captain taunted. "You've the look of a man well pleased with himself."

"I was merely hoping the ladies will enjoy the sights in Bath."

"Don't gammon me, brother. You looked positively moonstruck. And not for the first time this past fortnight, I might add."

Time to nudge Myles's thoughts in the right direction. And for a subtle warning as well. "You may as well know I find our cousin Abigail exceedingly attractive."

The captain swore, most colorfully. "You're daft! Fit for Bedlam. She's a nobody. Granddaughter of a—"

"Don't say it!" Jared barked. "Abigail Todd is as fine a lady as I have met. Indeed, she is more proper than nine-tenths of the *ton*. You'll keep your tongue in your head today and your thoughts to yourself. I'll not have the two of you quarreling."

The captain rapped on the panel behind the coachman. "Moorhead," he called, "stop the coach."

"Myles," Jared groaned. "Drive on!" he shouted to his confused coachman, who was pulling the team to a halt. "Myles, I need you," the earl confessed. "In my naiveté—never dreaming the old girl would send her own grand-daughter into such unpleasantness—I led the ladies into a questionable situation in Southampton—"

"Anyone foolish enough to take two ladies anywhere in Southampton—"

"Very well," Jared snapped. "I was hoodwinked by our grandfather's mistress, dazzled by a desire to be of service to Miss Todd, and bedeviled by the arrogance bred into an earl. *Mea culpa*. The truth of the matter is, I need you, Myles."

"For one old man in a city full of elderly hangers-on?" the captain scoffed. "Good God," he added in a rush, "you cannot mean to introduce her to mother?"

"No," Jared sighed. "Quite impossible, I fear. I have been

determined she know nothing of our cousin's visit. Now . . ." His voice trailed away into gloom.

"You cannot mean to marry the girl, Jare. I won't believe it. The Earl of Langley leg-shackled to the granddaughter of the old earl's mistress. No, brother mine, never. Absolutely never!" The earl remained silent, chin on his neckcloth, staring out the window. "So you've succumbed to our grandfather's disease," Captain Verney sighed. "Then set her up as your mistress, if you must, Jare. She's ripe for the plucking."

"Be glad I'm fond of you, Myles, and that men no longer carry swords, else you'd be bleeding all over my fine velvet squabs."

At that moment Moorhead brought the horses to a halt in front of Arbor Cottage. Daniel, the footman, jumped down to lower the steps. As the earl left the coach to bow over the hands of the two waiting women from America, Captain Verney murmured a heartfelt, "May this day end better than it's begun."

Chapter Eight

*B*oth Verney men had driven through Bath with a count-less number of women. Only the captain, however, was surprised by the Americans' enthusiasm, in such contrast to the reaction of the blasé beauties he was accustomed to escorting. *Provincial,* he thought scornfully as the women nattered on, even before they crossed the Pulteney Bridge into the heart of town.

"So light and bright," declared Mrs. Greaves.

"The flowers!" Abby breathed.

"A bridge with shops on it."

"Do look, Hannah. How odd those boats are. As skinny as a needle."

"The Avon is part of a canal which goes all the way to London," Jared explained. "It is quite narrow, so the canal boats must be the same."

Captain Verney, though still finding the ladies' excitement excessive, condescended to add to their enlightenment. "Bath is nearly as famous for the light golden color of its building stone as for its medicinal waters."

"Quite the most beautiful city I have ever seen," Mrs. Greaves admitted, far more enchanted by stones shaped into proper buildings than by the sorry-looking jumble they had viewed on their way back from Southampton.

Jared rapped on the driver's panel. "Go by way of Milsom Street," he commanded. "The ladies will wish to see the shops." He turned back to his guests. "As you have seen, the drive is short. You may wish to come back and do some shopping."

"It's wonderful," Abby breathed, a catch in her voice. "I have never seen a more beautiful city in my entire life. I am delighted Bath is one of the places we must visit!"

Myles felt the first chink in his armor of hostility slip open. How could he dislike a person who openly admired England's gem of civility, the city so ancient stone-age hunters had enjoyed its warm waters long before the Romans had claimed it for their own. Truth was, having lived near the city all his life, he had taken it for granted. Now, seeing it through the eyes of the Americans, he viewed the river, the architecture, the parks and gardens as if for the first time. *Bloody hell!* The Americans were going to turn him into blancmange! A fine state of affairs for a captain of the cavalry.

As they left a sparkling array of shops behind, Jared slid back the driver's panel. "Take us along Royal Avenue to the Crescent, Moorhead. Then back along Brock Street to the Circus."

"The royal treatment," Myles teased with the first grin Abby had ever seen on his usually disapproving face. "My brother is offering you a full panoply of the finest architecture of the modern age."

"John Wood designed the Circus where Lord Granby lives," Jared explained, "but died before he could complete it. 'Tis said he was so impressed by Stonehenge that he designed the Circus with the same circumference. In any event, his son was left to finish it. He then moved on to build the Royal Crescent, connecting the two with Brock Street. You will admire the area, I believe."

Admire was not a term Abby would have employed. Awe—as when she had viewed Stonehenge—was more like it. Surely the same inspired genius had built them both, though four millenniums separated the architects. Stretched out before them was a crescent moon of pale gold sandstone, each attached residence overlooking a lovely park. Astonishing. And then they were driving down an arrow-straight street where every row house was precise to a pin, the entry doors as lovely as the buildings into which they were set. Suddenly, their coach moved into a wide-open space and began to circle a central island of green. Abby looked around in disbelief.

"You said Circus, but I had not thought—"

"Completely round," the captain chortled. "Attached houses built in a circle. In London the fashionable live in squares. Here we have a circle, the first in the world, I'm told." Good God, he was as bad as Jared. He was enjoying himself. Myles Verney subsided back into a corner of the carriage. Miss Todd's joie de vivre was contagious. For a moment he had forgotten she was the enemy.

"Number Five, Moorhead," the earl told his coachman.

As they drove, the ring of houses in pale Bath stone was on their left, the circular park and gardens on the right, it seemed to Abby they had entered a separate enclosed world, sheltered from all of life's woes. A place almost as magical as Stonehenge which had provided the Circus its dimensions. Was it truly random fate, she wondered, that had brought her to these two places within days of each other?

"I had not thought," Jared murmured as the coach pulled to a stop before Number Five. "We are rather like an invading army, I fear."

"Four perfect strangers is rather a lot for a morning call," Mrs. Greaves agreed.

"Perhaps you should you go in first, Jared," Abby suggested, "as you did in Southampton." With a brisk nod, the earl descended, disappearing almost immediately into the three-storied structure. Shortly thereafter, a liveried butler came at a stately pace to invite them all into the house.

Jeremy Tomkin, Viscount Granby, was likely of an age with Mr. Aldis Kirkby. There the comparison failed. If Abby had not known the nobleman had to be a contemporary of her grandmother, she would have supposed him closer to the age of her father. She peered more closely at the man, dressed in the latest mode rather than in the garb of the last century, as was common among the elderly. Lord Granby faced them with one slender arm arrayed along the back of the couch on which he was sitting, a welcoming, if inquiring, smile on his nearly unlined face. Perhaps he used paint or powder, Abby speculated, but could see no sign of it.

"La Grande Clarisse," the ageless Lord Granby sighed. "I remember her very well, though I cannot imagine why she would send me a letter after all these years." As Abby stood to deliver the folded and sealed parchment, he added, "You have the look of her, child, but of a lady as well. Sending your father off to the colonies was a sound decision, I hope you realize that."

Jared had been busy in his few minutes alone with the viscount! Abby was not at all pleased to have her intimate family history shared, not even with one of Clarissa's old admirers. She bowed her head and retreated to her seat.

Lord Granby glanced at the brief missive in silence, a slow secret smile spreading across his face as he read. "How delicious," he murmured, carefully refolding the letter. "A fine woman, your grandmother," he said to Abby. "You can be proud to be an offshoot of such exemplary stock. She was far more of a gentlewoman than the witches who set themselves up as arbiters of the *ton*. My advice to you, my girl, is stay as far away from here as possible. Go back to Boston and be glad you have escaped our nasty British customs and conventions."

Though puzzled, Abby could only express her thanks for the viscount's reception of them and for his advice. Each of the four travelers allowed their eyes to stray as the butler showed them to the door. Even Abby's limited experience recognized that each of the viscount's collection of furniture, paintings and objets d'arts was of exquisite design and quality.

"Did you ever see the like?" Hannah Greaves declared as they settled themselves into the coach. "Not even Arbor Cottage has things so fine."

"True," Abby replied absently, "but what was in the letter? I am embarrassed to say, curiosity has me by the throat." She sighed. "I suppose we will never know."

"I can guess," Jared offered. Something close to a snort was heard from Captain Verney.

"Well?" Abby demanded.

"Are you quite certain you wish to know?"

"Quite."

"Do you want me to tell her, brother," Myles asked sweetly.

"Stubble it!" the earl said out of the corner of his mouth. He looked at the ladies, thought a moment, then shook his head. "How shall I put this?" he asked the air. As the coach began its careful journey downhill toward the river, Jared wiggled in his seat like a guilty schoolboy. Finally, he said, "I suspect that Clarissa was informing Granby that she had never told a soul about his failure with her."

Abby stared. Hannah gasped.

"I don't understand—" Abby began.

"And well you shouldn't!" declared Mrs. Greaves. "My lord, 'tis shocking that you could mention such a subject."

"She asked," Jared reminded Abby's chaperon.

"What subject?" Abby demanded.

"Good God, woman, you're not a child," Myles snapped. "You must know that there are men who do not care for women."

"Oh." Mortified, Abby studied her toes. She was naive, rather than ignorant. She had simply never realized . . . This was a world wholly outside her realm.

"We will visit the pump room before lunch," Jared pronounced. "Everyone who comes to Bath must have a taste of the waters."

The ladies welcomed the interruption. The same could not be said about the waters. Abby took one sip and put her glass aside. Hannah Greaves drank every drop, declaring she certainly hoped it lived up to its reputation, for this jauntering around was wearing her down to a grease spot. Abby was instantly contrite. The Verney gentlemen, who made no attempt at all to drink the waters, merely flashed identical smiles and ushered the ladies back to the coach.

"Perhaps you should come back and try the baths," the captain suggested blandly. "The King's Bath was built for the benefit of the sick by the Bishop of Bath in the eleventh century. It's said there was considerable mixing of the sexes, quite nude, in medieval times, but in these modern times there's a separate bath for ladies."

"Humph!" was all the reply the captain received from Hannah Greaves, though both Verney brothers thought they heard their cousin strangling on a chuckle.

"May I suggest a walk along the Parade?" the earl said as they ended a fine luncheon some two hours later.

"I think we must," Abby said, "for if we do not walk off some of this food, the horses will surely founder on the way home."

Jared offered his cousin his arm. "After a stroll along the river, perhaps a peek at the shops on Pulteney Bridge?" he suggested.

To Abby's surprise, the captain offered his arm to Hannah, who was looking appalled at the thought of walking so much as a step. Plainly, the older woman was stifling a wail of protest. "It's not far, ma'am," Myles assured her. "We'll be there in jig time."

"That's what I'm afraid of," Abby's companion moaned, sticking to her seat. "I should not have taken that last tart. I am so full I can scarce put one foot before the other. A jig is quite out of the question."

Myles Verney offered the doleful Hannah Greaves such a smile of sympathy and challenge, it almost forced Abby to be in charity with him. Heaving the older woman to her feet, he supported her steps across the private dining room, seemingly not at all put out about exercising his charm on a woman old enough to be his mother. Abby hardened her heart. She would not like him. Myles Verney was the enemy.

Their leisurely stroll soon brought them to a broad walkway along the river, much of it made even more scenic by a broad band of grass and beds of flowers. The sheer beauty and tranquility of the area made their feet seem to float the short distance to the shops that lined the sides of the broad Pulteney Bridge. The gentlemen eyed the many samples of fine leather at a bootery while the ladies lingered over a perfectly fascinating array of the latest bonnets and examined trinkets of every size and description from fans and hand

mirrors to miniatures of Bath Abbey, even a tiny replica of a
canal boat. There were masses of cut flowers . . . Abby
blushed as Jared handed her a long-stemmed yellow rose
from which every thorn had been removed. Turning her
head away, she ordered her pulsing heart to behave itself.
Abominable man! He played her as well as he played the
pianoforte. Just because he had presented a rose to Hannah
as graciously as to herself didn't mean that his gesture was
not intended for herself alone. What was to be done about it?
He was working his way into her heart and mind as insidiously as a worm into wood. An impossible situation. And
she was trapped in it by her equally abominable grandmother who had so carefully arranged these excursions.
Abby was beginning to wonder about Clarissa's motive. It
seemed quite possible the commissions had been designed
for something other than their ostensible purpose.

As they walked off the bridge, they found Moorhead,
Daniel, and the coach patiently waiting along the far bank.
Since Abby had supposed they were now beginning their
journey home, she was startled when the coach halted only
a few blocks down the road. She looked up to find Jared regarding her with an enigmatic grin.

"We cannot allow you to leave Bath without viewing
Sydney Gardens," he said. He turned to Hannah Greaves.
"Do you think you can walk a few more feet, ma'am? We
shall spare you the maze, but I believe you will find the gardens and waterways worth some small effort."

After a moment's hesitation, Hannah gave a decisive
nod. "Very well," she said, moving toward the coach door
where Daniel was now standing, holding out his hand. "But
I warn you I shall return to the coach if required to walk very
far."

"I believe you will not be disappointed," the earl assured
her solemnly, then spoiled the effect by tossing Abby a
wink. She had to clamp a hand over her mouth to keep from
chortling out loud.

True to his word, the earl had led his party only a short
distance into the pleasure gardens when they came upon a
dock at which was moored a smaller, less substantial version

of the narrow canal boats they had seen when crossing the Avon that morning. A grizzled captain and a jaunty young mate straightened from lounging positions near the stern. "I am Langley," Jared announced. "I trust my coachman spoke with you."

"He did," said the captain. "Step aboard."

"Oh, no, no, no!" Hannah wailed. "'Tis not a boat, but a needle. Put four more on that thing and it will surely sink."

"Nonsense!" Jared barked. "Myles, you go aboard first and see that Mrs. Greaves is properly settled."

Abby could see the debate chasing itself over her companion's face. If Hannah refused to go, Abby could not go. And Abby knew her shining eyes were betraying her keen desire to board the canal boat for whatever adventure Jared had planned.

"Very well," Hannah sighed, "but be it on your head, my lord, if we sink like a stone."

Unlike the working canal boats plying the waters between Bristol and London, this was an open boat with nothing more than a series of bench seats across the beam and a canvas canopy above their heads. Nor did it have a heavy plow horse waiting at the end of a tow rope. In a manner similar to the Venetian gondolas Abby had seen in a book, the craft's movement seemed to rely on two long poles and the muscles of the stalwart captain and his mate. This, then, was a boat specifically designed for the enjoyment of ladies and gentlemen on a lazy summer afternoon.

In her eagerness to follow Hannah and the captain on board, Abby stumbled over the gunnel, felt a surge of fire as the earl caught her around the waist and delivered her to a seat without so much as her toe touching the deck. Blushing furiously, she fixed her gaze on the river, presenting the earl with little more than a view of her stiff back.

The captain pushed off from the stern, his mate dipping down into the river near the bow. With almost ghostly quiet, the boat slipped smoothly through the quiet water. They were immediately engulfed in the shadowed world of tall greenery and tunnels passing beneath the many walkways that crisscrossed the gardens. It was lush and private, a hidden world tucked away on the edge of a city.

Each wooden bench seat on the narrow craft was equipped with a low back and bright canvas cushions. As they moved into the deep shadows beneath a bridge made of intricate white ironwork, Jared reached out and adjusted the cushion behind Abby's uncompromising shoulders. When his fingers skimmed her back, he felt a frisson of excitement he had not experienced in many a year, surely more than a decade. Abby's attention was firmly directed toward the light dappling the shore in front of them, her porcelain features hidden behind the rim of her high-poke cream silk bonnet. Seemingly, she was unaware of his existence, let alone his touch. He didn't believe it, of course. But had she felt as he did? Had she, too, been scalded by that brief encounter? By a touch that had seemed so much more intimate than walking by her side with her hand tucked through his arm?

Yet what a sight she was, even turned away from him, stiff-shouldered against any and all intimacy. Her gown of cream muslin sprigged in yellow was a perfect foil for her cinnamon hair, which insisted on sneaking below her bonnet and curling delightfully on the nape of her neck. Jared did not need to see her face to know that curls peeked out there as well. The reddish-brown tendrils had been etched in his mind since handing her into his coach that morning at Arbor Cottage. They had charmed him as she spoke to Viscount Granby, enchanted him throughout luncheon, where he had seated himself across from her so that he might not miss a moment of the view. Never had he been more in sympathy with his grandfather. The girl was a menace. If he were fool enough to marry her, the scandal would be enormous. His mother would disown him. Even Myles . . .

Oddly, it was Abby, with her stern New England conscience and her scorn of all things British, who would save him from himself, Jared realized dourly. Even if he could make her love him, willy-nilly she would go home. Come the third of September, she would be aboard the *Rose of Sharon,* setting sail for Boston.

As the tall greenery overhanging the stone sides of the canal suddenly fell away, the enchantment of the gardens overcame the surge of unwelcome emotion Abby had felt at Jared's touch. With something akin to relief, she allowed herself to be enveloped in the beauty of the moment. As far as the eye could see, there was nothing but colorful gardens, flowering trees, and soothing landscapes. The only sounds were bird calls and the distant rush of a fountain. Yet the call echoing in Abby's soul was quite different. That rebellious part of her was filled with a siren song so compelling she wondered how she would ever have the courage to go home. The vision of Sydney Gardens wavered. She looked at water, greenery, and flowers and saw only the man beside her. The arrogant British aristocrat. Her friend. Her would-be lover. Of the latter, she now had no doubt.

He was also the person who had arranged this special day in Bath. The man to whom she owed both thanks and the courtesy of polite conversation. For the first time since she had tripped over the gunnel, Abby turned to face her host. Eyes alight with genuine gratitude, she said, "It is a fairyland, Jared. I feel I have fallen into an enchanted realm. If I blink, I shall find myself back in Arbor Cottage or perhaps back in my classroom in Boston." She touched the tips of her gloved fingers to the back of his hand, making no objection when he twisted his wrist, clasping her hand in his. For both, the balmy temperature of the day turned uncomfortably, but excitingly, hot.

The narrow canal meandered through the gardens, the scent of flowers and fresh-scythed grass permeating the air. At one point they passed a watercourse tumbling down over a series of rocks. Shortly after, the canal opened into a pond, which boasted swans, both white and black.

"Be careful!" Hannah exclaimed as Abby reached out toward a black swan floating regally toward them. "You'll be nipped, Abby. Swans are not at all friendly."

Abruptly, Abby put her fingers back in her lap, suddenly, consciously, retrieving her other hand from Jared as well. "I wish I had known," she sighed. "I would have brought some bread from lunch."

Obligingly, the earl handed her a cloth sack of crusts. "The captain comes prepared," he said.

Delighted, Abby dived in, offering some of the bag's contents to Hannah Greaves. "No, thank you," that lady declared, "I've no desire to have my fingers snapped off."

Laughing, Abby threw out a crust, watched the black swan thrust his long neck forward into a dive, his pointed tail reaching toward the sky. He came up, dripping, swallowed the morsel, and made a regal inspection of the water, searching for more. When the bag's contents were gone, Abby softly apologized to the greedy swans, now floating serenely while never taking their eager eyes off the boat. Abby became aware of a feeling of well-being and contentment she had not experienced in years. With a small murmur of pleasure she turned to Jared. "I thought nothing could be better than Stonehenge, cousin, but this is quite the loveliest place I have ever seen."

Jared Verney looked down at the upturned face, the glowing green eyes framed in wispy curls of red, the soft curve of lips that seemed to demand to be kissed. Bewitched as he was, however, he was not unaware of his brother's disapproving glare boring into his back. Myles had not missed the clasped hands. Nonetheless, Jared allowed a smile to manifest itself. "If I call on you tomorrow," he murmured, bending his head so his words were for her alone, "perhaps you might be persuaded to grant me a suitable reward?"

A rush of heat once again enveloped her. Horrified, Abby turned away. The boat was moving again, drifting slowly through the scenic beauty of Sydney Gardens, but she no longer saw her surroundings. The Earl of Langley, sitting six inches away, blotted out the world. His presence overwhelmed her, addled her brain, suffocated her spirit. She was in grave danger of losing herself in him.

Was that really so terrible? whispered her insidious inner voice.

Yes! countered her New England soul. *It isn't marriage he has in mind.*

Five more commissions. Five more excursions with Jared Verney at her side. Clarissa Beaupré, Abby decided, was a wily old bird, far more clever than either she or her cousin had dreamed.

Chapter Nine

*A*bby escaped to the arbor directly after breakfast the next morning. Time alone to deal with her wayward thoughts was a dire necessity. She could tell no one of her dilemma, not even the kindhearted Hannah Greaves.

After ducking beneath a fragrant shoot of honeysuckle drooping over the entrance, she walked to the center of the bower, where she sank down onto one of the weathered wooden seats. The arbor seemed to close around her, protecting her from the outside world. Her personal hideaway from reality. Was she indulging in cowardice? Abby was unsure. She knew only that her basic beliefs and attitudes had been turned upside down, knocked helter-skelter by what she had discovered in the few short weeks since she had landed on British soil.

The English were not the devil incarnate. Nor was the Earl of Langley. Not even his military brother Myles. Nor were the Deerings, the staff at Arbor Cottage, the recipients of her grandmother's letters, nor any of the other people they had encountered on their journeys. Indeed, the countryside was exquisitely lovely, the antiquity of some of its artifacts breathtaking. Yet that archenemy George III, though mad, was still king; his son, the Prince Regent, a profligate fool. Of course, it was possible that was her American prejudice talking, Abby conceded. It was all immensely confusing. Taking away a person's basic beliefs in the structure of the world was disconcerting, to say the least.

And what about Jared . . . grandson of the man who kept

Clarissa Beaupré in luxury but would not deign to marry her? Jared, who showed no sign of being The Indifferent Earl when he had looked at her on the canal boat. In fact, the light in his eyes had nearly stopped her breathing. When he touched her, her body sang. Her heart as well, she feared. *Impossible. Quite impossible.* If he would not resist the attraction, she would have to be strong enough for both of them. Her world was Miss Todd's Academy for Young Ladies. His, an elite British realm in which earls did not marry American schoolmistresses.

As if her thoughts had conjured him, a shadow loomed in the arbor's arched entrance. "Good morning," Jared said, bowing before her. "Mrs. Greaves said I might find you here."

Hannah, her dragon of a chaperon, had sent the earl to the arbor. If Jared had charmed his way past her last ally, it was only because Hannah Greaves had wished it so. This was blatant matchmaking indeed.

The arbor benches were made for two. Boldly, Jared moved a fold of her spring-green muslin skirt before seating himself beside her rather than on the bench across the shaded pathway, a much more socially acceptable position for a single gentleman calling on an unmarried lady. Abby summoned the determination that had kept her ancestors going while crossing the Atlantic to the New World. It wasn't as if she hadn't expected him. Why else had she donned one of the fine new gowns so recently arrived from London, a soft muslin trimmed with yards of lace-edged flounces? And left off her bonnet, confining her masses of hair with nothing more than a satin ribbon that matched her gown? Scandalous for a spinster of her years to be so vain. And senseless to deny it. The days when she willingly played the dowd before the Earl of Langley were vanished as if they had never been.

He was smiling at her, rather like a cat eyeing a dish of cream. If her thoughts had been disconcerting before, they now verged on chaotic. "I wish to thank you once again," Abby babbled. "I have seldom, if ever, enjoyed anything so much as our trip to Bath. You are a true gentleman, my lord."

Jared raised an elegant brow. "My lord?" he questioned.

"We are without chaperon," Abby pointed out, dropping her eyes. "Formality seems in order."

"Puritan," he taunted softly. "I thought we were friends."

"Indeed, sir, we are," Abby responded hastily. "I merely—"

"Wished to emphasize the limits," the earl finished for her.

Abby nodded, her hands clasped tightly in her lap. Jared gazed at her for some time in silence. He longed to run his hands through the glowing embers of her hair, to tilt up her chin, experience the enticing softness of her lips. "Barriers, Abby?" he said at last. "I thought we were past all that."

"We met but a fortnight since," she protested. "There are proprieties which must be observed—"

He succumbed to temptation. Taking her chin in his hand, he lifted her face to his. "No," he told her gently. "We are friends, possibly cousins—"

"Possibly?" Abby pounced on the word.

"We cannot be sure," Jared told her. "How old is your father, Abby?"

"Three and fifty. Why?"

"Because I do not believe my grandfather met your grandmother until close on to fifty years ago."

Abby's eyes widened, but the earl gave her no time to think about the implications of this startling remark. "Therefore," he said, "I believe you can have no objections to my claiming my reward for what you have assured me was a delightful day in Bath."

Abby was not an innocent when it came to kisses. Jonathan Blaisdell had not spent all his days at sea. Moreover, she knew quite well what the earl intended when he informed her he would call on her to claim a "suitable reward." Nonetheless, the reality was stunning. The lips of the Earl of Langley were like a weapon cutting through to her soul. Warm, gentle, persuasive. Stunning. Abby's hands stole upward, one pressing tightly against his back, the other fisted in his hair. When she became conscious of what she had done, her eyes flew open, encountering a wicked, knowing smile. She jerked back, anchoring her hands firmly in her lap.

"Silly goose," Jared chided. "You've as much fire in you as Clarissa, and well you know it. Someday you must tell me how you have escaped marriage all these years."

"You need not remind me of my age!" Abby snapped. "I assure you I am well aware of it." *Good Lord, she could not have said that!*

Jared, well satisfied with his morning call, rose nimbly to his feet. "May Myles and I call on you at teatime? I fear we must open Clarissa's letters as quickly as possible, as one or more may involve journeys of length."

"Yes, of course," Abby replied coolly. "You are quite correct. I shall tell Cook to prepare for two hearty male appetites."

Even in the gloom of the arbor, Abby could see the gleam of satisfaction in the earl's silver-gray eyes before he bowed with almost mocking formality and took his leave. She buried her face in a handful of green muslin and burst into tears.

When the last Sèvres teacup had chinked gracefully into its matching saucer and Captain Verney was swallowing his third damson tart, Abby signaled for Deering to bring the next of Clarissa's letters.

"Are we off to Scotland?" Myles quipped as Abby broke the seal, "or perchance the wilds of Dartmoor? Care to wager on it, brother mine?"

"No," was the damping reply. "Well?" Jared demanded, skewering his American cousin with a frown.

"I am beginning to wish I had listened to my father and stayed in Boston," she sighed. "Somehow I had thought to be involved in a series of simple bequests, such as the locket for Mr. Kirkby. I must admit I cannot like the sound of this one, even though I confess it would be very fine to know more—"

"Abigail!" the earl warned. "Get on with it."
She commenced to read aloud:

My dearest child,
    *Yes, I know you are no longer a child, but to
someone nearly fifty years your senior, you are a
veritable infant. It occurs to me that you have a right
to know more about your family. Though I will go to
my grave without acknowledging the lot of them, you
should know what strange creatures lurk on your
family tree. (With the possible exception of my cousin
Eleanore.) I often think that, in spite of what you will
find in Oxford, you and I must take after Duncan
McKenna, who, you will discover, is our mutual
Scottish ancestor."*

A chortle, swiftly strangled, was heard from Captain Verney. "Red hair, by God," he muttered. "So that's where it
came from. Good thing you didn't take the bet, Jare. Beg
pardon, Miss Todd. Please continue."

    *I have attempted to draw one of those charts so
popular with those who wish to study their ancestors.
I fear I have failed quite miserably. Hopefully, your
cousins Eleanore and Margaret can make all clear.
At least I hope you find Eleanore still alive. She is
my cousin, daughter of my mother's brother. We have
exchanged an occasional letter since we each grew
more mellow with advanced age, and she clearly
seems to be the best of the Tyndales. I have never
met her, however. My family is as dead to me as I am
to them. Yet I do not hesitate to send you into the
lion's den, as long as Jared is by your side. He has
my permission to lord it over our Oxford relatives as
much as he likes. Our noble ancestor, Sir William
Tyndale, was a mere baronet, so I trust the family
will be suitably cowed.*

This time it was Jared who was hard-pressed to control his mirth. "The old witch," he grinned. "It appears we are off on crusade."

"That seems to be all." Abby turned to a second sheet, which she studied with some consternation. "Clarissa is right," she declared. "She has indeed failed quite miserably. I can make neither head nor tail of this."

"Let me see." Jared held out his hand. Silence reigned as he frowned over Clarissa's family chart. "It would appear," he said to Abby, "that you and Clarissa are descended from a Sir William Tyndale. Two generations down, there was a Dulciana Tyndale who had a child, Clarissa, by a Duncan McKenna, though where she met a Scotsman I cannot say." The earl scowled at the shaky lines. "As far as I can tell, Dulciana then married a Clarence Bivens, giving his name to his wife's child."

"So she was not truly a Bivens," Abby breathed.

"Meanwhile, Dulciana's younger brother Thomas married and became father to the Eleanore Clarissa mentions in her letter. Eleanore married a Jerome and has a daughter Margaret, now married to a Quentin Farleigh. It is their home in Oxford where we are expected to visit."

"You are a genius," Abby declared. "How you fathomed all that from Clarissa's hen-scratches, I cannot imagine."

"Very knacky, my brother the earl," Myles declared, "though it pains me to admit it."

Abby fingered the letter addressed to Mrs. Eleanore Jerome or Mrs. Margaret Farleigh, which was lying in her lap. "I wish to know what happened, of course," she confessed, "but I am not eager to subject myself to my relatives' scorn, which is what I fear we shall find."

"Turning tail, are you?" Captain Verney scoffed. "I must say, cousin, I had not thought you fainthearted. Particularly now you have discovered nobility among your ancestors."

"It is my American ancestors who give me courage, Captain," Abby informed him coolly. "I will go, of course, as I am expected to do. I merely say that I cannot like it. I fear that, influenced by my grandmother's scorn, I may be less than polite to my Oxford cousins. And that would not do at all. It has been borne in on me," she added quietly, "that not all Britons are the enemy."

"Merciful heavens," the captain mocked, "the world may be coming to an end. Shall I stay home then, so I may not witness your humiliation before these dirty dishes Clarissa declares are your relatives?"

"Dirty dishes?" Jared repeated, "I think not. Oxford is home to academics, an acceptable occupation for a younger son. So I doubt we'll have need of your strong right arm, Myles, if you do not care to join us. Eleanore Jerome cannot be much younger than Clarissa, and her daughter well into middle age. The possibility of menace seems unlikely."

"Granby was such an ogre," the captain murmured provocatively.

Abby giggled. "You are wicked, sir."

"Oh, quite," Myles grinned. "Well, Jare, do I go or stay?"

"You do as you wish."

"Then I believe I shall go," said the captain. "After all, I went straight into the army after Eton and did not have the advantage of years of wine, women, and song in the hallowed halls of Christ Church."

"Not quite within the walls," Jared said with a quelling look at his younger brother.

"You were at Oxford," Abby cried. "Famous! Then we may be sure of visiting all the best places of interest."

"Do not expect Bath," the earl warned. "Oxford is a university city, the buildings Gothic, the citizens never quite sure they are comfortable with a myriad of young men, most seemingly more bent on frivolity than on their studies."

"And you," Abby laughed, "were you frivolous as well?"

"Indubitably."

"Do not believe him," Myles said. "He took a double first in history and Greek."

"You are betrayed, my lord. Must I assume you are the male equivalent of a bluestocking?"

"Indeed," Jared admitted. "Except that as long as a man knows how to drive to an inch, hunt with the Quorn, and does not fuzz the cards, he may be as scholarly as he wishes. Therefore, there is no male equivalent of a bluestocking."

"Naturally," Abby ground out. "How could I have thought otherwise?"

Ignoring her grumbling, Jared suggested they take a day of rest before beginning their journey to Oxford. "Agreed," Abby declared. "Will you dine with us tomorrow?"

The Verney brothers expressed their delight and took their leave. Abby was left staring at the letter in her hand, wondering how the great-granddaughter of a baronet became La Grande Clarisse, toast of London's *demimonde*.

The Gothic towers and quadrangles of the university buildings at Oxford were so familiar, Abby could almost believe she was back in Boston or, more precisely, across the Charles River in Cambridge. Here was a culture that had been transplanted, en masse, to the New World with little outward sign of the rebellion against the mother country which had sprouted in England's recalcitrant colonies. An environment of academia, providing a safe haven from outside cares. In addition to her father's other duties, Dr. Lucian Todd occasionally lectured to aspiring young doctors at Harvard. As a very special outing, Abby and her mother had sometimes accompanied him, lingering in Harvard Yard to feed crumbs to the pigeons and the squirrels while Dr. Todd put forth his views on his particular specialties, including the vital importance of cleanliness in medicine.

Nostalgia gripped her as the coach rolled past endless buildings of golden sandstone, with an occasional view of sheltered green lawns glimpsed through Gothic-arched entrances. The hallowed halls of academia were her world. She was Abigail Todd of Miss Todd's Academy for Young Ladies, an environment of challenge and satisfaction that she truly loved. She was a woman of substance, a woman who garnered respect from Boston's finest. A woman whose opinion was not ignored. She was, therefore, far better off than most of her contemporaries.

Why then did she feel her heart crack when she saw a woman with a baby in her arms? Even a nursemaid seated on a park bench, placidly watching while her charges rolled hoops or raced each other over the grass, set off a yearning she had thought repressed long since. She had made her life what it was, Abby told herself sternly. After losing Jonathan, she had eschewed marriage, forever pilloried herself in the halls of learning. She *loved* teaching! Adored watching young minds grow. Was most particularly satisfied by watching young *female* minds grow. She had a calling, as some did to the church. She was content. More than content, she was happy.

But the day the *Rose of Sharon* set sail for home, her heart would break.

After spending the night at a pleasant inn obviously accustomed to catering to the quality, they set out to find the Farleigh residence, soon discovering it was tucked, cheek by jowl, under one of the college walls and built of closely matching sandstone.

"A don, by God," the captain ventured. "Too fine a residence for anything else."

"They may be living on the glory of earlier times," his brother countered, "though 'tis true homes like this are frequently tied to a university position."

"I will accompany you," Abby said as Jared prepared to leave the coach. "They are, after all, *my* relatives. They can scarcely turn away someone who has come all the way from America to see them."

"I doubt they'll turn up their noses at an earl, either," Jared murmured provocatively as he handed her down.

"Too easy," Abby retorted. "I'll not hide in the carriage, as if I were not good enough to be seen."

In a grand gesture, Jared swept his hand through the air, ushering his cousin before him.

The combination of a visitor from across the Atlantic and an honest-to-goodness earl on the doorstep at half ten in the morning was enough to fluster the housekeeper to the point of stuttering. Jared stepped past her, loftily examining the foyer as if he were considering a purchase. Abby had difficulty keeping a straight face. The housekeeper finally found enough voice to inform them that, yes, both ladies were at home. Would they be pleased to step into the parlor while they waited?

Jared was swept by a sudden urge to shock the occupants of this house. Why, he could not have specified. Perhaps because the place felt stultifying, as if no one had opened a window to either fresh air or a fresh idea in more years than one cared to count. Spotting a maid peeking out a door at the end of the hall, he summoned her with an imperious wave of his hand, sending her scurrying out to tell Myles and Mrs. Greaves to continue their drive through the streets of Oxford. Abby shot him a look but did not protest. He rather thought she was experiencing the same atmosphere herself. Additional guests would not be welcome. They followed the flustered housekeeper into the parlor.

Within a few minutes a man came bursting into the room as if he could hardly wait to prove his servants liars. Stopping short a few feet into the parlor, he stared at his guests with haughty surprise. Of medium height and medium age, his hair sprinkled with gray and a figure that was edging from well-fed toward portly, he was precise to a pin, his clothing almost a caricature of the Oxford don. "My lord." He bowed. "I am Quentin Farleigh. To what do we owe the honor of your visit?"

"Mr. Farleigh," the earl nodded, "may I present your wife's cousin from America, Miss Abigail Todd of Boston?"

Abby sank into a curtsy she knew this man would expect, even though it went considerably against the grain as he was looking at her as if she were a worm.

"America!" Farleigh pronounced the word as if it were the Black Plague. "I know of no family in the colonies."

"Former colonies," Abby corrected automatically, then wished she had held her tongue. This man could deny her access to her relatives, and would certainly do so if she were not careful. Fortunately, he was so enchanted by having an earl come to call that he seemed not to have heard her. "That is why we are here, Mr. Farleigh," she said with as much obsequiousness as she could manage. "I have brought a letter to my cousins from my grandmother, explaining the relationship. I have come a long way and would be most pleased if I might speak with them." Before entering the house, Abby had had Hannah tuck every stray red curl under her bonnet. She now lowered her eyes, hoping she appeared properly demure and eligible to speak with Mr. Farleigh's wife and her mother Eleanore Jerome.

For long moments Quentin Farleigh looked her up and down. Abby's anger mounted with each passing second. She dared not peep at the earl, for fear they might incite each other to riot. She doubted Jared Verney had ever had his eligibility as a visitor questioned before in his life.

"Very well," Mr. Farleigh declared at last, and signaled the hovering housekeeper to find the two ladies of the house.

Chapter Ten

Try as she might, Abby could find no resemblance to her grandmother in the two women who soon ventured into the parlor. The face of Eleanore Jerome, a stylishly garbed if rather plain lady of well over sixty, was suffused with ill-repressed excitement and curiosity. Abby liked her on sight. Her daughter, Margaret, however, looked as if she had scented something quite vile and could not wait for it to be gone. In the face of this hostility, Abby transformed her curtsy into little more than a regal nod. Later, she would wonder at herself. It was as if she had taken on Jared's in-born arrogance, treating her Oxford relatives as if she were a countess. The Countess of Langley. A shocking encroachment that seemed to have crept up on her unawares. Worse yet, the thought brought strange flutterings to her insides rather than hot denial.

At the moment, however, she readied herself for battle while wondering, rather vehemently, how Clarissa could have placed her in such an awkward situation.

"Mr. Farleigh," the earl declared with suspicious heartiness, "family history can be tedious for those not involved, perhaps there is some place where we might talk. I confess I would like to know if the traditions I once knew still exist here in Oxford."

He was deserting her!

He was using his power to rid her of a stuffy professor who would likely interrupt them a dozen times with his pontifications, further exacerbating Abby's temper and possibly ending this opportunity to learn about her grandmother's family. Abby managed a gracious nod as the two gentlemen bowed themselves out.

"You are alone, Miss Todd?" Margaret Farleigh huffed the moment her husband and the earl left the parlor.

"Alone, ma'am?"

"You, an unmarried woman, are traveling with the Earl of Langley. Alone," Margaret Farleigh clarified in frozen accents.

Abby stared at her hostess, examining every sour irregular feature as if the don's wife were a museum specimen. No wonder the lady was hostile. That Margaret Farleigh had a cousin, no matter how far removed, who was a raving beauty must be a continual thorn in her side. And now, to be confronted by Clarissa's reincarnation . . .

Although Abby's own fortitude was considerable, she consciously imitated the Earl of Langley at his most arrogant. "I cannot imagine why it should be of interest to you, ma'am," she said to Mrs. Farleigh, "but in view of the private nature of a family reunion, my companion and Captain Myles Verney, the earl's brother, are touring Oxford at this moment, leaving me to the sole escort of the earl. I trust this meets with your approval."

"As if Margaret could ever question the comings and goings of an earl," declared Eleanore Jerome, even as her daughter's countenance grew more dour. "The ways of the quality must always be a mystery, I fear. We live in our little backwater, cut off from the world, scarce a ripple in our lives beyond the changing of term and an occasional schoolboy prank." Mrs. Jerome beamed upon Abby. "Now, do tell us about yourself, my dear. You have come all the way from America, I'm told. How delicious! Have you seen any Red Indians? Come, come, we must hear all."

"Ma'am," Abby laughed, "I have come to deliver a letter from my grandmother and to discover what you can tell me about her family. But if you truly wish—"

The elderly lady clapped her hands. "We do, my dear, I assure you we do."

"Speak for yourself, Mama," Margaret Farleigh snapped. "I have no desire to hear about savages."

"I fear I know no savages, ma'am," Abby replied lightly. "Indeed, we are quite civilized in Boston, though Indians once showed kindness to my forefathers."

"Truthfully, Miss Todd," Mrs. Farleigh declared, "I can only wonder at the temerity of your visit. I am not ignorant of your ancestry, and, I assure you, Clarissa Bivens is a person I never cared to know."

"Margaret!" her mother chided. "Clarissa was my first cousin, the child of my father's sister."

"She was a—" Mrs. Farleigh paused, swallowed what she was about to say. "She was not the child of Clarence Bivens," she declared primly.

"Indeed not," Eleanore Jerome agreed. "How else would she have had that glorious red hair but from Duncan McKenna?"

"Did you know him, ma'am?" Abby inquired eagerly.

"Alas, no," the elder lady sighed. "He was here as a student while my father was still a child, but the stories I've heard. A braw and hearty lad, everyone said. 'Twas no wonder Dulciana lost all sense—"

"Mama!"

"And he simply left her?" Abby asked.

"The way of the world, my child," Eleanore shrugged. " 'Tis possible he never knew. He was off to Scotland at end of term, and when he came back, Dulciana was gone, married off to Clarence Bivens, who was nothing more than a merchant. My grandfather Tyndale, younger son of Sir Arthur Tyndale, offered him enough to establish his own bootery in London, and so he did—"

"Enough!" Margaret Farleigh groaned. "Must you wash our dirty linen in public, Mama?"

"Miss Todd is family," Eleanore declared. "You have only to look at her to see she is Clarissa's direct descendant."

"Mama, you cannot possibly know that." Mrs. Farleigh, suddenly looking stricken, forged on. "I mean, you cannot possibly have seen Clarissa."

The older lady's lips curled in a smile of reminiscence. "Oh, but I have," she said. "One year I coaxed Preston into taking me to the opera during the Season. I hoped Clarissa might be present that night. The *on dits* which made their way here from London were so intriguing I was quite determined to see her." Eleanore clasped her hands before her, supporting her chin, eyes sparkling. "And she was there. In one of the finest boxes with quite the most handsome man I had ever seen, the perfect foil for her own beauty, which was startling. She was the most exquisite sight I have ever seen."

Margaret Farleigh sat mute, evidently too stunned to speak.

"The Marquess of Stafford, that's who he was," Eleanore sighed. "I had to ask. They made such a striking picture, I confess I have no idea what was onstage that night."

"Do you remember what year that was?" Abby asked.

"Oh, goodness me," Eleanore frowned, "sometime in the seventeen-sixties, my dear. I fear my memory is not what it once was. Except for the sight of the two of them in that golden box, looking as if they owned the world, finer than royalty itself. That is clear as a bell. I can tell you exactly what she was wearing, if you wish. And the diamonds . . . ah, I've never seen anything so grand."

"Good heavens," Abby exclaimed, "I have completely forgotten the letter." Jumping up, she delivered Clarissa's missive to Eleanore Jerome.

"How kind of her to remember me," Eleanore murmured as she read. She ventured a glance at her daughter. "You did not know, Margaret, but many years later, when I heard that Clarissa was settled at Arbor Cottage in Vernhampton, I wrote to her. We corresponded occasionally after that, though of course she never thought it fit that we meet. I confess that after Preston passed on, I was tempted to go, but somehow I never did. I am sorry for it now."

Eleanore turned to Abby. "I believe she has sent you as her messenger, my dear. You are so much like her that it is almost as if she herself were here. Oh, I am sure she wished you to meet the family and learn the history which has been denied you for so long, but I daresay it is more than that.

You are her emissary, a bridge to reunite the diverse branches of the family." Eleanore Jerome tapped the letter in her hand. "She says as much here. She herself can never forgive the family for rejecting her mother and forcing her into a marriage which was so far beneath her, but she hopes that you, who are of such irreproachable character, may be accepted and treated as an honored guest."

With a flourish, Eleanore handed the letter to her daughter. Mrs. Farleigh read in silence, then set the letter aside with two fingers, as if she could no longer bear to touch it. "Clarissa Beaupré," she declared, "is a family skeleton I would prefer to keep well hidden. However, I concede that you are blameless, Miss Todd. I can only hope your resemblance to my unfortunate cousin is not a pit into which you may fall to your doom."

"Margaret!" her mother gasped.

"Mrs. Farleigh," Abby retorted, "I can only assure you that I am beginning to feel that Clarissa led a much more interesting life than mine." Later, Abby would wonder how her anger manifested itself in such an outrageous statement, but at the time the words brought her great satisfaction.

Having fired her parting shot, Abby gave her elderly cousin an impulsive hug, then took her leave, sending a hovering servant to inform the earl of her departure. If she had to stand alone on the street while waiting for the coach, so be it. The air outside the austere residence would, at least, be fresh.

But the coach was waiting. Daniel rushed to help her inside, with the earl arriving almost on her heels. As the coach rumbled into motion, Abby could only feel sorry for her lively elderly cousin who must live out the remainder of her life with Quentin and Margaret Farleigh.

"Farleigh is an ass," Jared pronounced in response to a questioning look from his brother. "A veritable ass. I am uncertain how I survived the minutes we spent without giving him a sharp set-down."

"You deserted me," Abby accused. "You deserved to suffer."

"It was a kindness," the earl responded austerely. "You

had a right to privacy without that pompous nitwit interfering with every word."

"I declare I am famished," Hannah Greaves interjected. "All this rambling about the streets has brought on a fine appetite. Do you think we might have nuncheon early, my lord?" The other travelers promptly subsided, hint taken.

As Jared passed along the order to Moorhead, Abby wondered at the intensity of her reaction to her relatives. *I am beginning to feel that Clarissa led a much more interesting life than mine.* Had she actually said that? She, the Abigail Todd of Miss Todd's Academy for Young Ladies, had told the wife of an Oxford don that life as a *demi-rep* might be better than life as a schoolmistress.

More interesting did not necessarily mean *better,* Abby corrected meticulously. But she had said it, she'd actually said it. It was mortifying. Unconscionable. She had no secret wish to emulate Clarissa Beaupré. Not even with the present Earl of Langley. Truly, she did not.

Liar!

For much of the long trip home, the four travelers managed a conversation distinguished by a variety of topics and considerable lively wit. But beneath it all, Abby was worried. Her grandmother had invaded her life. At times, she almost seemed to be taking it over, infusing her head with startling new thoughts, her body with physical reactions she had thought lost to her forever. She did not want to be Clarissa Beaupré. She did not want to allow emotion back into her life. She did not want to care for Jared Verney. She simply wanted to go home, to be enveloped once again in the safety and security of her life's work in Boston. She must cling to the tried and true, to the strict mores and standards by which she was raised.

Yet for a moment there, in Oxford, she had slipped. It was Clarissa's voice that had issued from her mouth, not her own. She was Abigail Todd, upright spinster of irreproachable character, mentor of young women. The company of the Verney brothers must be seen for what it was, the polite attentions of gentlemen raised in a world of studied good manners. In a little over four weeks, she would once again don the cloak of invincibility of the dedicated teacher. The summer's aberration would be over. Gone. *Fini.* Never to return.

When the earl asked her if something was wrong, Abby informed him she had a bit of dust in her eye. Fishing out her handkerchief, she proceeded to wipe away a surreptitious tear.

The ladies were delivered to Arbor Cottage in mid-afternoon of the next day, the gentlemen receiving their now customary invitation to dine the following evening. But the next morning as Abby sat in the bright morning room she now termed the Wicker Room, engrossed in a copy of *Emma,* Deering interrupted her relaxation. "Captain Verney, miss," he intoned.

"Myles . . . what a pleasant surprise." Abby was startled to discover she meant it. During the trip to Oxford their sparring had mellowed to the point where the captain had ceased to be an ogre.

"I trust you do not believe in shooting the messenger," Myles said as he sank into one of the inviting white wicker chairs. "I fear I am the bearer of bad tidings."

Abby's heart somersaulted. Breathless, she cried, "Pray do not tell me some disaster has befallen Jared—"

"Beg pardon," the captain hastened to say. "Nothing so dire. 'Tis merely that our mother has descended on us with a house party of six. My brother finds himself a trifle occupied. I fear we must cry off from dinner tonight."

"Of course," Abby acquiesced, aware only of the thudding of her heart. She should be insulted. Instead, she was overwhelmed by relief that nothing had happened to Jared. The implication was staggering. Just when she thought she had convinced herself . . . *Enough!* It was time to call upon her stiff New England pride.

Under normal circumstances she and Hannah should have been invited to dine with the houseguests at Langley Park. The omission, particularly by an earl who prided himself on his correct behavior, was glaring. For the first time in Abby's sheltered life, she felt the humiliation of not being

acceptable. Her indignation on her grandmother's behalf
was startling, her temper soaring far worse than it had under
Margaret Farleigh's scorn. Fortunately, Abby recalled that
the messenger was indeed not guilty. She looked up to discover Myles was clearly aware of the awkwardness of his
position. That Jared had not come himself, or at least penned
her a note, was a greater insult than not being invited to meet
his mother.

"I—we very much regret . . ." The captain tripped over
his tongue. "You would not care to meet my mother, Abby,"
he burst out. "Truly you would not."

Abby stood, signaling that the captain's visit was over.
Myles bounded to his feet. "You may inform the earl," she
proclaimed, "that I perfectly understand the situation. I
thank him for the generosity of his time and assure him I am
quite capable of executing the remaining commissions on
my own." She dropped into a stiff curtsy, which failed to
hide the blaze in her eyes. "You, too, have my thanks, Captain. It has been more of a pleasure knowing you than I had
expected. Good day."

"Abby—"

"Good day, Captain Verney."

Tempted to salute before taking his leave, Myles confined himself to executing a military turn and marching
from the room, as if Wellington himself were watching.

"Deering," Abby snapped as soon the captain was out the
door, "bring me the next letter. At once!"

Jared Reignald Fitzroy Verney, Earl of Langley, had been
swearing under his breath for most of the hours since he had
arrived home from Oxford to discover his mother and guests
already ensconced in his best bedrooms. There were few un-
used curses left by the time his brother tracked him down in
the library. When he heard Miss Todd's message, the earl
surpassed his previous profanity, calling upon words that
had not passed his lips since he had eavesdropped on the
conversation of the stable hands in his formative years.
Jared's solid oak desk rattled from the force of his fist. Pa-
pers flew in all directions. "The situation is intolerable," he

roared. "Mother is quite frank about it," he informed his brother. "She did not write that she was coming because she knew I would find some excuse to keep her away."

"The young ladies are quite charming," Myles ventured, knowing he was adding fuel to an already raging fire.

"The young ladies are intruding on my life," Jared ground out. "And their bloody parents as well."

"Lady Christabelle is accompanied only by her mother," Myles pointed out, taking a side step out of range of his brother's fists.

"Lady Mablethorpe," the earl declared gloomily, "is a worse dragon than Mama, if such is possible."

"Lord and Lady Pierpont seem tolerable," Myles said, playing devil's advocate, "and Lady Lavinia suitably sweet and pliable."

"Pliable! Since when have either of us wanted a sweet mealymouthed pea-goose!"

"Ah," said the captain, "but I had thought that was the desire of every man. A pretty twit to gaze on us with worship in her eyes, listen breathlessly to our every word, and declaring her greatest desire is to please us."

In anyone but a nobleman of high rank the noise Jared made would have been called a snort. "There was a time when I might have agreed. It now seems part of some distant boyhood. As, I suspect, you will agree."

"Indeed," Myles admitted. "I have long found namby-pamby misses boring. I just had not realized how much until I met Miss Abigail Todd."

"Not you, too!" Jared groaned. Resting his elbows on the desk, he dropped his head into his hands.

"Cut you out with the new Clarisse? Not likely, brother. But I confess, American or no, I cannot help but like her. She grows on one, rather like acquiring a taste for ale or brandy or fine wine."

"A delightful analogy, I'm sure," Jared mocked. He ran his hands through his chestnut hair, disarranging his valet's careful efforts. "I confess I am at *point non plus*. Suggestions would be welcomed, Myles."

"I never thought to hear myself say this," the captain

replied, "but it seems to me that in this case your obligation to Clarissa outweighs your obligation to our mother. You may do the pretty with whatever females Mama drags before you at any time. You have only four weeks to finish the work Clarissa set for you."

"The cool head of a captain of cavalry," Jared murmured. "I had not realized how engaged my emotions were until this impasse was dropped upon me. Suddenly I, who am so accustomed to making decisions, find myself caught in a whirlpool, my head swimming 'round and 'round the problem, unable to fight its way out."

"Filial responsibility is ingrained since birth, Jare. 'Tis not an easy thing to cast off, particularly for the head of the family. But in this instance I think you must."

"So I'm to set the cat among the pigeons?"

"Yes," said Captain Verney. "Needs must when the devil rides."

Chapter Eleven

*A*bby struggled up from sleep with a sense of deep foreboding. Something was wrong. As memory returned, her eyes snapped open, then squeezed shut in anguish. The earl's desertion should not matter so much. Truly it shouldn't. Yet with only half their commissions completed, he was lost to her. Lost to a world she could not enter.

Because her grandmother was La Grande Clarisse, *courtisane extraordinaire*.

Scrambling out of bed, Abby strode toward the infamous painting and pulled the silken cord, revealing Clarissa Beaupré in all her glory. It was true, she sighed. *Extraordinary* was the correct word for this glorious creature who, incredible as it might seem, was her father's mother. From the tumble of cinnamon curls to the rosy tips of her perfect breasts to the soft pink of bare toes, she was exquisite. In comparison, Abigail Todd was a pale ghost. Her features might be similar to her grandmother's, but she lacked the élan to make the similarity complete. She could not imagine displaying herself in such a fashion. Not even to a lover, let alone to an artist.

Whatever had put such a thought in her head? The sooner she got back to Boston, the better. And yet . . . perhaps she would leave her hair down this morning. Who was there to see but Hannah and the servants? She would don one of her frivolous new morning gowns, perhaps the soft French blue with embroidered flowers and flowing flounces on sleeves and hem. A gown she had chosen with her heart instead of her head. Then, draping herself *à la Clarisse* over the couch in the Wicker Room, she would read more of *Emma,* while dreaming she was posing *au naturel . . .*

Shocking! Abby glared at her grandmother. *You are a conniving witch, Clarissa. You thought to catch an Earl of Langley at long last. And you've botched it badly. Again. I doubt he'd have me as a gift, even if I were willing. Which I assure you, I'm not! The first sign of trouble, and he cries craven. I don't think much of your choice of men, old girl. Nor your legacy! It's back to Boston for me, where the men look up to me, not down. For shame to try your tricks on your grandchild. For shame!*

Abby jerked the cord, obscuring her grandmother's exposed flesh behind its curtain of pink silk. Standing with fists clenched, head bowed, she castigated herself for an idiot. She had not lost the Earl of Langley because she had never had him. He was performing his duty to Clarissa, as she was. Jared was a well-manned gentleman who might be her cousin, that's all there was to it.

If only she could make herself believe it. Until last night's defection, she had not realized how far her secret thoughts had soared. It was humiliating. Worse than that, she feared her heart was involved. The thought of not seeing Jared again was unbearable. Yet even more terrible was the thought he might have to sneak away from his family to speak with her. Far better she should never see him than be reduced to the level of her grandmother.

Chin up, Abby headed for Clarissa's vast dressing room, where, struck by a sudden frisson of New England conscience, her fingers hovered over a serviceable gray poplin before moving on to the French blue sarcenet. The temptation proved too much. Feeling haunted by the courtesan who refused to go away, Abby donned the sinfully becoming French blue gown, then untwisted her night braids to allow her hair to fall free, unencumbered by so much as a ribbon. Decadent, that's what she was. *I hope you're satisfied, you wicked old tart,* Abby grumbled, glancing toward the swath of pink silk as she made her way to breakfast.

*   *   *

Emma was not so interesting this morning. The heroine's
snobbery offended Abby's egalitarian ideals, and the author's comments about the local academy for young ladies
were quite beyond the pale. Abby found herself unable to
wish for anything other than a firm comeuppance for Miss
Emma Woodhouse. In addition, she had found Hannah
Greaves's determined cheerfulness exceedingly irritating. In
fact, her companion had been positively chirpy, effusive in
her compliments about Abby's hair and her gown, going on
at length about how impressed dear Jared and Myles would
be if they could see her. Abby had, at last, reminded her
neighbor from Boston that the Verney brothers had deserted
them, that it was quite evident the residents of Arbor Cottage
were not worthy of the attention of the aristocrats of Langley Park. Mrs. Greaves had bent her head to her embroidery
and not uttered a word since. Tension in the bright and usually cheerful morning room was high.

"The Earl of Langley," Deering announced in a tone
more portentous than his usual polite pronouncements.

How extremely aggravating, Abby fretted, even as her
heart soared, that the servants always seemed aware of what
was going on. And then Jared, solemn-faced, was bowing.
Breathless, she clutched her book to her bosom.

"My lord," Hannah Greaves nodded complacently. "I
was just thinking how lovely the courtyard is this morning.
I believe I will find the sunshine more illuminating for my
embroidery." She stood, offered the earl her best curtsy, then
turned to Abby. "I will leave the door open, my dear. If you
should need me, I shall be right outside." The admonitory
look in her eyes, however, told Abby quite clearly that she
did not expect to be called. Forgiveness, not quarreling, was
in order.

Abby, who had been stretched out on the sofa in a pose
remarkably similar to Clarissa's portrait, quailed from the
unabashed sweep of the earl's eyes over her recumbent
form.

"No, please," Jared said, "do not disturb such a charming
picture." He flashed a smile that he probably thought winning. Abby found it lecherous. She sat perfectly upright,

back stiff and straight, both feet on the floor, hands clasped in her lap.

Jared seated himself in a wicker armchair across from her, his mouth gone as grim as her own. "You are angry," he said softly. "Myles said you were, but I had thought we were friends, that you would understand."

"I understand perfectly," Abby told him. "You have houseguests. Your time must be given to them. Therefore I will continue the commissions on my own. Exactly as I informed the captain."

"Abby, that is not what I intended—"

"You may fulfill your obligation to Clarissa by loaning Moorhead and Daniel to me, along with your coach. If that is not possible, then I shall, of course, go post."

"You'll go with me, by God!" The silver eyes flashed lightning.

"You must realize that is not possible," Abby replied in accents as cold as his anger was hot. "You cannot desert your houseguests, and the remaining commissions will not wait."

"They are my mother's guests, not mine."

"And what excuse will you give?" Abby shot back. "Jared," she added more softly, "you know it is not possible. None of it . . . is possible."

The earl sat for a moment, staring stonily out the open door to the courtyard, where Hannah Greaves could be seen, head bent over her embroidery. "Oddly enough," he said at last, "I seem to have forgotten the reason I came."

"I had thought you driven by my words to Myles."

Jared shook his head. "I did come to make up a quarrel which I had not realized I had started," he admitted, "but somehow I have not made myself clear. I am here to invite you to dinner at the Park tonight. I would like you and Hannah to join our party. Is seven convenient?"

Abby stared. "You are mad!" she hissed. "You cannot possibly mean it."

"I assure you, I do. I shall not flaunt your antecedents, Abigail. I shall merely tell my mother you are two visitors from America, living in Arbor Cottage for the summer. That

Myles and I have enjoyed your hospitality and are pleased to have a hostess at Langley Park so we may return the obligation."

"Of course," Abby murmured, her insides writhing at the truth of his words. That's all she was to him. A minor social obligation. Not to mention that he was prevaricating, foisting on his mother someone she would not wish to know. "And your guests?" she managed coolly. "Will they not be insulted?"

"I doubt they will make the connection. Clarissa has not appeared outside Vernhampton for a quarter century or more. You are eminently respectable, Abby. They will recognize that."

She narrowed her eyes. "And what else will they recognize, Jared? I cannot help but wonder if you have an ulterior motive."

"Ah, yes, of course I must have a secret reason for inviting a neighbor to dine. Let me see." The earl raised an elegant black brow, spread steepled fingers to tap against his lips. "Perchance I wished my mother's guests to discover that the nubile young ladies being paraded before me have some competition, a rather spectacular beauty already on the scene and too well ensconced to be easily ousted."

"Jared!" As if the situation weren't awkward enough! But her heart was singing, almost enough to drown out her anger. "Let me make sure I understand you," Abby said with deliberate emphasis. "You wish the granddaughter of the old earl's mistress to display herself before your mother and her guests as some kind of latter-day Clarissa Beaupré in order to frighten away your mother and the families with whom she is attempting to establish a match."

Jared considered her words. "I suppose you could say that was a desirable side effect," he nodded. "Though, truthfully, I merely wish to invite a neighbor to dine."

"I don't know whether to throw something at you or laugh," Abby declared roundly. But what a conversation to be having, when she had thought his companionship lost forever.

Hope shone on the earl's ruggedly handsome face. "You will come, then?"

"To be perfectly honest, my lord, it sounds a dreadful evening." Abby sighed. "But I cannot resist the challenge. Clarissa would never forgive me if I said no."

"Quite right." The earl stood, looked down at her, his silver-gray eyes full of something that held her gaze. Abby's heart pounded as unspoken thoughts flew between them, shattering in their intensity. But all Jared said was, "You've opened the next letter, have you not? Where are we to go?"

"To Salisbury Close. And, truly, I shall not need you, though I would be grateful for the loan of your coach. I am to visit a retired bishop, you see. The Right Reverend Chauncey Merriwether. There can be nothing exceptional in that. With the assistance of Moorhead and Daniel, all will be well."

"We will discuss it further tomorrow—"

"I had hoped to leave for Salisbury tomorrow."

"You have time," the earl decreed. "I will call upon you in the morning." Jared Verney, very much Earl Langley, bowed himself out.

Come the earl over her, would he? Just wait. Abby jumped up and dashed to the courtyard, eager to give Hannah the news.

Shades of his grandfather, he was undone! Jared allowed his stallion to find its own way back to Langley Park while his thoughts stayed behind at Arbor Cottage. Not even the most voluptuous of London's *demimondaines* had ever been as enticing to him as Abigail Todd stretched out on the couch in that softly flowing gown, her masses of red curls falling onto her shoulders, then down over her sinfully rounded bosom, which she had attempted, unsuccessfully, to hide behind a leather-bound book. His mouth had gone dry, his head tossed so badly awry that he could only react like an automaton to Abby's taunts. He had almost forgotten the dinner invitation altogether.

About which he must now inform his mother.

Could he tell his mama of the invitation without mentioning Arbor Cottage or Clarissa Beaupré?

Highly unlikely.

Had his mother ever gotten a good look at Clarissa? As he recalled, his mama's few years at Langley Park had been marked by a concerted effort to ignore her notorious neighbor. Nor had she known Clarissa in her heyday. The resemblance could very well pass unnoticed.

Only if no one mentioned Arbor Cottage.

His goose was cooked. Even if his mother failed to make the connection, she would be incensed by his inviting an unknown raving beauty to dine when she was trolling two proper young maidens beneath his nose. His mother never suffered the vapors. There had been times he wished she did. Lady Langley was made of hearty stock. She would rant, rave, give in because she had to. Because he was Langley. She would retreat into cold formality, freezing Abby and Hannah with the full force of a woman who had been daughter of a duke before becoming a countess at age eighteen.

Was he wrong? Should he save Abby's sensibilities by excluding her from his home? Or was it better to stand like a man and say, "This is Abigail Todd, my friend." Put that way, he had no choice. Abby was no fragile blossom incapable of fending for herself. Common sense be damned! He wasn't going to let her go. Best to begin as he meant to go on. Jared put spurs to his horse and broke into a canter. His mother must be told to set two more covers for dinner.

"How kind of his lordship to send a carriage," declared Hannah Greaves for the third time that evening as the ladies waited in the drawing room at Arbor Cottage.

"The gig would have sufficed," Abby responded, also for the third time.

"But how gracious for him to send a note saying he had quite forgot to mention it when he was here earlier."

"I fear our earlier conversation was not conducive to graciousness."

"More like the poor man knows not if he's coming or going," Hannah stated firmly. "Love addles the brain."

"Love!" Abby scoffed. "Do not be foolish, Hannah. Kindly remember his high-and-mighty lordship's first reaction to his mama's visit was to disown our acquaintance entirely. Indeed, I fear we are in for a most uncomfortable evening."

"My dear, if you could see the way he looks at you . . . why, I daresay 'tis no different from the way his grandpa looked at Clarissa. It's a wonder to behold. I cannot believe you are so foolish as to scorn the possibility of such a fine match."

"Match! Can you possibly mean as in wedding, my dear Hannah? It is you who are foolish, if you think that. If Clarissa was not good enough to rise above her station in forty years of supposed bliss, then it is unlikely the present earl will offer more to her granddaughter. Let us not dwell on it, if you please. I find the thought quite spoils my appetite."

"Oh, my dear," Hannah moaned, "I should have realized . . . should have known. Your feelings have been trod upon quite dreadfully. I am truly sorry." She brightened. "But dear Jared has made amends, surely. You are invited to meet his mama."

"It will be torture," Abby declared. "Sheer torture. I should have stood on my pride and refused to go."

"Do you know who the other guests are?" Hannah asked, concealing the fact that her customary optimism was wavering ever so slightly.

"Captain Verney was kind enough to send 'round a note this afternoon, a gallantry I had not expected from him, I confess. He detailed the party, for which I am grateful. I am sorry, Hannah," Abby apologized. "In my agitation I forgot to tell you." She opened her reticule, took out a much-folded piece of paper. Glancing at its contents from time to time, she informed her companion: "In addition to Lady Langley—who is Charlotte Verney, by the way—the highest-ranking lady present is Henrietta Charnley, Marchioness of Mablethorpe. She is showing off her daughter, Lady Christabelle Charnley. We will also have the happy privilege of meeting Viscount and Lady Pierpont, doting parents of

Lady Lavinia Gordon—Myles's words, I assure you, not mine."

"Lady Langley is matchmaking," Hannah nodded, "no doubt about it. No wonder his lordship was wary of introducing you into the mix."

Abby glared at the older woman but chose to suffer in silence. Too much had already been said on the subject. "The sixth guest," she enumerated, "is a Mr. Thaddeus Stanhope, described as a man about town who moves from house party to house party, being suitably charming to everyone. And then, because Lady Langley nearly had the vapors over an unbalanced dinner table, she has invited Mr. Hadley Rutherford, who, you will recall, is the local vicar. A widower for the past two years, according to the captain, though not sufficient to even the table unless he were triplets."

"Merciful heavens," Hannah breathed, "yet another reason for Lady Langley to be distressed."

"*Distressed,*" Abby mused. "I believe *distressed* might not be quite adequate, Hannah dearest."

That lady moaned. "Perhaps we should not go after all," she whispered, but her soft tones were lost in the clip-clop of approaching hooves.

"Ah," said Abby, "I believe that is Moorhead now." She held out her hand to her friend and companion. "Courage, Hannah. Let us be off into the lion's den."

Mrs. Greaves pried herself off the couch. "Did I ever mention my palpitations?" she inquired dryly.

"No," was Abby's unfeeling reply. "I fear you must lock them away before we set foot in Langley Park. As must I," she added softly as the two ladies from America walked toward the front door, which Deering was holding open, his eyes sparkling with delight as the residents of Arbor Cottage, for the first time in its fifty-year history, set off for a dinner party at Langley Park.

Abby was grateful for Moorhead's familiar face and Daniel's as well. Somehow, as she readied herself for entrance into the Verney's grand country home, the coachman and footman had become her only friends. She flashed Daniel such a brilliant smile as he handed her down that the young man blinked, later declaring that he'd felt warmed all over. Moorhead, older and wiser, merely nodded and wondered how it would all end. Mighty queer doings when the spit and image of Clarissa Beaupré was to sit down to dine with the family. Mighty queer indeed. He'd best stand by to take the Americans home at any moment, for the young one wouldn't take no sass from nobody. He wouldn't put it past her to walk out, leaving them all with their forks in the air, their pointed tongues hanging out like the serpent itself.

Abby had suffered over her dress for this occasion. Though sorely tempted to present herself as a reincarnation of Clarissa Beaupré, common sense had prevailed. With the aid of one of the maids from Arbor Cottage, her unruly hair had been coaxed into an upswept arrangement, twined with dainty silk flowers. Only two long curls had been allowed to escape, emphasizing the slim and graceful lines of her neck. At least that was what the maid had told her. Her gown was a half dress of rich teal-blue, with larger puffed sleeves than she was accustomed to wearing and a vandyked hem with seed pearls and brilliants scattered among a band of ruching just above. Filling her décolletage, which displayed far more flesh than she could be comfortable with, were the pearls Jonathan had given her as an engagement gift. Abigail Todd was entering the halls of Langley Park armed in her best. If, that is, it were possible for a twenty-eight-year-old spinster to compete with two shockingly young and titled maidens.

Vanity, she chided herself, as she ascended the broad front steps of Langley Park. *All is vanity.*

Chapter Twelve

*M*iss Todd's vanity did not outlast her first view of the people assembled in the drawing room at Langley Park. The earl's guests glittered, the gems in the men's cravats and on their long elegant fingers almost rivaling the sparkle of the women. Moreover, an aura of wealth and breeding enveloped them, the supreme confidence born of centuries of equally elegant ancestors living out their lives in the comfort of castles and sprawling country mansions. Never had Abby felt more the outsider. She and Hannah should not have come. It was a mistake.

But Jared had seen them and was striding their way, a broad smile of welcome lighting his aquiline face. As he held out both hands to her, the room fell silent, the chattering cut off as if by a knife. All eyes turned their way. Abby wanted to sink. Instead, she steadied her shoulders as the earl gave her hands a quick squeeze before offering a hearty welcome to Mrs. Greaves. He led them forward toward nine pairs of eyes that, Abby was certain, were looking straight through her, instantly cognizant of who she was and of the scandal let loose in their midst.

In truth, the guests' reactions were mixed. Captain Verney, aware of all the nuances of the situation, was enjoying the intrigue of the moment. Almost anything could happen. He hadn't found a situation so interesting since he'd sold out of the army. Mr. Thaddeus Stanhope, who had made a life of being the extra man at dinner parties in town and house parties in the country, immediately sensed the tension. Deli-

cious. Lady Langley was dangling two beauties in front of
her sons, and the earl had just covered the bet with a beauty
of his own. Lady Mablethorpe and Viscount and Lady Pierpont were outraged. Competition of this nature was not at all
what they expected when they had accepted the dowager
countess's invitation to Langley Park. Lady Christabelle, an
astute young lady who had remained heart-whole through
three seasons, accepted defeat of her mother's hopes on the
spot. In any event, she rather thought she preferred Captain
Verney's stalwart good looks, even if he were a younger son.
Lady Lavinia's good nature was undisturbed by the two
newcomers. Anything the dear earl, or any other man, chose
to do must always be acceptable.

Mr. Hadley Rutherford, the vicar, was privy to the secret
that had contributed to the crackling atmosphere surrounding the earl's guests. Clarissa Beaupré had been a resident in
Vernhampton throughout the entirety of his tenure; he could
not fail to recognize the resemblance. Although Miss
Beaupré had never shown her face of a Sunday morning,
Mr. Rutherford was not an unkind man. He was also pru-
dent. The Earl of Langley held his living in the palm of his
hands. Mr. Rutherford offered the Americans a half smile
and a nod that was only faintly condescending.

Lady Langley, now fully realizing the extent of her eldest son's perfidy, swelled with indignation. She might never
have set foot in Arbor Cottage, but she had found the copy
in miniature that the old earl had ordered for himself. When
she had shaken this betraying object under her husband's
nose, George Verney had instantly named his father rather
than have his dear Charlotte think the portrait his own.
George could not, however, boast the strength of character
of his father, nor of his son. It had taken less than five minutes for his wife to discover the shockingly displayed lady's
name. And now the tart's exact image was here, under her
own roof, and she, Lady Charlotte Verney, Countess Langley, was expected to dine with the encroaching American
upstart. Incredible! Jared might not have the look of his
grandfather, but in this he was the very reincarnation. Except, she amended dourly, the old earl had had far too much

sense of what was proper to ask his family to sit down with
his mistress.

Charlotte Verney, the Dowager Countess of Langley, was
everything an English noblewoman should be: tall, well pro-
portioned, regal in bearing, with classic patrician features
and English rose complexion, well turned out in the most
tasteful mode. In truth, Lady Langley considered her ancestry superior to that of the present monarch and his profligate
son. Her own sons, ever a shining contrast to the Prince Regent, were her greatest pride and joy. And her greatest weak-
ness. That did not, however, mean that she could always
agree with their fits and starts. This was one of those times
when her faith in bowing to her eldest son's position as head
of the family was sorely tried. Earlier that day, when she had
informed the earl, in deadly accents, that if he chose to add
two unaccompanied females to her dinner table at the last
moment, he could rearrange the seating himself, he had
done just that. She had not spoken to him since.

Miss Todd had no trouble recognizing Lady Langley's
pique. Alas, however, she had no hint of the earl's good intentions as she watched him offer his arm to Lady
Mablethorpe and lead the party, in strict order of prece-
dence, into the dining room. Myles followed with the dowager countess on his arm, then Viscount and Lady Pierpont.
With the insouciant smile that was his stock in trade, Mr.
Thaddeus Stanhope offered an arm each to Lady Christabelle and Lady Lavinia, receiving a gracious nod from the
former and wide-eyed awe from the latter, who had previ-
ously known Mr. Stanhope only from the frequent mention
of his name in society columns of the *Morning Chronicle*.

"Ladies?" Mr. Hadley Rutherford, well coached by his
host, offered his escort to Abby and Hannah.

Grateful they had not been left to follow the procession
like females at the tag end of an army, Abby ignored her suspicion that the vicar had been prompted in his duty. Holding
her head high, she accepted his arm. When the three swept
into the dining room, they were struck by the silence. A silence bristling with emotions Abby could not identify. She
did, however, recognize that they did not include approba-

tion. The vicar slowed to a halt, obviously puzzled by the problem of where to seat the ladies at his side. One of the three remaining seats at the lengthy table was to the earl's right, a privileged position reserved for the most honored guest. Obviously, Mr. Rutherford was not the only person who found this peculiar. Nor, in a roomful of titled nobility, could Abby or Hannah imagine themselves in such a favored position.

"Miss Todd," the earl said with a nod toward his right, "if you would be so kind."

As Abby's feet took her the length of the spacious room, her mind was functioning just well enough to feel the daggers aimed at her back. She had wanted to be invited to Langley Park. She had wanted to be one of Jared's guests, but for him to single her out in such conspicuous fashion was too exceptional. It was likely to be interpreted as a declaration of intent. He had just made every other woman in the room, except for her own dear Hannah, into the enemy. Surely, Abby told herself, this must be a perfect example of *be careful what you ask for.*

Jared himself pulled out her chair while Mr. Rutherford seated Hannah before taking his own place beside Lady Pierpont on the far side of the table. Down the length of the table—set with Wedgwood, glittering crystal, and a stunning array of silver—the earl returned his mother's glare with a look of remarkable innocence. When Lady Langley did not relax her icy mien, he signaled his butler, who was standing at attention near the hall to the kitchens. As if by magic, a steaming tureen of soup was brought to a sideboard, and a small army of footmen proceeded to ladle out the chestnut soup, placing bowls before each guest.

"You are from America, Miss Todd?"

Dazed, Abby had not noticed that Mr. Stanhope was on her right. Another example of Jared's kindness, she was sure, because the open friendliness of this man of about her own age could not be misconstrued.

"From Boston, Mr. Stanhope. I am headmistress of an academy for young ladies."

"Indeed." His eyebrows rose. "Surely you are much too

young." Clear blue eyes and a sweet smile signaled that the words were a compliment rather than a criticism.

"I was fortunate enough to have the means to pursue my calling at an early age," she responded quietly. "I take great pleasure in educating young minds."

"Then you are a disciple of Mary Wollstonecraft?"

Abby paused, a spoonful of soup almost to her mouth. "Yes, I suppose I am," she admitted. "I cannot like her views on marriage—although her reasoning is perfectly sound—but education for women is essential. On that I cannot agree with her more."

Mr. Stanhope's eyes twinkled as he replied: "Ah, then you are not averse to marriage?"

"For others, no. For myself, I have long since ceased to consider the matter. I have my school. That is enough."

"But, my dear young lady, you cannot allow such a loss to the world," Thaddeus Stanhope protested. "You are quite the loveliest woman here. Indeed, the finest I've seen in years. You must not waste yourself on a bevy of silly young things."

Abby gave her attention to her soup. How perfectly awful that she was flattered by a man whose particular gift was saying the right thing to everyone. Not that Mr. Stanhope could be faulted for so agreeable a trait, of course. When Abby's bowl had been whisked away by a hovering footman, she said to her dinner partner: "I thank you for your kind words, sir, but I must forever feel that I do far more good training young women to know something beyond embroidery and the correct cut of a gown than by settling into a conventional situation where my fortune as well as my person is subject to a husband's whims."

With a charmingly winsome smile, Mr. Stanhope shook his head. "Ah, but I think the earl cannot agree with you on this."

"The earl," Abby declared more loudly than intended, "has nothing to say on the matter."

Conversation around them wavered. She could feel Jared's eyes on the back of her neck. Abby wished to wake up in her own bed, finding this dinner party only a nightmare.

"A dragon," murmured Mr. Stanhope provocatively. "A veritable dragon. So that's what it takes to snabble The Indifferent Earl."

Abby was saved from a reply by the presentation of the fish course. From under lowered lashes she watched the guests bend their heads and ill-concealed curiosity to the dressed crab. *The Indifferent Earl*. Would that he were indifferent to her!

Ah, no, she didn't mean it. Could never mean it. That half a day when she thought him lost to her forever had been pure anguish. She was Abigail Todd of Boston, and she would not let these *British* intimidate her. Abby stabbed her fork into her dressed crab and brought it to her mouth. Undoubtedly, the crab was a gourmet treat. Tonight it tasted like sawdust.

Mr. Stanhope, recognizing that he had pushed Miss Todd as far as good manners would allow, selected more innocuous topics for the remainder of their conversational allotment, but he could not quite restrain a sigh as he was forced to turn his attention to the nearly inarticulate Lady Lavinia, whose occasional girlish effusions were punctuated by long moments of blushing incomprehension, requiring all his masterly aplomb while revolting his quick wit and ready humor.

"You should not have done this!" Abby scolded as soon as she had Jared's undivided attention. "You have singled me out, and the others will eat me alive. Even if they do not know about Clarissa," she added, leaning toward him to make sure no one else heard the dreaded name.

Lady Langley looked up to see her son's dark head nearly touching Miss Todd's. Only years of rigorous training kept her from barking a reprimand down the length of the table. An impossible situation! She could not allow it. Yet her son was Langley, she a mere mother. There was little she could do but make every effort to ensure the Americans hastened home, never to be heard from again.

If the dowager had been privy to Miss Todd's conversation with Mr. Stanhope, she might have been more sanguine. As it was, she could scarcely wait to lead the ladies into the drawing room, where she planned to strip the young American of her encroaching pretensions.

At the opposite end of the table, the earl's attention was still turned to his guest of honor. "Just be yourself, Abby," Jared advised. "You are a lady of irreproachable character. I am privileged to call you friend. I trust I have made that clear to all present."

"Oh, you've done that, my lord," Abby retorted. "I expect to be greeted in the drawing room by knives at the ready. My knees are all a-quake."

"Abigail Todd cry craven? I doubt it."

"I am petrified, I assure you. If you linger long over the port, you may glimpse me running for my life."

The earl laughed out loud, bringing heads up around the table, ears on the prick, for no one had failed to note the two heads so close together, the one so forceful and dark, the other so elegant and fully alive. Soft strands of red, glowing in the candlelight from the multifaceted chandelier, topped Miss Todd's porcelain skin, the finely sculptured features the goddess of love herself might have envied. A knowing look passed between Lady Christabelle and Myles Verney. A wise woman, the captain thought. No illusions there. Lady Lavinia, who found the earl both old and intimidating, was relieved. Surely her mama could not expect her to attach the earl when the competition was so far beyond her touch. Lady Mablethorpe and Lady Pierpont, however, now had confirmation that their hopes had turned to dust. Mr. Thaddeus Stanhope could not recall the last time he had enjoyed a dinner party so hugely. Viscount Pierpont and Mr. Hadley Rutherford returned to their Florentine of veal and potato pudding. Food was far less complicated than the intricacies of romance, particularly when a nobleman seemed determined on a shocking misalliance.

When Lady Langley rose from her chair, signaling the ladies' departure from the dining room, Abby felt her stomach clench. The small amount of food she had managed to eat threatened to rise in her throat. She had thought she was

made of sterner stuff, that it did not matter what these
British aristocrats thought of her. Reality was a darkness
where pride and knowledge of her own worth could not
overcome the deep-seated feeling that these ladies, according to the teachings of their own peculiar culture, might well
have a valid reason for being incensed. Even if the guests
did not know about Clarissa Beaupré, they were well aware
they had been invited for the express purpose of matchmaking and had discovered a cuckoo in the nest. An intruder
who seemed to have snabbled the quarry right out from
under their noses. It was all most unpleasant, Abby decided,
coming to a belated appreciation of Jared's hesitation in
inviting her to his home.

As she followed in the wake of the other women, with
only Hannah to keep her company, Abby's ears were already
burning. She greatly feared she might be the topic of the
men's conversation over port as well as cynosure of all the
ladies. That the topic of conversation in the drawing room
would be Miss Abigail Todd, her life and antecedents, Abby
had no doubt. The whole sorry situation would be revealed,
for she simply knew not how to lie. Her grandmother would
be exposed for what she was, the old earl's forty-year infat-
uation as well. As the ladies seated themselves in the drawing room, Abby felt disaster barreling toward them with the
heedless onslaught of a runaway carriage. There was nothing to do but maintain her dignity as best she could and attempt to save Jared from the wreck of her own reputation.

Lady Mablethorpe, sitting stiffly upright in a Sheraton
armchair as if it were a throne, began the attack, forcing her
hostess to snap her mouth closed over her own intended
words. "Miss Todd," the marchioness demanded, "what
brings you to Somerset?" The question was overly direct for
after-dinner conversation, but ladies of Lady Mablethorpe's
age and rank were accustomed to saying anything they
pleased.

"I am here to settle my grandmother's estate," Abby
replied without rancor. "She wished me to spend two
months in her home and perform several commissions on

her behalf. Lord Langley, as executor of her estate, was designated to assist me."

"And who was your grandmother?" the marchioness asked, looking down the length of her patrician nose as if expecting Abby to name the local laundry woman.

"Clarissa Bivens, my lady. A neighbor to Langley Park, she resided in Vernhampton for close on to fifty years. Hence, her acquaintance with Lord Langley and her desire that he should execute the provisions of her will." Good. She had managed that quite well, Abby thought.

"You have been in the area how long?" Lady Mablethorpe continued her interrogation, while all the other ladies, including Hannah Greaves, looked on with awful fascination.

"Nearly a month, my lady. Lord Langley and I have completed half the commissions assigned to us. There are four left." Again, nothing but the truth.

Hannah Greaves could no longer contain herself. Abigail Todd was too fine a woman to be treated as if she were a prisoner on the block. "Miss Todd's father is a noted Boston physician," she declared, "and a lecturer at Harvard. She herself is owner and headmistress of an academy for young ladies. Therefore, we will be returning to America as soon as she has fulfilled the terms of Clar—her grandmother's will."

"Mrs. Greaves and I will sail on the *Rose of Sharon* on the third of September," Abby confirmed, and could feel the collective sigh of relief which swept the room.

"Then you and my son have been forced into close association by your grandmother's will," Lady Langley pointed out for the benefit of her guests.

"Yes, indeed." Abby brightened at this unexpected aid. "Lord Langley and Captain Verney have been most helpful. I could not have managed without them." She lowered her lashes, hoping she looked suitably appreciative of the Verney brothers' condescension.

"Bivens . . . Bivens," Lady Mablethorpe muttered. "I do not believe I know the name. Who were your grandmother's people, Miss Todd?"

It was bound to happen. Abby had known it would. But her feelings were not aided by a slight moan from Lady Langley.

"We visited her relatives in Oxford last week, my lady," Abby replied evenly, though her pounding heart was drowning the sound of her own voice in her ears. "My grandmother was, it seems, descended from a Baron Tyndale of Kent, her grandfather an Oxford don. I was pleased to converse with her cousin Eleanore Jerome and that lady's daughter, Mrs. Margaret Farleigh, whose husband is also a don."

Undiverted by these obviously acceptable connections, the marchioness continued her attack. "But your grandmother, Miss Todd, was she in society? I do not recall a family named Bivens."

The end was near. Abby knew how the losers in a battle must feel when it became apparent they were not destined to carry the day. "Her mother married a Clarence Bivens and moved to London," she replied, head high. "I fear I do not know any details." Which was as close to a lie as Abby could come. Revealing that Mr. Bivens owned a bootery was unnecessary, even for Miss Todd's stern New England conscience.

Help came from a second unexpected source. "I think it delightful that the earl is helping Miss Todd with her commissions," declared Lady Lavinia. "It is quite like a knight-errant carrying out quests for his lady." Shining blue eyes swept the room. "Do you not think so?"

"He has been most helpful," Abby agreed before any acerbic responses could cut the young lady down.

"Clarissa . . . Clarissa," Lady Mablethorpe mused. "How close a neighbor did you say she was, Miss Todd?"

"Quite close, my lady. She resided at Arbor Cottage, not more than a half mile from Langley Park."

"Good God!" gasped Lady Pierpont, who had been a mere spectator up to this point, "You cannot be talking of Clarissa Beaupré!"

"I believe she was also known by that name," Abby concurred, wondering if she and Hannah should make their adieus before the servants were called to escort them to the door.

Later, Abby would wish she had the talent to draw the expressions on the older ladies' faces. Shock for Lady Pierpont. Anguish for Lady Langley. Triumph for Lady Mablethorpe. Lady Christabelle and Lady Lavinia merely looked puzzled, aware they had missed something but having no idea what.

And then Lady Mablethorpe's face changed. A bark of laughter startled them all. "My dear Charlotte," she said to Lady Langley, "I shall dine out on this story for the next year. The Indifferent Earl caught in the same clutches as his grandfather—"

"Henrietta, you would not dare!"

"It is delicious, truly delicious. Miss Todd, you cannot sail on third September. This is a tale which must be allowed to continue to its end."

"It will indeed, my lady," Abby assured her grimly. "Its end is our sailing back to Boston as planned."

"Oh, no, no, no," the Marchioness of Mablethorpe chuckled, "I very much doubt it. I think it highly unlikely indeed."

Chapter Thirteen

After shaking off a bevy of disdainful but curious pea-cocks, Abby plunged into the shelter of the arbor. She sank down onto one of the center seats, clasped her hands tightly in her lap, and waited for the peace of this special place to settle over her. But her insides continued to shiver, her spirit hovering somewhere around her toes. Sunk beneath reproach. Last night . . . last night she had been revealed as the granddaughter of a courtesan, and not all the fine wrapping of her respected position in faraway Boston could remove the stigma. No matter how delighted Lady Mablethorpe was with the discovery, no matter Lady Langley's forbearance or the tight-lipped tolerance of Lady Pierpont, the names of Abigail Todd and Jared Verney were now linked in everyone's mind. A scandalous *on dit* that would titillate the *ton* for months to come.

My dear, have you heard? The very image of the old earl's mistress. Young Langley caught in the same trap, don't you know. The Indifferent Earl and the Reincarnated Clarisse. Snapped him up right under our noses. Upstart American, no better than she should be. You may take my word for it, he'll never marry her!

Poor Jared. She'd ruined him. And he'd looked so very fine in his black jacket and knee breeches, immaculate white linen, with his gray vest shot with silver, catching the color of his eyes. A diamond had sparked in his cravat and on each cuff, a lock of chestnut hair fallen over his noble brow. His lips, when they smiled, drew her in . . .

Dear Lord, she was becoming maudlin! And as fanciful as Lady Mablethorpe. Abigail Todd of Boston did not tolerate such idiocy. An earl was an earl and could easily survive his name being associated with a descendant of Clarissa Beaupré. Indeed, men being what they were, his reputation would probably be enhanced rather than shattered. And the determined mamas and fluttering young things would pursue him all the harder, believing—perhaps rightly–that this evidence of interest in a female indicated that The Indifferent Earl was ripe for a wife.

"Dare I enter?" Jared's silhouette filled the archway.

A listless, almost ungracious, wave of her hand, and Jared moved into the lion's den, meekly accepting Abby's designation of the seat across from her, although he had a strong inclination to sweep her into his arms and vow that everything was going to be all right, truly it was.

"Mea culpa," he murmured, "but would it not have been much worse to bar you from the door?"

"As you originally planned!"

"Do not give me worse traits than I already have, Abigail. My thought was to spare you."

"It is done, Jared, and cannot be undone. In a month I will go home, and the wonder of it will be gone as if it never was. You have been a good friend. I am sorry to so cut up your peace."

"Abby . . ." The earl clamped his teeth over what he had been about to say. Instead, he asked, "Can you not stay longer?"

Her head shot up. "Do not be absurd, my lord. I would go tomorrow if I did not feel an obligation to Clarissa. Gladly would I sell Arbor Cottage to you for whatever price you wish and be on the next ship back to Boston."

"I don't believe you," Jared responded, softly and unsmiling. "You cannot tell me you have not enjoyed this past month, the time we have spent together. I will not believe you wish to run away and never look back."

"I did not say I would not look back." Her admission was barely audible "No! Do not touch me. I could not bear it."

Jared subsided onto his bench, silently swearing. The

very qualities he most admired in her would be the architects of his downfall. Courage, intelligence, strength of purpose, high moral fiber—all would combine to take her from him. His only hope was to attach her feelings with bindings so strong she was unable to pull away. This he could not do with a houseful of guests requiring his attention. *Bloody hell!*

"When do you wish to leave for Salisbury?" he inquired.

"*Hannah and I* will leave in the morning, if your carriage is available."

"I will accompany you."

Abby sat up straighter, barbed her voice with steel. "We have had this conversation before, my lord. You know quite well you have an obligation to your guests. Give us Moorhead and Daniel, and we shall be fine."

She was right, though it did not sit well with him to admit it. Her commission must be fulfilled, and until he could convince his mother her machinations were hopeless, he was trapped at Langley Park with the houseguests.

"Myles will travel with you," Jared stated, unwilling to concede the issue entirely. "He will be glad enough for an excuse to quit the house."

"I had thought him to have an eye for Lady Christabelle."

Jared considered the matter. "She might do for Myles," he conceded, "but he likes being pursued as poorly as do I. You may depend on it, he will leap at the opportunity for a journey to Salisbury."

"Very well," Abby murmured, "but please do not insist the captain do something he cannot like."

But Jared's thoughts had leaped beyond his brother. "A bishop, you say? Rather an odd note for Clarissa, is it not?"

Abby offered him a winsome smile that twisted his sorely tried feelings into knots. "I confess to being intrigued," she said. "A bishop is not at all what I would expect to see numbered among her correspondents."

"I shall be eager to hear the tale when you return." Jared stood. "Shall I send the carriage at nine? You must plan to stay the night in Salisbury. If you visit the bishop the next morning, you should be back in time for supper the same day."

Abby thanked him most sincerely. As he scattered the peacocks with his long strides back to his horse, Jared fervently wished that Abby might have his own certainty of mind. Besotted as his grandfather, he was determined to have her. Yet 'twas obvious she was fixed against it. Hell and damnation, what a coil! Foolish girl, to turn her back on love.

Love. Foolish earl, to so forget his manners that he was ready to accompany his love to Salisbury, leaving his guests to fend for themselves. He was a sad case. A very sad case indeed.

Two mornings later, Jared escaped his guests—few of whom had yet descended for breakfast—by shutting himself in his private study and closing the door. Although he was long accustomed to having his own way, guilt hung heavy as he attempted to fulfill his duties as host at Langley Park. His body went through the motions, his lips opened, his voice spoke, but his thoughts were with the party traveling to Salisbury. More specifically, with one of those on their way to visit a retired bishop. His agitation over not seeing Abigail Todd for two full days brought home the reality of what life would be like when she was gone. Intolerable! He wouldn't allow her to leave.

Arrogance, nothing but arrogance. This was the nineteenth century, and he was no medieval Scottish laird raiding over the border to carry off a bride. Neither rank nor power, command nor entreaty were going to win Abigail Todd. Even love might not do the trick. For Abby's scruples were strong, her devotion to her calling as a teacher far more dedicated than he could like. Surely, there must be something more . . . some other reason. Surely the possibility that they shared a common grandfather was not sufficient. Another man? The intensity of the surge of jealousy which shot through him was astonishing. And brought yet another bout of guilt.

He was not living up to the expectations of his heritage.

To the expectations of his mother. To what had once been his expectations for himself. Abigail Todd was totally outside his world, a woman who would only be acceptable if the *ton,* following the lead of Lady Mablethorpe, chose to be amused. If Abby's beauty and gracious manner could outweigh the shock of such a misalliance.

It did not matter. They would live in seclusion, as his grandfather had lived with Clarissa Beaupré. Except, of course, that he would dignify their relationship with wedding vows.

Yet how could he even think of asking the woman he loved to give up the world? No matter the angle from which he viewed the problem, there was guilt. He was letting down his mother, his class, his own convictions—not to mention Abby and her convictions, as well as the young ladies in Boston who were awaiting her return.

A soft sound at the door. Jared wiped a grimace of annoyance from his face and bid the person enter. He rose as Viscount Pierpont's rotund figure glided in on surprisingly light feet and, with remarkably little perturbation, announced that he and his family were forced to cut short their stay. They would, he hoped, have the pleasure of seeing the earl in London during the Little Season. Lord Pierpont then tarnished this gracious speech by giving Jared a wink and assuring him his admiration for his lordship's taste was considerable. He would not think of putting a rub in the earl's way. And, besides, his dear puss could not hold a candle to Miss Todd. He and his family would be gone on the morrow.

Jared's guilt soared still higher, warring with relief. News of the fall of The Indifferent Earl was about to spread throughout the *ton.* If, indeed, the process had not already begun with the letter Lady Mablethorpe had asked him to frank that morning. He suspected that lady might stay the course, not wishing to miss what would happen when the travelers returned from their mysterious sojourn in Salisbury.

Late that evening, after the others had retired and he had endured yet another scalding scold from his mama, the earl paced the floor of his library. The French doors to the terrace were open, his jacket thrown carelessly onto a chair. Hair mussed, cravat askew, he appeared exceedingly grim. Hell and damnation, where were they? The journey to Salisbury was an easy one. They should have returned by dinner time. Flashes of carriage accidents, highwaymen, Abigail thrown into a ditch, bleeding from a gunshot wound, running off to Gretna Green with his perfidious brother, warred for supremacy in his mind.

He was Langley! His world revolved around him. His world did as it was bid. This could not be happening. He would not allow it. Jared poured a brandy, tossed it off. He peered at the decanter, idly noting how far it had gone down since he had begun his evening's vigil. Not good. A drunken sot was of no use if he had to ride to the rescue. Grasping the cut crystal decanter, he moved it from his desk to a small table on the far side of the room. When he turned, his brother was framed by the open French doors.

"Good God, Myles, where have you been?"

"Sorry," his brother muttered. "Coming back made me feel like a lamb returning to the slaughter. Couldn't face the music." The captain shrugged. "So I dropped the ladies off and treated Moorhead and Daniel to dinner at the Ploughboy. Seemed the least I could do for all their extra work."

As Myles wended his way across the room, Jared became aware that his brother had probably imbibed even more freely than himself. A fine pair they made. An earl of the realm and one of his majesty's finest, brought low by women. A whole slew of women.

"Moorhead and Daniel are being well compensated for their extra duties," Jared began sternly before realizing he sounded like a self-righteous prig. He shook his head, waved his brother to a comfortable wing chair. Taking a seat opposite him, he asked in a considerably milder tone, "How did the ladies like Salisbury Close?"

"They declared themselves enchanted, envying the clergy for having residences so sheltered from the world. In fact, they seemed quite determined to promote a similar cloistered environment for retired teachers when they return to Boston."

"And the bishop?"

Myles grinned, tapping his thumb beneath his chin. "Ah, the good bishop. You know, brother, sometimes I wonder about the old girl's motives. I understand Sentiment, Nostalgia, Family, but I think this can have been nothing other than Mischief. When the poor old man, well fed as he was, read her letter, he turned quite purple. I swear to you I've never seen such a color except in a piece of cloth. A fit of the apoplexy at any moment, I thought. But he recovered, informed us that Miss Beaupré wished to thank him for a past service he was able to grant her, thanked Miss Todd kindly for delivering the letter, and did we plan to return to Vernhampton today?" Myles stretched out his feet, flashed a rueful smile. "'Twas plain we were dismissed. Undoubtedly, the old boy was anxious for a restorative nip at the brandy. So we thanked him for his kind attention and took our leave."

"A service?" Jared inquired, amused.

"I suspect the only service rendered to Clarissa Beaupré was that of a stallion to a mare."

Jared did not bother to stifle his bark of laughter. "I suspect you are right. This was out and out mischief. Torment for a peccadillo of his youth. A wagging finger: *Dear Bishop, I have not forgotten.*"

"Jared?" Myles paused, scowling at the toes of his polished Hessians.

"Yes?"

"Have you ever considered that Clarissa had another purpose in mind when she set up these commissions?"

"Ah . . . you're beginning to wonder, are you?"

The captain groaned. "Second to big brother again, am I? And how long have you doubted the lady's motives?"

"I could say, since the moment I first saw Abigail Todd," the earl mused. "But, truthfully, only after our trip to Bath were my suspicions fully aroused."

"The old witch is matchmaking."

"I believe so," Jared agreed. "Oh, some of the letters serve a purpose. Abby has a right to know about her father's family, but the others? . . . I have to agree that her purpose was to throw Abby and myself together. But whether for sentiment or revenge, I cannot tell. Very clever was our Clarissa. A woman to be reckoned with."

"Revenge?" Myles murmured. "Why revenge?"

His brother simply looked at him. After a moment, the captain's eyes fell. "The arrogance of the Verneys," he conceded. "All these years and it never occurred to me she might have minded not being offered marriage."

"Quite impossible. Just not done, old boy," Jared mocked.

Myles sunk his head into his hands. "I confess my head's not up to clever thought at the moment. Suggestions, Jared? What happens next?"

"I strongly suspect Clarissa has anticipated our difficulties," the earl returned dryly. "We have a month's time and three commissions yet to be fulfilled. Surely, somewhere in Clarissa's little game there has to be an answer."

My dear Abigail (and do not chide me for calling you so),
   You may wish me in Hades for inviting you to drive out after so much journeying these past weeks, but I wish to speak with you in private. Will three o'clock be convenient?

                                             Your friend, J

Abby could not help but smile. The arrogant earl was making progress in addressing an independent American lady. And the opportunity to speak with him in private after the alarms of the past few days was a prospect she found all too attractive. As much as she disliked to admit it, she had missed him. Myles had been all that was helpful and amusing, but it was not at all the same. Damping the flare of eagerness in her eyes, she looked up, addressing the patiently waiting Deering quite coolly. "You may inform the messenger I shall be pleased to see Lord Langley at three o'clock."

She would wear her pale green muslin sprigged in white, Abby thought as the butler left to convey her response, and she would not even need a spencer. The waning days of July

were not as hot as Boston, but there was little doubt high
summer was upon them. She would leave her hair down,
Abby decided. It was, after all, quite respectable when confined by her bonnet.

A shameless decision, as wanton as Clarissa! She could
not have him. Would not have him. Yet a glorious anthem
was racing through her, her heart thumping in rhythm with
a heavenly chorus. Jared Verney wished to speak with her in
private. Even if it were nothing more than to set a time for
their next task . . . By the time the earl's curricle came up the
drive, Abby's thoughts had skittered from the mundane to
ultimate disaster. He was crying off from their commissions.
Ah, dear God, he was coming to tell her he had offered for
Lady Christabelle!

Jared took one look at Abby's face and instantly recognized her smile of greeting as false. "We are still friends, are
we not?" he inquired, standing very close just before handing her up onto the seat. But her murmured reply was somehow lost beneath the broad brim of the straw bonnet with
the peacock feathers. Making a wise decision to stick to the
commonplace for the moment, Jared said as they exited the
gates of Arbor Cottage, "Myles tells me you and Mrs.
Greaves found Salisbury Close charming."

Abby visibly brightened. "Oh, indeed. For a moment I
was quite tempted to the cloistered life. How very fine to
live behind walls, with only those of a like mind around you.
It is quite the first time I ever understood the attraction of the
convent. Surely there must be a great competition among the
clergy to be allowed to retire to such tranquility."

"So I understand," Jared agreed, "but not you, Abby. I
cannot see you finding such a life attractive for long."

"Very true," she sighed. "It was so lovely, so marvelously
sheltered from the world. In a way, it reminded me of Arbor
Cottage. So beautiful . . . yet so unrealistic. In truth, I should
go mad in a month. Though, perhaps, when I am old and
gray, I should be more pleased to retire from the world," she
added thoughtfully.

Holding this confidence for further reference, Jared
moved on to another topic, telling her of the departure of

Lord and Lady Pierpont and their daughter. That Lady Mablethorpe and Lady Christabelle would stay on as guests of his mother only, freeing him to be of use to Abby in her three remaining quests. "I believe," he added blandly, "that Lady Mablethorpe is consumed with curiosity."

"She fancies herself the witness to a carriage running out of control toward a gorge," Abby responded, equally neutral. "She does not wish to miss the wreck."

"Will there be a wreck, Abby?" Jared inquired softly. "Surely we are too wise to allow that to happen."

Chapter Fourteen

*T*he earl cursed the invention of the bonnet. If he tried to peer around it, the wreck was likely to be sooner rather than later. "They will be cutting this field next week," he commented casually as they drove past waving stalks of pale gold wheat.

No reply. Abby's shoulders were so stiff Jared feared she was being badly jounced about. He allowed silence to reign until they had gone a half mile down a narrow lane and he had pulled the horses to a halt by an idyllic grassy hollow where a large willow hung out over a small stream. Water gurgled over modest-sized granite boulders, cooling the air around them. At the edge of the clearing, which was shaded by sturdy oaks, was a granite boulder about two feet high, its surface worn smooth by all the times it had been used as a seat in the aeons since nature had tossed it there.

Jared helped Abby down, then ordered his groom to walk the horses. Startled, Abby watched the curricle turn round a bend and disappear behind a hedgerow. When the earl had said he wished to speak with her alone, he evidently meant exactly that. In spite of the warmth of the day, she shivered. Whatever his topic, it must be very serious indeed. Their situation was most improper, even for a woman of her considerable years. They were completely alone in the middle of nowhere, not a house, a barn, nor even a sheep, in sight. Undoubtedly, the groom had been instructed not to return for some length of time known only to the earl.

Somehow Abby found herself seated on the boulder with

strong hands deftly at work beneath her chin. "Jared!" she exclaimed.

"I wish to talk to you, not your blasted bonnet," he retorted, tossing Abby's prized confection onto the mossy green grass.

Abby tried to focus on the sunlit splashing of the stream, but they were seated hip to hip, her heart somehow stuck in her throat. How could she possibly talk about anything? The sharpness of her mind had been snuffed as easily as a candle. She was about as capable of a serious discussion as Lady Lavinia. May God forgive her for such an uncharitable thought!

"Abby, I wish to know why you have never married."

Merciful heavens, was that it? Was this, then, the cause of all her suffering since she'd scanned his note that morning?

Abby gathered her resources, forcing herself to hear the sound of the moving water, the varying notes of the birds, the underlying hum of insects. She was sensible, capable Abigail Todd of Boston. After all these years, she could speak of what was never mentioned. Of the personal tragedy that had changed her life. She could tell this titled English gentleman, her friend Jared, of her greatest pain, of the loss that refused to go away.

"I was affianced at seventeen," Abby said, her gaze fixed on the gloved hands in her lap. "To a young man I had known all my life. Jonathan Blaisdell. He was first mate on a ship out of Boston. We were to be married as soon as he got a ship of his own, and I was to travel with him 'round the world." Abby paused, carefully pleating the folds of her gown. "On the last leg of his voyage home from China, his ship went down with all hands in a hurricane off the Bahamas."

"I'm sorry," Jared said. Firm fingers touched her hand. "Truly I am."

"I know I must sound overly dramatic," Abby continued, without acknowledging the comfort of his touch, "when I tell you that my life ended before it ever began, but that was how I felt. I asked my father to allow me to use my dowry to set up a school, for I knew that was what I must do to make use of my life now that all my hopes and dreams had been dashed."

"And he gave it to you?" Jared wondered. "Did no one tell you you were so very young and lovely that love must certainly enter your life once more?"

A rueful smile, a shake of her head. "There were times I thought half Boston must be of a like mind. The opposition . . . the admonitions. Scolding, pleading, outright shock. Believe me, I heard it all."

"You would not heed them."

"I was nearly nineteen by then. And headstrong."

That he could well believe. "And you were never tempted?" Jared asked. "You could teach other people's children and never desire to have little ones of your own?"

Abby's head dipped lower, her voice declining to a whisper. "You have found me out," she admitted. "There are times when it has been . . . difficult."

Jared laid the tips of his fingers under her chin, gently raised her face to his. His heart clenched, for her eyes brimmed with tears. He longed to declare himself. To say, "Stay with me, Abby. Marry me, bear my children," but the timing was impossibly wrong. Jonathan Blaisdell, long years dead, loomed between them as solid as the granite on which they were sitting. Not to mention her dedication to all those silly young ladies back in Boston.

When planning this drive, Jared had thought to snatch a kiss. Truthfully . . . a bit more than a kiss. Not that he had intended a seduction in this sheltered glen, but surely he could not be faulted for dreaming of something more than a few short seconds of a chaste embrace. Could he? After all, his Abby was no longer the young girl Blaisdell had known. She was a woman with all a woman could offer. All a woman could want. Somehow, some way she would be his. Yet for the moment he must hold his peace. Only for the moment. If Jared Reignald Fitzroy Verney, Earl of Langley, could not compete with an American sailor, gone these many years, then he did not deserve Miss Abigail Todd of Boston.

The drive back to Arbor Cottage was marked by a strangely companionable silence, each willing to respect the other's privacy, each caught up in regrets for words spoken and thoughts unspoken.

Had she, perhaps, dramatized her love for Jonathan beyond all reason?

He'd have her, by God, if he had to go to Boston and drag her back to Langley Park!

My dearest granddaughter,

I hope that by now you are becoming more familiar with the world that comprised my life. Dear Chauncey, I suppose he denied he had ever known me. Poor man, he never could quite come to terms with the fact that clergymen are also human.

You have met some of your relatives by now, and I trust you survived the encounters without too much difficulty. I fear, however, that there are dirtier dishes on the family tree. If fate is kind, Myles will have returned from his adventures and be available to accompany you and Jared to London, for your next task will be daunting. If the captain is not available, then I suggest Jared find another stout arm to bear you company.

"I cannot like it," Abby declared, lowering the letter, which she had been reading aloud.

Jared stifled a most ignoble groan. "I had hoped we'd seen the last of her relatives."

"Get on with it," Myles instructed. "This begins to sound interesting." A long-drawn sigh echoed from Hannah Greaves.

I have a niece, Betty Bivens, daughter of a half brother born after my mother's marriage to Clarence Bivens. She married an Edward Mapes and bore him several children. The youngest, to everyone's amazement, has turned out to be a throwback to her Tyndale ancestors, gifted with the dainty face and

*figure of an aristocrat. She is exquisite, I am told.
Petite, blond, blue-eyed, graceful. What some men
call a pocket Venus. Her mother has made a
particular effort to raise her with proper speech and
manners, fortunately, something not totally lost
through the generations.*

*The child's name is Lily. At the time of this
writing, she is just turned sixteen. Her father, I am
told, is already making plans to take advantage of
her beauty. He thinks to make his fortune presenting
her as the natural successor to La Grande Clarisse.
<u>Abigail, this must not happen!</u>*

"That last is underscored three times," Abby informed
her audience. She resumed her reading:

*I count on you to rescue the child. Even if she has
already been launched on the path to notoriety, I beg
you to save her. Few women of my kind are fortunate
enough to acquire a lifelong love and considerable
wealth, and even then the price was too high. Never
to believe myself good enough for a wedding ring.
Never to feel the approbation of my neighbors. Never
to know the joy of children and grandchildren at my
knee. These are tragedies I must live with. Tragedies
I will not allow for Lily.*

*You cannot know, dearest Abby, how proud I am
of all you have accomplished. Of my delight in
knowing what a remarkable and upright woman you
are. Or how proud I am of your father and what he
has made of his life. I take great satisfaction in
knowing I did the right thing when I sent him away
with the Todds.*

*And now I address you and Jared together. Please
go to London and rescue my great-niece Lily. I am
unable to offer suggestions on how this may be
accomplished, but I beg you to find a way. Abigail, if
other means fail, perhaps you could take her back to*

*Boston with you. Since she is such a beauty, surely
some nice young man will want to take her to wife.*

*I hasten to assure you that this is your last
unpleasant commission. The final two are—shall we
say?—quite different. I believe you will find them
fascinating. So do this thing for Lily, and then you
will be free to enjoy the remainder of your time at
Arbor Cottage.*

May God go with you. Your loving grandmother,
Clarissa

"London," Myles pronounced with great satisfaction.
"When do we leave?"

"Fortunately, we have time to investigate this situation
before leaping into the carriage," Jared declared.

"Time!" Abby sputtered. "Indeed we do not. I leave in a
month, and who knows what has happened to the poor child
since this letter was written." She rustled the pages, searching for a date. "See here," she said, shaking the missive
under the earl's nose, "'twas written nearly a year ago. We
must be off immediately!"

"We," declared the earl in godlike tones, "will not be off
anywhere. If you think for one moment I would allow you
to march into such a situation—"

"Abominable!" Abby cried. "Then I shall go without
you. Will you accompany me, Myles?"

"You'll both go when I go," the earl roared.

"I left off my short pants a long time ago, brother," the
captain declared. "If Abby considers the situation desperate,
then I am ready. At your service, cousin," he told her.

"The girl's been waiting for months on end," Jared
snapped. "Another day or two won't matter."

"Barnyard cats!" Hannah Greaves interjected in the
voice she had perfected while raising four boys and two
girls. "I am ashamed of all three of you. You, Abigail, for
being so headstrong and unaware of your obligation to the
earl for his remarkable kindness to us. And you, sirs, for forgetting that you are gentlemen. One would suppose you both
back in the schoolroom."

Shamefaced, Abby ducked her head, but not before noting Jared had hidden his face behind his hand, his reaction to Hannah's scold a mystery. The captain's shoulders were shaking. Abby rather thought he was laughing.

"Now," Hannah said, "I wish to know why you want to delay the matter, my lord. The situation seems dire."

"Fools rush in, Mrs. Greaves," the earl murmured. "The situation cannot be remedied if we do not fully understand exactly what it is."

"Ah. Most sensible, I'm sure, my lord. Do you not agree, Abigail? Captain?"

Abby, accustomed to settling disputes among her pupils, was mortified to find herself being offered a similar treatment by her companion. Good Lord, she was twenty-eight years old. The captain must be close to the same. How could they be sitting here like schoolchildren receiving a scold from the governess?

"And when would you wish to leave, my lord?" Hannah inquired of the earl while Abby ground her teeth.

"I will send to my solicitor immediately and have him make inquiries. Hopefully, the task will not be difficult."

"May we not go to London in the meanwhile," Abby proposed, "so we will be ready when the situation is clear?"

Myles chuckled as Jared scowled. If his brother accepted a leg-shackle from this independent American, his life would never be peaceful. Then again, it would never be boring. And his nights . . . Ah, yes, he had come full circle in his opinion of Abigail Todd. She was almost enough to convince him that marriage was not anathema.

"Very well," Jared sighed. "We will leave two mornings hence. I shall direct my solicitor to send word to Langley House rather than here."

"Oh, dear," Hannah murmured. Abby's eyes flew to her companion's face and found . . . dismay. "The impropriety, child," Mrs. Greaves pointed out.

"What impropriety?" Abby demanded, genuinely puzzled.

"We have been misled by all our jauntering about without criticism, when, in fact, none of our travels were quite up to snuff. A young woman traipsing about the countryside with two unmarried gentlemen can never be acceptable. But we were in the country, you see, and I felt my chaperonage adequate. But in London, my dear . . . to stay at the earl's townhouse in full view of the *ton* . . . looking as you do . . ." Hannah's voice trailed away as words failed her.

"Perhaps we should stay in an obscure inn," Abby offered in a small voice.

"Nonsense!" Once again, Jared was close to shouting.

"Much worse," Myles agreed. "Then everyone would be sure we were hiding something. Neither of us is unknown in town, you know."

Abby and Hannah sighed in unison. "I cannot like it," the latter said.

"It is fortunate, is it not," said Abby on a wry note, "that we are returning to Boston in a month. Hannah and I may escape, leaving the two of you to face the music. Chivalrous gentlemen that you are."

"Ruined," the earl intoned.

"Sunk beneath reproach," his brother concurred.

"Hannah and I will stay at the Clarendon," Abby announced. "The gentlemen may stay at Langley House."

"My dear child," Hannah declared, "do you not recall the outrageous bill when we were there for a mere three days? A shocking waste of funds!"

"She's quite right, you know," Myles added, grinning hugely. "Not practical at all, when we've all those rooms and a multitude of servants growing fat with so little to occupy their time."

"I believe it's settled then," the earl declared, getting to his feet.

"If we set out quite early, may we make the journey in one day?" Abby asked.

Jared and Myles groaned in unison. "Must we?" the earl sighed.

"I think we must. I fear for my young cousin."

"You ladies have proved yourselves excellent travelers," the earl conceded. "A half hour after daybreak, it is," Jared agreed.

The Verney brothers took their leave. Myles, eager for action, for an opportunity to show his metal. Jared, feeling very much as if he'd lost control of the entire business. It was not a feeling he could like. Instead of sitting safe at home, while he and Myles took care of the matter, Abby was once again charging off into the unknown. Joan of Arc begging for the stake. No, he could not like it. Could not like it at all.

Solemnly, Deering held out a silver salver on which rested a single calling card. Abby, who was seated in the Wicker Room, attempting to finish *Emma,* peered at the card. Her green eyes widened. "She is here? Now?" Abby breathed.

"All three of them, miss," Deering intoned. "I put them in the drawing room."

"Deering," Abby asked, "to the best of your knowledge, has Lady Langley ever set foot in this house?"

The butler forgot himself enough to blink. "Oh, no, miss," he replied in shocked accents. "Never!"

Abby drew a deep breath. "Bring whatever refreshments you deem appropriate," she told Clarissa's loyal major-domo, "and please inform Mrs. Greaves we have guests." Deering, full of news which would shock his spouse and the kitchen staff as well as Hannah Greaves, set off at as fast a pace as a proper butler could allow.

Abby put a marker in the copy of *Emma.* That the shocking little snob, so overly attached to her papa, should actually be rewarded with the noble and sensible Mr. Knightly seemed remarkably unfair. The silly chit should have been forced out into the world to earn her own keep instead of winning such a fine prize. Indeed, his love of Emma seemed to be Knightly's only fault. But perhaps the author had it right. Men were very strange creatures. There was no accounting for their tastes.

Abby tucked in stray curls, smoothed the folds of her sprigged muslin—pink rosebuds on cream with a fichu of matching lace—and set off for the drawing room, wondering fleetingly if Jared and Myles had any idea of their guests' whereabouts. She strongly suspected that if they had, they would have accompanied the ladies.

Abby swept in, head high, a smile fixed firmly in place. "Lady Langley, Lady Mablethorpe, Lady Christabelle," she pronounced. "How very kind of you to visit us." The ladies had arrayed themselves on Clarissa's very fine Louis Quinze chairs. Abby joined them. "I understand you have not been to Arbor Cottage before," she said to Jared's mama, taking the bull by the horns. "Perhaps, before you leave, you would wish to see some of the cottage and then walk in the gardens. The arbor is of particular interest, I believe."

"You are most gracious," Lady Langley replied stiffly. Abby suspected she was here only she had been bullocked into it by Lady Mablethorpe.

"Did you enjoy your journey to Salisbury, Miss Todd?" Lady Christabelle inquired.

"The Close, the cathedral, the cloister courtyard—all were exquisite," Abby told her, grateful for the neutral topic. "Well worth the trip, but I apologize for taking Captain Verney from you. My grandmother, you see, stipulated in her will that Lord Langley must assist me on the commissions she set. In this instance the captain was kind enough to act in his stead."

Lady Christabelle blushed, suddenly appearing far less the sophisticated town beauty and more the vulnerable besotted maiden. Oh, dear, Abby thought, hoping Myles would not break the girl's heart. Her own heart, however, gave a thump of satisfaction. Evidently, Jared was in no danger from the strikingly attractive and self-confident Lady Christabelle.

There was a flurry of greetings as Hannah Greaves joined them, looking nearly as flustered as Abby felt. The approbation indicated by a call from these three sterling members of the *ton* was far more than she had ever expected.

"These commissions," Lady Mablethorpe said, "what is their nature?"

There were times, Abby thought, trying not to wince, when the marchioness seemed to believe she had the privileges of royalty. In this instance Abby decided not to take umbrage. It was only a moderate invasion of privacy in a situation so strained that she was willing for almost any port in a storm.

"She set eight commissions, my lady," Abby informed Lady Mablethorpe. "The personal delivery of a token, the return of old letters, a visit to cousins I did not know I had. The tasks appear to range from Sentiment to Compassion to Family and Duty. In one case"—a tiny smile lit her face—"in one case I might almost say she was up to Mischief, a bit of teasing from the grave." The ladies were staring at her, utterly fascinated. "There are three commissions left," she continued. "Deering and his wife are the keepers of our letters of instruction from Clarissa, but even they have no idea what is in them. We do know, however, that our next task takes us to London, and Clarissa was quite firm that both Lord Langley and Captain Verney should accompany us. I am truly sorry to be so disaccommodating, but I have only a few weeks left in my stay here, and we must make all haste."

"What, pray tell," declared Lady Mablethorpe, "could Clarissa Beaupré have to do with anyone in Salisbury Close?"

"We walked through the Close, my lady. I did not, I believe, say that I visited anyone there." And that was the honest truth. If only the good bishop Chauncey Merriwether could know how close to mendacity Abigail Todd had come to preserve his good name.

Lady Mablethorpe's "Humph!" echoed through the room just as Deering and a footman arrived with the tea tray and several silver dishes filled with delicacies more suited to high tea. Abby's lips twitched. What consternation there must have been in the kitchen.

Conversation was somewhat less stilted over tea, but Abby never lost her awareness of the enormous condescension being shown her by this visit. Therefore, she would be gracious, showing no sign of the turmoil that was shaking her insides. She expected the ladies to bolt for the door as soon as the last cherry tart disappeared from the plate. In fact, Lady Langley shot a significant look at Lady Mablethorpe, only to have that lady sink farther into her silk brocaded armchair as if she planned a visit of some duration. Lady Christabelle, looking puzzled, peered at her mother from under modestly lowered lashes.

"I believe I promised you a tour," Abby said brightly, rising to her feet. "You will like the Wicker Room, I think, and then we may go out into the courtyard and gardens."

Lady Mablethorpe did not budge. "Indeed, Miss Todd, that sounds very fine, but I must tell you that we have come to see the portrait. Since the earliest days of my marriage to Mablethorpe, I have heard of Clarissa Beaupré's painting. It *is* here, is it not?"

Ah . . . the quid pro quo, Abby thought as shocked gasps echoed from Lady Langley, Lady Christabelle, and Hannah Greaves. Well, why not? That the ladies would also be looking at Abigail Todd in the flesh was a fact she refused to contemplate. Perhaps Mrs. Deering could show the portrait. . . . Ah, no, Abby sighed. It was *her* house. Her responsibility. This was not a task to be foisted off on the housekeeper. She could, of course, simply say *no*. But if there were to be any future for her here, there must be no surprises left. *Absurd!* Her only future was the *Rose of Sharon* on third September.

"Very well," Abby declared. "If you will kindly follow me . . ."

"Abigail!" Hannah warned. And was ignored.

The procession moved down the hallway into Clarissa's bedroom, where Abby allowed sufficient time for the ladies to gape at the ornate room before she moved to the wall opposite the bed and drew the pink silk curtains.

Lady Mablethorpe stared, Lady Christabelle blushed. Lady Langley staggered backward, collapsing onto Clarissa's crewel-embroidered quilt. "Doomed," she groaned. "My poor Jared. My poor besotted boy." She continued to murmur to herself. The only words Abby caught were "hopeless, absolutely hopeless."

Chapter Fifteen

$\mathcal{B}$orn and raised in Boston, Abby had never known anything but city life until her long days at sea followed by the past month at Arbor Cottage. Although London was larger, older, more elegant than the younger American city, its ambience was a familiar friend. The clatter of carriages, the rumble of wagon wheels, the shouts of vendors, the bustle of crowds, the lively hum of thousands of people packed into residences ranging from hovels to palaces, brought home to Abby how very different it all was from life in the country. And yet, for the first time she saw the dirt. Her nose wrinkled at the smells. She had seen poverty and its effects when she accompanied her father to his weekly clinic on the waterfront, but she was so accustomed to the underbelly of her own city, she suddenly realized she had never actually *seen* it.

Nor had she truly seen London when she was there at the end of June. It had been merely another city. The enemy's capital. She had tried not to be dazzled by the fine shops, even as she patronized their services. She had compared the imposing residences of Mayfair to the homes on Beacon Hill and found the latter's relative modesty appealing. Americans didn't need all those fences, fancy gates, and private parks. Boston Common was good enough for all. And if American dress was more practical, less ostentatious, then she could thank her sturdy Pilgrim ancestors who had turned their backs on their mother country and founded a New World of less pomp and circumstance.

But today, with dusk fast approaching as they drove past every kind of decadence on their way to Langley House on Berkeley Square, Abby saw and smelled it all. One month in the country and, like a siren song, it had her in its grip. Merciful heavens, she liked it! The bucolic beauty so silent it had kept her awake her first nights at Arbor Cottage was suddenly an ideal much missed. The soothing sigh and soft scent of the gardens. The tinkling splash of the courtyard fountain. The honeysuckle and roses twining over the arbor. Even the raucous squawking of the peacocks.

How very odd. One month, and she knew she could spend the remainder of her life in the country quite happily, with only an occasional trip to the city for a dash of shopping and the brightening spark of an opera, a play, a visit to a museum. Yet she had not realized it until this moment when she looked on London with eyes that might as well have been blind when she passed this way before.

Horrified, Abby drew back into a corner of the coach and closed her eyes. *This could not be happening.* She could not actually prefer the country, particularly the *English* countryside, to Boston. Her life was in the new England, not the old. On third September she was going home. Back to everything that was near and dear. There was nothing for her here in this ancient land from which both her father's and mother's ancestors had fled.

There were vast amounts of forest and fields outside the city of Boston. Far more than the puny remnants left in England now. Perhaps she and her father could find a cottage . . . or even build one. Papa should get more rest, have a quiet place to spend an occasional weekend. Yes, that was the very thing. She would begin a search for a suitable property as soon as she got home.

Abby was in a much better frame of mind by the time Moorhead stopped the coach before an elegant townhouse in Berkeley Square. Yes, indeed, she had found an admirable solution to the dichotomy of her feelings. She would ignore the traces of mocking laughter echoing from some hidden recess of her mind.

*   *   *

Since Lady Langley made frequent visits to town, Langley House was well staffed and ready for occupancy on little notice. It was, indeed, one of the expenses the earl would have preferred to do without, but deny his mother both pleasure and consequence he could not. And his own pride would have suffered, he had to admit, if he had succumbed to the temptation of selling the Verney family's traditional town residence. Built with all the opulence of the early eighteenth century, the rooms were spacious, the furnishings elegant, if showing occasional signs of wear. The earl could be quietly confident that Abby and Hannah would find their rooms to their liking.

Myles joined his brother for a brandy after their long day's journey. "The ladies are safely tucked up?" he asked as he entered the library.

"I trust so," Jared sighed, nodding toward the bottle that was sitting on his desk. He was slumped in a comfortable wing chair, his booted feet resting on an upholstered stool.

Myles eyed the letter lying open on the leather-topped desk. "You've had word?" he asked as he sank, glass in hand, into a matching chair across from his brother.

"Yes."

"Well?"

"Not good," Jared sighed. "Smallwood had no difficulty getting information. The chit's being touted all over town as the Beaupré's niece, a successor worthy of La Grande Clarisse's name. As far as I can tell, she's not yet been sold, but the bidding's fierce, the bets in the clubs already enough to ruin her forever."

Myles swore. "Exactly so," Jared intoned, tossing off his brandy. He sat up just enough to stretch out a long arm to his desk and pour a refill.

"So do we hire an army and go in and get her?" Myles inquired, eyes gleaming with an odd mix of eagerness and amusement.

"An army, Myles?" Jared chided softly. "Captain Verney needs more than Langley at his back?"

"You add new meaning to 'pistols for two,'" his brother mocked.

"Diplomacy, I think, Myles," the earl murmured. "'Tis likely gold will get us farther than lead."

"And spoil all the fun?" the captain protested.

"Patience, dear boy. It may come to pistols yet. We will explore negotiation first."

"You know," Myles said slowly, "it's possible the girl doesn't want to be rescued. Seventeen is a damned stupid age."

"You should know," his brother agreed. Provocatively.

The captain ignored him. Neither of their careers at seventeen could bear much scrutiny. "So it's will-she, nill-she," Myles said.

"Possibly. I am hoping for a sensible compromise."

"Wrought with gold you can ill afford."

"You forget, I am executor of Clarissa's estate. She may not have had as much stashed away as I had presumed, but she died far from penniless. The estate will stand the expense of this enterprise."

"Oh, happy thought," said the captain. Holding his snifter up to the candlelight, he rotated the contents, studying the warm glow as if it contained the answers to life's questions. "I used to find you highly annoying," he told his brother thoughtfully. "But I find, now that I am older, you are not so bad. For a brother, that is."

"Your approbation unmans me," murmured the earl.

Another brandy for each was immediately indicated, lest the brothers be betrayed into any further maudlin sentiments.

Abby and Hannah stepped out of the earl's town carriage, a somewhat old-fashioned landau with the top full open, and stared at the front of the shop whose brass plate proclaimed, "EDWARD MAPES, FINE LINENS." "No," Abby declared, looking up at the earl, who had leapt out to hand them down, "we shall not need you. As we agreed, I shall introduce myself and invite Miss Mapes and her mother to tea. They can scarce refuse an invitation to the townhouse of an earl."

"That may be so," Jared said, "but I cannot like the sound

of Mapes himself. And I suspect you will find him behind the counter inside."

"And what can he do in a public shop, pray tell?" Abby scoffed. They had picked this bone over before leaving Langley House. She saw no earthly reason to renew the argument. "I believe we agreed on subtlety. I even promised to leave the letter until the ladies come to tea. It is, in fact, atop a dresser in my bedroom. Does that satisfy you, my lord?"

Jared shook his head, the silver eyes gone nearly to charcoal. "Clarissa was not given to alarms over nothing," he told her.

"We will go in, request to see Mrs. Mapes and Lily, and extend our invitation. If they are not home, I have written out an invitation for tomorrow. We shall not be above ten minutes, I assure you."

"He may consider you a rival," Jared pointed out, playing his trump card.

"Rival!" Abby echoed. "Whatever do you mean?"

"You are Clarissa's image. You have come to London all the way from America. Mapes may well conclude you're here to be the next Clarissa yourself. He could turn hostile, I should think."

Abby blanched. "You might have mentioned this earlier," she breathed.

"Quite frankly, I didn't think of it earlier. Omnipotent I'm not."

There was a snort from Myles, who was standing next to his brother. Hannah Greaves looked grave. "So we wait right here," the captain said to Jared. "If the ladies are not out in a quarter of an hour, we'll go in to find them. I doubt even Mapes can have sold them into slavery in that length of time."

"Young man—" Hannah declared, swelling in outrage.

"Come along," Abby instructed her companion. "We are blocking the walk."

The inside of the linen-draper's was shadowed, the great stacks of cloth cutting off the light from the glass windows at the front. Abby paused to allow her eyes to adjust. It was an establishment of some size, with linens and muslins for ladies' clothing on one side, a sea of white damasks and other fine fabrics suitable for tablecloths, napkins, and sheets on the other. Near the far wall Abby spotted white goods of lesser quality, undoubtedly intended for servants' bedding and aprons. The stacks were neat, no sign of dust. It appeared that Edward Mapes was a successful and respectable merchant. She could not help but wonder if Clarissa had gotten the situation wrong.

Abby nodded to the young clerk who had come out from behind his counter to greet her. "I am Miss Abigail Todd of Boston, Massachusetts," she told him. "I am looking for a Mrs. Edward Mapes. I believe she resides above? I am a cousin, visiting from America."

The young man, seemingly flustered by having an American come to call, mumbled something incoherent and dashed toward a back room. In less than a minute a barrel-chested man of medium height, whose vest buttons appeared ready to pop at any moment, came striding down the aisle. "Edward Mapes," he barked. "You know my wife?" His face was choleric, veins bulged in his forehead. Abby could see suspicion progress to hostility as his dark eyes peered at her from beneath shaggy brows. She experienced a frisson of fear. All in her head, she scolded herself. Clarissa's warnings, then Jared's, had set her teeth on edge.

"No, sir," she replied gently, not wishing to exacerbate his temper, "but I believe she is a cousin of sorts, and I should very much like to meet her." She turned mild expectant eyes on Mr. Mapes, while holding her breath.

He looked her over from head to toe. The nerve of the man! Abby fumed. How dare he? But if she lost her temper, she might never meet her young cousin. Nor would she be able to carry out her grandmother's intentions.

"You've got the look of her," he growled. "Saw a picture once, some toff's sketch, done from memory of a grand night, he said. Come to set yourself up, have you?" he challenged. "Plannin' to push my chick into the shade?"

"My dear sir—" Hannah Greaves cried.

Abby clutched her companion's arm, drew herself up into all the dignity of Miss Abigail Todd of Miss Todd's Academy for Young Ladies. "I am here to settle my aunt's estate, Mr. Mapes. I am booked to return to Boston in early September. I assure you I am not, and never will be, a member of the *demimonde*."

"Ah-h," said the linen-draper, rubbing his chin. His eyes took on an avaricious gleam. "Then perhaps there's a legacy, what? Did the old girl leave our puss a nice dowry, perchance?"

"I don't think so," Abby said, taken aback because the thought had not occurred to her. Surely Jared would have mentioned it if there had been a bequest to Lily in the will.

Mapes scowled. "A pity, the old girl must have had a nice bit of blunt," he grumbled. "Still and all, I suppose there's no harm in your meeting the wife and Lily, seeing as you're going home so quick like. "Come along, come along, I'll take ye up."

Though she would never admit it to a soul, Abby's knees were wobbly as she followed Mapes up the stairs to the second floor. She recalled all too clearly the disaster of the letter she had delivered to Broderick Wetherby in Southampton, the old hostilities stirred up in Oxford. Surely this was worse. For this time she was deliberately setting out to do something contrary to the family's intentions. For, after meeting Edward Mapes, she no longer doubted Clarissa's judgment.

Betty Bivens Mapes was a shadow creature. Abby instantly suspected her husband beat her on a regular basis. Her features, once likely quite fine, were now faded, perfectly in accord with the droop of her shoulders, the hesitation of her movement. The shock of discovering she was receiving a visit from an American cousin seemed to freeze her to the floor. But Mrs. Mapes's incomprehension went unnoticed, for, when standing next to her daughter, the former Betty Bivens became totally invisible.

Lily Mapes was stunning. There was no other word, Abby thought. She was suddenly very glad she had insisted Jared and Myles stay with the carriage. *Bloody hell!* whispered the imp inside. She had been warned, but somehow she had not expected . . .

"Oh, how delightful," the vision cried as waves of silver-blond hair tumbled over her fashionable gown, while failing to conceal the hourglass figure no seventeen-year-old should be able to boast. Her face was heart-shaped, her eyes a glowing violet, thickly lashed, wide and luminous with excitement. Her fashionable gown of lavender-blue, the hem trimmed in double rows of scallops, was more suitable for paying a morning call in Mayfair than for a young woman at home in a residence above a linen-draper's shop.

"Cousin!" Lily cried, dashing forward to take both Abby's hands in hers. "How truly wonderful that you have come to visit us."

Abby blinked, fought to recover her aplomb. A diamond of the first water, her young cousin. If Lily Mapes had access to the *ton,* she would take it by storm. "I am pleased to meet you as well," she declared, recalling her manners enough to include Betty Mapes's still figure in her smile of greeting. "We do not wish to intrude. We have come only to extend an invitation for you, Mrs. Mapes, and for Cousin Lily to join us for tea tomorrow when we may have the opportunity to indulge in a comfortable coze. Mrs. Greaves and I are staying at Langley House in Berkeley Square. Would four o'clock be convenient?"

"Langley House!" Edward Mapes exclaimed. "And what would you be doing there?"

Dear Lord! Abby could imagine what he was thinking. "The earl is the executor of my grand—of Clarissa Bivens's estate," she told him. "He has been aiding me in fulfilling the commissions she set for me to do."

"I just bet he is," Mapes muttered.

"Oh, Papa," Lily cried, "say we may go! Langley House—I cannot believe my good fortune."

"And will the earl be taking tea?" Mr. Mapes inquired.

"I would think so," Abby replied, wondering if she were saying the right thing. "His brother as well, I should imagine."

She could see Mapes considering the possibilities. Two well-breeched young gentlemen. A display of his daughter's wares not to be missed. Distaste warred with triumph as it appeared their scheme was going to work. Silently, Abby uttered a few dire imprecations against her grandmother for thrusting her into such an anomalous situation.

"Very well," Mapes agreed. "You may go." Lily squealed and clapped her hands. At her daughter's display of school-girl manners, Betty Mapes winced. So, Abby noted, gentil-ity had not completely faded along with the looks of Clarissa's niece.

The American ladies made their farewells and followed the linen-draper back down the stairs to his shop, only to find the Earl of Langley and Captain Verney pacing the floor before the counter, each looking as if he were counting the moments until he might charge up the stairs to the rescue. Upon being introduced to his visitors, Edward Mapes visi-bly brightened, wringing the gentlemen's hands and hasten-ing to offer a discount anytime the gentlemen had need of linens. Any friends of his wife's dear cousin . . .

The earl offered a regal nod, grabbed Abby by the arm, and headed for the carriage. Grim-lipped, nose twitching as if he smelled a bad odor, the captain did the same for Han-nah Greaves.

"Good God!" Jared burst out as Moorhead put the car-riage into the traffic and started back to Berkeley Square.

"Clarissa said he was a dirty dish," Abby pointed out, most reasonably. The earl's scowl grew darker.

"Well," Myles demanded, "what is she like?"

"You will not wish to miss tea tomorrow." Hannah's voice was tart, but her eyes gleamed with humor.

"Oh, I agree," Abby assured him. "You will both wish to be there. Horrors!" she added as an awful thought struck her. "You do not suppose Mapes will come?"

"He might," Jared told her. "He will wish to see what Myles and I think of his darling child."

"I most sincerely hope not," Abby said. "The whole idea was to be able to speak with the women in private."

"Perhaps we can contrive something," Jared mused. "Take him off somewhere, as I did with Farleigh."

"He'll think you wish to negotiate," Myles pointed out.

Jared swore, begged pardon. "Not at all," Hannah said, shaking her head. "I feel a bit like swearing myself. I've raised too many children to believe this quest is going to be a success. That girl's a handful, if ever I saw one."

"I've spent the last decade dealing with girls her age," Abby reminded her.

"Not like that one you haven't. The only solution for Miss Lily Mapes is a fast marriage. Preferably to a farmer who lives miles from the nearest neighbor and is gifted with a remarkable amount of stamina."

"Hannah!" Abby was shocked. Jared and Myles laughed so hard the landau rocked.

"Mark my words," Mrs. Greaves declared. "That one is trouble."

"Bloody hell!" The captain's words surprised them all. One moment he was shaking with laughter, the next, he looked as if he had seen a ghost. The earl, following his gaze, groaned.

"What?" Abby asked as they slowed to a halt short of the portico at Langley House, which was already taken up with a ponderous old traveling coach with the Langley crest upon the door.

"*Mother,*" Myles said in a voice of doom. "It's our mother."

"Oh, good God!" Abby breathed. Perhaps she should send a footman to inquire about the next coach for Plymouth. She and Hannah could make a run for the coast, take the next ship home. Enough was enough. Surely Clarissa could not have expected . . .

But, of course, a Todd did not run. A Todd held her head up and did her duty, come hell or high water. At the moment, it seemed she'd been thrown into both.

Chapter Sixteen

Abby nodded her thanks to the maid who had escorted her to a room at the back of Langley House. As the girl hastened off down the hall, Abby took a deep breath, squared her shoulders and rapped lightly on the jamb of the open door. Less than an hour short of the time to dress for dinner, she had been summoned by Lady Langley. Whatever the reason, Abby was quite sure it could not be good.

"You may enter." Charlotte Verney, Dowager Countess of Langley, sounded no less formidable than Abby had expected.

After a curtsy worthy of the older lady's rank, Abby seated herself in the chair indicated by Lady Langley. "I trust you had a smooth journey, my lady?" she inquired.

"Indeed," the countess conceded coolly. "The roads are considerably better than they were in my youth."

"And Lady Mablethorpe and Lady Christabelle—did they come to town as well?" Abby asked, determined to demonstrate that Americans knew how to make polite conversation.

Something close to annoyance crossed the dowager's face. "Why Henrietta Charnley would wish to be in town when not a soul of consequence is about, I can only imagine," she sniffed. "It is quite unthinkable to be in town in August." The earl's mother eyed Abby with distaste. "I hope you realize, young lady, what a sacrifice I am making on your behalf."

"My lady?"

Charlotte Verney regarded Abby as if she were viewing something long and slithery slinking out from beneath the rug. "My sons may have lost their minds, Miss Todd, but I am not so lost to what is right and proper that I can allow them to host an unmarried female beneath their roof without better chaperonage than an unknown American of uncertain years."

"Ma'am!" Abby protested. "I assure you Hannah Greaves is among the most respectable women in Boston."

"That's as it may be," the dowager retorted, "but who's to attest to it but the two of you? I'll not have Langley brought down because he could not recognize a menace when he saw it. Men are all alike. Quite lose their heads over a pretty face. But I am not so blind. The conspiracy concocted by you and your infamous grandmother is quite plain. So let me assure you Langley will not be forced into marriage by any scheming red-haired wench, young or old. I'll not allow it."

"You cannot think—" Abby sputtered, jumping to her feet.

"Sit down, sit down," said Lady Langley. "I have not finished with you yet." Abby hovered, chin tucked under, eyes blazing. "Don't be any more foolish than you already are." Charlotte Verney made a shooing motion with her hand. "Sit, sit."

Abby remained standing, struggling to remember these outrageous accusations were coming from Jared's mother. "This is much ado about nothing," she told the countess. "In one month's time I am returning to Boston."

"Somehow I doubt it," Lady Langley sighed. "Jared has never hesitated to use his consequence to acquire whatever he desired. He has been all that is gracious to me, but he's had a will of iron since the day he was born." The older lady shook her head. "Please sit down, my dear. We have much to discuss."

With an obvious show of reluctance, Abby resumed her seat. She had not come all the way from America to be berated by a member of the once-despised English nobility. Yet there was no doubt that, as mother to Jared and Myles, she owed Lady Langley respect.

Charlotte Verney hitched up her heavily embroidered silk shawl, played for a moment with the drooping black fringe. "I believe you forget that I recall my father-in-law well," she said. "His devotion to Clarissa Beaupré was an established fact through all the years of my marriage to George. I know how he looked when he spoke of her. And I have some idea of how much time my own Jared spent in her company. Even after he was grown, he would visit her, saying that his grandfather's death had caused such a void in her life that he felt obligated to continue their friendship. In truth, I believe he liked her very well. Yet I sensed, even then, that nothing good could come of it, but I never expected . . . this."

Almost, Abby felt sorry for her. Lady Langley, the sum product of her culture, could not be expected to throw off fifty-some years of strong convictions. "My lady," she said, "I truly have no intention of entrapping your son."

As if she had not heard Abby's words, the countess continued: "Have you any idea of the scandal if you two should marry? Unthinkable! I could not hold up my head. I should have to retire to . . . Yorkshire . . . perhaps as far as Scotland. It would be as bad as a man marrying his mistress."

"And that," Abby snapped, "I assure you I am not!"

"No, no, do not run away!" the dowager cried as Abby gripped the arms of her chair. "I am a weak old woman, afraid of any upset in her life." Abby sank back. "It may be that I have spoken amiss. Certainly, I know that my son will do as he pleases in this matter. And if you are to marry him, I wish you to be aware of the consequences."

"I am *not* to marry him, my lady!"

"You may think not," Lady Langley sighed. "And even if that is so, I doubt you have much say in the matter."

"I have every say in the matter," Abby retorted. "That, I believe, is why my ancestors took ship for the New World, to be followed by a tidal wave of others looking for more equitable treatment in their lives. I am not a thing to be bandied about as my lord wishes. I am myself, a woman with a life of my own. No man, certainly no English lord, is going to tell me what I may or may not do."

"Oh, my dear," cried Lady Langley, doing a remarkable *volte-face*, "you will break his heart!"

The dowager countess was not the only one who was surprised. Over the past month Abigail Todd, headmistress, had retreated further and further into Abby's consciousness. Her sudden resurrection at this critical point took Abby herself by surprise. Until this moment she had not realized how far down the primrose path she had been led by the Earl of Langley. For all her protestations, she had actually been considering . . . *Impossible!* Lady Langley was entirely right. Abigail Todd had no place in her eldest son's life. Clarissa's attempts at meddling had come all too close to being successful. It was time to deal with the possible and leave futile dreams behind.

"My lady," Abby said, plunging into further provocation, "I fear I must bring up another awkward topic." She told the countess of the relatives who would be coming to tea the next afternoon, ending, "If I had known you would be here, my lady, I would not have invited them, but it is done, and we have a good deal of family business to discuss." Abby allowed her voice to trail off, waiting hopefully for the reply dictated by good manners.

"I have invited Henrietta and Christabelle to tea tomorrow afternoon as well," Lady Langley said. "May I assume your relatives are persons they would not wish to know?"

Good God, could it be worse? "I fear so," Abby admitted. Thoughts of Edward Mapes accompanying his wife and daughter gave her chills. As if Jared's mother were not already convinced her son was determined on a shocking misalliance.

"As much as I would like to see the look on Henrietta Charnley's face," the dowager mused, "I will not indulge her desire to play the voyeur. You may entertain your guests in the drawing room, Miss Todd. I shall greet mine here in the morning room."

"You are most gracious, my lady. I am truly grateful." Abby hesitated. "May I have your permission to leave?" she asked, granting formal respect to the woman who had has-

tened to protect the virtue of an American of doubtful ancestry, no matter how doubtful her motives might be.

Lady Langley waved a vague hand toward the door. But
as Abby reached the threshold, the sound of the dowager's
voice caused her to pause. "Miss Todd"—Abby turned—"I
am glad we had this talk. It is possible my son has better
judgment than I had supposed."

Startled, Abby sketched another curtsy, and fled, her head
so full of conflicting emotions she got quite lost and had to
seek a housemaid to guide her back to the staircase at the
front of the house.

"Your house is very fine, my lord," Lily Mapes trilled,
turning in a complete circle in the middle of the drawing
room, her violet eyes avidly examining everything from the
plasterwork on the ceiling to the Aubusson carpet on the
floor.

"I am glad you like it," the earl returned, subtly guiding
Miss Mapes to a place beside her mother on one of two
couches placed before the fireplace. Abby, who had stood to
greet her guests, sat on the opposite couch, the earl taking
his place beside her. Hannah Greaves was already seated
nearby, calmly working on her embroidery. Captain Verney
leaned against the mantel, openly enjoying the delectable
sight presented by Lily Mapes, although Abby strongly suspected his thoughts were filled as much with mischief as
with admiration.

Both Mapes women were dressed in their best day wear,
in fine silk instead of linen or muslin, the very picture of
fashionable respectability. Abby suspected Betty Mapes had
risen above herself long enough to dictate what should be
worn. At the moment, however, Clarissa's cousin was as
cowed and silent as she had been in her own home, raising
her eyes only enough to take an occasional peep at the won-
ders around her. But Lily, Abby noted with some misgiving,
was fascinated by this glimpse into the world of the nobility.
Totally unabashed, the girl seemed to revel in her surroundings, as if she had always expected to be here. As if this mi-

lieu was her *due*. Abby felt a frisson of what she feared was to come.

Tea was enjoyed to the accompaniment of Miss Mapes's odd combination of girlish enthusiasms and sophisticated flirtations, indiscriminately offered to both Verney brothers. Although Abby tried to make allowances for her cousin's youth, she found herself cringing at the child's blatant use of her charms. She no longer felt relief that Mr. Edward Mapes had not accompanied the women of his family, for his presence in the room was as apparent as if he had been sitting there before them.

"If you will excuse me," the captain said, "my mother also has guests this afternoon and wishes me to pay my respects."

Lily Mapes fluttered her thick golden lashes, violet eyes raised in seemingly innocent appeal. "La, Captain, but we shall miss you quite prodigiously." She held out her small gloved hand. "I do hope we shall meet again?"

"Undoubtedly," Myles murmured, brushing a kiss just above her kidskin glove. With a wicked wink directed straight into Lily's upturned eyes, the captain left the room.

The devil! Abby fumed. Encouraging the little minx when the opposite was needed.

The earl did not budge. As executor of Clarissa's will, he was obliged to remain. And, besides, he growled to himself, his presence was needed to balance his brother's demmed insouciance.

Abby removed Clarissa's letter from her reticule. Interestingly enough, it was addressed to Lily Mapes, rather than to her mother. "My grandmother wished you to have this," she told the young beauty. "I have some idea of its contents because of what she wrote to me. I hope you will pay close heed to what she has to say."

"You may read it now," Jared instructed as Lily sat there, looking blankly at the letter.

For the first time, a sign of life flickered across Betty Mapes's face. "Yes, indeed," Lily's mother offered, "read what Clarissa has to tell you, child."

With a shrug, Lily broke the seal and began to read. By

the time she finished, her exquisitely lovely features were twisted into a fearsome scowl. She tossed the letter onto a side table. "She is an old fool," the girl declared. "Too ancient to remember the glory of it."

"There is no glory in selling yourself to the highest bidder!" Abby snapped, then wished she had bitten her tongue instead. Criticism of Lily's chosen path would get her no farther than Clarissa's letter had done.

"You wish me to become my mother?" Lily asked, with a grand sweep of her hand toward the shadow woman who was Mrs. Edward Mapes. "I was born for gaiety, for laughter. To be showered with fine silks and jewels. To sit in a box at the opera, drive out in a carriage lined in pink silk. To dine on pheasant and the finest wines—"

"To sleep with any man who offers you coin." Hannah Greaves had been unable to keep her mouth shut a moment longer.

Lily Mapes turned on the older woman with scorn. "I will not be a woman of the streets, I do assure you. I will have a house in St. John's Woods and a noble patron who caters to my every whim. I shall enjoy myself hugely, then do what Aunt Clarissa did—find a lover who will keep me in comfort for the rest of my life. And what, may I ask, is wrong with that?"

"What is wrong with that," said the earl, "is that Clarissa was unusually fortunate. It is also possible your patron may beat you or give you a disease. You may have a child which you would loathe to give up, but give it up you must if you are to continue in your profession."

"You would not have a true family of your own," Abby added. "Husband, children, the joy of watching them grow. I realize you are too young to understand what you are giving up, but there are alternatives to this life you think you want."

Lily Mapes thrust her small perfectly shaped nose in the air and fixed her gaze on the elaborate plasterwork of the fireplace's overmantel.

"As executor of Clarissa Beaupré's estate," the earl said, "I am prepared to offer the sum of two thousand pounds as a dowry. This would be paid," he emphasized, "only upon your marriage to a man acceptable to the estate—"

"To you?" Betty Mapes interjected, actually showing some animation.

"To me," the earl agreed.

But her daughter regarded the earl with scorn. "Two thousand pounds," Lily repeated. "My papa has already received offers as high as five. Surely, you cannot believe I could be bought for so little."

"Young lady," declared Hannah Greaves, "respectability is not to be cast aside so lightly."

"Oh, yes, it is," Lily retorted. "'Tis the only way I can gain entrance to the *ton,* and I choose to take it."

"A house in St. John's Woods and bearing a child on the wrong side of the blanket is scarcely being part of the *ton,*" the earl pointed out, his temper exacerbated beyond the limits of polite conversation.

"I do not care," Lily Mapes responded with a snap of her fingers to emphasize her point.

Abby stifled a groan. "Miss Mapes . . . Lily," she said, "I am prepared to take you back to Boston with me. There, you could marry well with a dowry of two thousand pounds." Although the offer was made, Abby could not help but have misgivings. Lily Mapes was more of a responsibility than even Abigail Todd, headmistress, wished to have. *Clarissa, I hope you appreciate this sacrifice!*

"Boston? 'Tis the end of the world," Lily declared in horrified accents. "I would not be caught dead in Boston."

"Oh, my dear," Betty Mapes moaned, seeing her final hope dashed.

Silence descended. "Lily," Abby said at last, "I confess to finding myself at an impasse. Please allow me until tomorrow to think on the matter. Perhaps the earl and I may yet find some compromise. Will that be acceptable, ma'am," she inquired, turning to Betty Mapes.

"Very kind . . . very generous, I'm sure," that lady replied from beneath her bonnet. "I am sorry," she added, "so very sorry." Mrs. Mapes rose and turned toward the door. Her daughter, with a laugh and a last come-hither glance directed at the earl, sauntered out behind her.

Abby dropped her head into her hands. "Good God," she murmured. "I never thought . . . never expected."

"Depressing, that's what it is," said Hannah Greaves. "But she's made her bed. Let the little fool lie in it."

"An alternative?" Jared inquired softly. "Are you a magician then, Abby? I doubt Merlin himself could fix this mess."

"But Clarissa expects it."

"The chit was right. Clarissa was an old fool," the earl retorted. "And she's gone these ten months past. You have done all you can, Abby. It's time to turn your back."

Abby's gaze flew to his face. "Surely not?"

Jared held her look with his, a slow smile beginning to light his grim features. "Of course," he conceded, "if you were to stay and keep an eye on her? . . ."

Chapter Seventeen

Stay in England? Preposterous! Yet Jared's taunt echoed in Abby's head. As did his assurance, a few moments later, that her efforts to rescue the stubborn ungrateful little wretch were enough to fulfill her mission. She did not have to succeed with Lily Mapes in order to claim Clarissa's estate.

So they had quarreled over his intimation she might be motivated by money. That the fate of Lily Mapes might possibly be less important than the acquisition of Arbor Cottage. The earl had thrown up his hands, scowling mightily, muttering words Abby couldn't quite catch. At that point she had dashed off up the stairs to her spacious bedroom, which overlooked the green expanse of Berkeley Square, and thrown herself onto the bed, heedless of crushing her amber silk gown.

Never would she give up her independence. Never! Even without Clarissa's estate, she was comfortably fixed. But marriage would see her stripped of everything that was hers, from control of her money to decisions about the way she lived her life. She could not, would not, do it. Yet it was becoming increasingly obvious that the earl was contemplating an arrangement of some kind, though the nature of it was still questionable.

There was a time, Abby thought sadly, when the concept of love had not been so frightening. Yes, there had been a time when she was young and foolish, when she had rushed, eager and excited, toward giving up her freedom. But since then she had had a decade of being her own mistress. She now knew what she would be giving up.

What would Jonathan think of all this? she wondered. The answer popped into her mind with stunning clarity. Jonathan would want her to be happy. To live the full life they had once intended to have together. She had known this for some time now, Abby realized. The thought had lain there dormant, shoved to the back of her mind. But it was true. Jonathan would never have expected her to wear the willow for the rest of her life. She could almost hear his voice, asserting in no uncertain terms that the spinsterhood of Abigail Todd would be a shocking waste.

But marriage so far from home? What could possibly compensate for thousands of miles of distance between her new life and her old? Ah, but she had not been offered marriage, Abby reminded herself. She was agonizing over nothing more than a gleam in the earl's eyes, a certain warmth. If he were to make her an offer, it would likely be of the same kind his grandfather had made to Clarissa.

Which inevitably reminded her of Lily. And at the moment Lily's problems must be more important than her own. Somewhere, deep down, Abby had to admit to a sneaking admiration for the startlingly sophisticated seventeen-year-old. Using her great-aunt as a role model, Lily Mapes had set a goal for herself. She would cut a swath through the gentlemen of London, and perhaps in the end she might better her grandmother's record. She might indeed persuade one of her lovers to wed her.

And what was young Lily giving up? Except for respectability, she was giving up nothing but what Abby herself had turned her back on. *No!* Lily was giving up less than Abby. For all the risks of the life she had chosen, it was likely Lily Mapes would experience gaiety, desire, laughter, the warmth of companionship, perhaps even the children Abby so longed to have. And, if Lily were fortunate, she would eventually find a life's companion, possibly even a husband.

While Abigail Todd, fool that she was, had persisted in

her celibate existence, determined to eliminate love from her life.

Abby pushed herself up, sitting on the edge of the bed, oblivious to the room's fine appointments. She could not miraculously conjure an alternative for Lily Mapes. Even if they could somehow lead the headstrong chit to the altar, no ordinary marriage—the only kind available to a linen-draper's daughter—would last out the month. Lily was destined for greater things. Even if those things were contrary to everything Abigail Todd had been taught. The truth was, she and Lily were both independent women, each working at very old professions. At occupations considered *suitable* for females.

Abby sighed. Reality could be ugly. And what about herself? She was two months shy of turning twenty-nine, so firmly on the shelf that the earl's interest seemed astonishing. Perhaps his mother was right. He was merely infatuated by the legend of her grandmother. When he looked at her, he saw Clarissa Beaupré, not Abigail Todd. Yet in spite of all her doubts, how would she feel when she boarded the *Rose of Sharon* en route back to Boston? Truthfully, she would be beyond tears. She would sit on her bunk or stand at the rail, staring into space. Lost in what might have been. And when she was home in Boston, she would be a heartless wretch with her students because her soul would have remained behind. In Somerset. With a man whose way of life was totally foreign to her own, yet oh so dear that he had been able to displace Jonathan from the pedestal of honor in her heart. And she no longer doubted that Jonathan had gladly made room, for Jonathan Blaisdell had always been a man of great good sense. Far more so than his foolish fiancée.

Abby dragged herself off the bed and made her way to the delicate escritoire set near the windows above the street. She would write to Betty Mapes, begging her to do her best to delay Lily's entrance into the world of the *demimonde*. She would assure Clarissa's cousin that she herself would continue her quest for an alternative solution and would write again from Arbor Cottage. Yet even as Abby wrote, doubts flooded over her. Should she let Lily Mapes set her own course? The girl was the age Abigail Todd had been when she'd pledged herself to Jonathan Blaisdell, completely certain of her own mind. She had been only a bit older than Lily when she set out to found a school. She strongly suspected both Clarissa and her mother Dulciana had been equally certain of their goals. Her family, it seemed, did not run to weak women.

If only she knew her own mind about Jared Verney . . . Even if his intentions were honorable, his country was the Enemy. She would have to live out her life separated from everything that had comprised her world for nearly thirty years. She would be giving up country, father, her Todd grandparents, her students, Hannah Greaves and her many other friends in Boston. Oh, yes, she knew she *could* do it—had she not just reaffirmed that hers was a family of strong women?—but did she *want* to? Was her love that strong?

Was Jared's? And if he offered *carte-blanche*—would she turn him away? For unlike Clarissa Beaupré, who had been dependent on her protector, Abby was not. Accepting *carte-blanche* would allow her to express her love and still not be ruled by Jared Verney. *Horrors!* She could not have thought such a thing. There must be some other way out of this twisted coil.

Two more commissions. Perhaps, miraculously, a solution lay with one of them. Slowly, Abby folded the letter to Betty Mapes, dripped on a blob of wax, and sealed it with a pretty star-shaped press. With a sigh she tapped the letter against the desktop, her vision filled with Lily's finely shaped features, the toss of her head, the surety of her expression. If only . . .

Abby bounded to her feet, jerked on the bellpull. She would have a maid take the letter to the earl and request that it be sent around by messenger immediately. At the moment, there was nothing else to be done.

Abby cracked open her bedroom door, ears on the prick for the slightest sound. All was quiet in the Langley's London townhouse. The earl had insisted they spend another day in town, enjoying a few of the marvels of the world's most influential capital city. So Jared and Myles, with the somewhat surprising addition of Lady Christabelle, had spent the day showing Abby the sights of London, from the Tower and the Elgin Marbles to Carlton House and St. James Palace. A fine day, Abby had to admit. One expressly designed to emphasize how very agreeable was the companionship of a charming gentleman. No matter how certain he might be of his own predominant position in the world.

So when the earl had bent his head to hers for a moment after dinner, issuing a soft but distinct invitation to meet him in the library after everyone else had gone to bed, it had seemed the most natural thing to nod assent. Now, however, as she eased out the door and tiptoed down the hall toward the staircase, an assignation at nearly midnight seemed quite wicked. Something Abigail Todd of Boston would never do. But Miss Todd seemed to have faded into the British mists. Abby could only wonder if that prim-and-proper New England spinster could ever be resurrected. Lately, there were times when she was certain that Clarissa Beaupré had entered her life so thoroughly that the headmistress of Miss Todd's Academy for Young Ladies would never be the same again.

Abby started to creep down the stairs one step at a time, then decided it would be better to descend as fast as possible, trusting to the thick stair carpet to muffle the sound. She arrived, breathless, at the library door, where she paused to gulp in air, pat down her severely confined coiffeur, and smooth the folds of the deep blue silk gown she had donned for dinner.

She should not have come.

Wild horses could not have kept her away. Inside this room was an alternative future.

Inside this room was the forbidden.

Inside this room was her friend Jared. Who had asked her to meet him at an hour when she should be sound asleep in bed. Her lonely bed.

Abby opened the door and walked in.

"I feared you might not come." Jared, smiling, rose to his

feet. He had arranged two comfortably upholstered chairs so they were nearly touching. After escorting Abby to one of them, he sat back down in the other. "You feel quite wicked, do you not?" he teased, his silver eyes reflecting the light of the candles in the wall sconces above.

"I am unaccustomed to midnight rendezvous, yes," Abby conceded with a prim nod.

"But you came. Clarissa would be pleased. In fact, I believe I may hear faint sounds of the old girl singing her own version of 'The Hallelujah Chorus.'"

"I cannot think Mr. Handel would appreciate the analogy."

"Handel is long dead and does not care. And don't go missish on me now, my girl," Jared warned. "It doesn't suit you."

Abby folded her hands in her lap, did her best to reconstruct the solemn and confident expression she used in the classroom. "I believe you wished to see me about something?" she suggested coolly.

Jared eyed her with some amusement. No one could ever accuse Abigail Todd of hunting either a fortune or a title. Almost any other woman he knew would be taking advantage of this private moment, making every effort to capture The Indifferent Earl. Abby was sitting there, grim and stiff-shouldered, as if she would screech and run if he so much as laid a finger on her. Not the attitude he had hoped for, at all. Leaning back in his chair, Jared willed himself to fade into the upholstery, to become as little of a menace as it was possible for an earl of the realm whose height topped six feet. "There are only two commissions left," he said, deciding to approach the object of his intentions from an oblique angle.

"I do not consider Lily's problem closed," Abby retorted. "Therefore, there are three left."

"As I told you this afternoon," Jared pointed out with careful patience, "as far as the estate is concerned, the matter is closed."

"You may toss the girl aside if you wish. I shall not."

Inwardly, Jared winced. Things were going badly, not at all the way he had planned. "Abby . . . I mentioned the remaining commissions only to show how much I am aware that time is flying. It is something else altogether which I wish to discuss. May we leave the problem of Lily Mapes for the moment?" Abby nodded her agreement, though her chin remained remarkably stubborn. Perhaps, Jared thought, he should forget the whole thing. Wait until they were back in Somerset. But, no, privacy was difficult to come by. Now, when they were both under the same roof, was the perfect opportunity. She was wearing her pearls again, he noted, their pristine beauty warm against her fair skin, emphasizing the deep décolletage, the voluptuous swell of her breasts highlighted by the dark silk that barely hid—

"You may raise your eyes, my lord."

Coming close to his first blush in more than a decade, the earl jerked his eyes upward. "You are very lovely," he offered with a smile. "Surely you cannot blame me for looking."

"The situation itself is wicked enough," Abby told him sharply. "Pray do not add to it."

"My intentions are purely honorable," Jared assured her, seeing his opening at last. He leaned forward in his chair, looked her straight in the eye. "Don't go back to Boston, Abby. Stay here with me. As my wife."

Wife! Her green eyes seemed huge, twice their normal size, as she stared back at him. Her lower lip quivered. "Jared . . . I cannot," she whispered, the words anguished. "You know I cannot."

"Why?" he demanded. "Jonathan Blaisdell or no, I will not believe you do not care for me."

Abby raised knuckled fists to her mouth, slowly shook her head. After long moments of silence, she lowered her hands and said, "You are quite right. The thought of never seeing you again fills me with dread. And, yes, I admit I have thought about what I would do if you should make me an offer."

"What could possibly be unacceptable?" Jared demanded. Although he had never before made an offer, the thought that the Earl of Langley could be refused had never entered his head.

"*If*"—and Abby emphasized the word—"*if* I were willing to give up my American life and all the people in it and move to a country which has been the enemy for as long as I can remember—and I must tell you I am not sure I can do that—I fear we would face ostracism from the world that is yours." She managed an exceedingly brave smile. "I would not mind for myself, but for you . . . for our children. No, Jared, it is not possible."

Abby pressed her fingers against his lips, shushing his protests. "I am instantly recognizable as the granddaughter of a courtesan. There can be no question."

"Lady Mablethorpe was amused, not shocked."

"Lady Mablethorpe is a law unto her herself. Others will not be so kind."

"My dearest Abby, I am not so fainthearted. Trust me. No one would scorn the wife of the Earl of Langley."

Abby shook her head. "I did not think you such a fool, my lord."

"So much the fool," Jared declared with mock solemnity, "that the finest ring Rundell & Bridges had to offer is burning a hole in my pocket."

"Social suicide," Abby ground out, ruthlessly quelling her surge of curiosity. Maybe just a peek . . . No, indeed. One peek and the ring would make a miraculous leap onto her finger and all her good intentions would be for naught.

"It will keep," Jared told her, patting the breast pocket of his jacket. "I'll not press you further tonight. Just think about it, my love. Think about gladdening Clarissa's heart. I can practically feel the old girl hovering over us. Can't you hear her? *Say yes, Abby, say yes!*"

Abby cocked her head to one side, listening intently. A mischievous smile played over her lips. "I will say yes to a kiss," she said. "I am not averse to a bit of persuasion."

That's what he liked about Abigail Todd, Jared thought. She could stand toe to toe with a British earl and be his equal. No die-away miss, this strong-minded American. He found himself on his feet, pulling Abby up to meet him. Their lips touched, and his blood surged. Here, by God, in his arms was the only woman for Jared Reignald Fitzroy

Verney, Earl of Langley. And he would prove it. He tightened his grip and asserted his mastery.

He was winning. With Abby clinging to him in most satisfactory fashion, he deepened the kiss. Waves of warmth engulfed him, exciting every part of his body far beyond the desire he had known with other women. One hand crept to her waist, moved slowly up toward the luscious curves above. For a moment Abby melted into him, their bodies nearly one. Then with a sound between a sob and a snarl, she jerked away so abruptly the chair behind her teetered wildly before moving back six inches, allowing her room to escape. Jared stood stock-still as she ran for the door.

He looked upward, shaking his fist. "Clarissa, you old tart," he growled, "you want this union, I know you do. So you're going to have to find a way out of this mess, for it seems I'm unable to do it myself."

Candles glowed, illuminating the tall stacks of books, the leather-upholstered furniture, the empty fireplace, the rich reds and blues in the carpet. But the night was silent, with not so much as an echo of laughter from above. Jared stalked to a side table, poured himself a tot of brandy. He was caught in a trap of Clarissa's making—no, that analogy would not work. Twisting in the wind was more like it. Dependent on the whimsical wishes of a courtesan to straighten out his life.

"This makes no sense," Abby declared two days later when they were all gathered once more at Arbor Cottage. In vain she turned Clarissa's letter over, searching for more words, another page.

"What is the problem?" Myles demanded, for Captain Verney now considered himself a permanent part of their expeditions.

"There are only two lines," Abby told her eager audience.

"Read them," Jared ordered, perhaps not as politely as he might have.

Abby flashed an indignant glare, then turned her attention to the nearly empty page. "It says," she announced:

Clarissa's glory marks the place
Where Abigail and Jared meet face-to-face.

"Good heavens," said Hannah Greaves, "whatever does it mean?"

"Cryptic is not an attribute I associate with Clarissa Beaupré," the earl commented dryly.

"A game!" the captain declared. "I do believe it's a game." Everyone stared at him.

"You mean like a treasure hunt," Abby asked, puzzled. Suddenly, all eyes shifted to her, momentary disbelief blossoming into eager speculation.

The earl strode across the room, seized the paper from Abby's hands. Slowly, he repeated the words.

"It makes no sense," Abby mused. "We meet face-to-face all the time."

"Clarissa's glory," Myles murmured.

"Clarissa's glory," his brother repeated, frowning.

Abby made a strangled sound. Her gaze locked with Jared's. The same thought seemed to occur to all four occupants of the room at once. "I'll check on it," Abby said, making for the door.

"Oh, no, you don't," Myles declared. "We're coming with you."

"Captain!" Abby protested, much shocked as everyone seemed intent on following her to her bedroom.

"We've seen it before, Abby. Don't make a fuss," the earl informed her.

"But—"

"Abigail," said Hannah Greaves, "there's no sense pretending Clarissa wasn't what we know very well she was. Lead on, if you please."

Chapter Eighteen

When their small cavalcade entered her bedroom, Abby slunk to the far side of the bed, effacing herself behind one of the silk-draped bedposts. No one seemed to notice her embarrassment. The others rushed to stand before Clarissa's portrait, with Myles winning the race to pull the cord. Abby blanched as her own voluptuous figure, every naked inch of it, flaunted itself before the Verney brothers. As the come-hither green eyes in her very own face beckoned them closer. She swallowed hard and buried her face in the rose silk hangings.

She heard the earl's authoritarian tone. "Deering," he called to the butler, who was hovering discreetly in the doorway, with his spouse peering over his shoulder, "is there anything different in this portrait? Any additions in recent years? Mrs. Deering, what about you? You'd know if any changes had been made."

"Nothing, my lord," the Deerings replied, almost in unison. "The portrait is as it's always been," Susan Deering asserted. "Not a hair different from what it was when Deering and me came here twenty-six years ago."

"Clarissa's glory marks the place," Myles murmured. "This has to be it." The two brothers glanced at each other, then moved purposefully toward the portrait.

Jared and Myles each took an end of the six-foot painting, fussed a bit to disengage it from a double set of hooks, then gently lowered it to the carpet. "Ah!" the earl exclaimed, peering over the edge to the painting's back.

"Abby, come remove these letters, if you please. Abby?"
Keeping a good grip on the portrait, Jared turned his head,
found his love still clinging to the bedpost. Their eyes met,
and she read his chagrin. He truly had not realized how mortified she was. "Hannah," the earl amended, "if you would
be so kind?"

With an apologetic glance at Abby, Mrs. Greaves moved
forward, gently peeling away two folded pieces of paper that
had been glued to the back of Clarissa's portrait. She held
them tightly while Jared and Myles, with the guidance of
Deering, struggled to get the huge painting back on the wall.
When, with a firm hand, Jared had pulled the pink silk
draperies closed, he turned to Abby. "My apologies," he
said. "I have become so accustomed to the painting through
the years that I thought nothing of our invasion of your privacy. She loved to show it, you know. We—none of us—
associate it with you. I swear it."

He appeared so truly contrite that Abby's distress began
to fade. Even Myles appeared subdued, his excitement thoroughly dampened. "I suppose we must continue this farce,"
she murmured, wondering as soon as the words left her
mouth if she sounded like a sulky child.

"There's a letter each," Hannah said. "One for Abigail,
one for Jared." She held them out.

Abby moved away from the bed, accepting the folded
paper with her name on it. She looked up at the earl. *"Where
Abigail and Jared must meet face-to-face,"* she mused. Sage
nods from the four observers. "Shall we?" Abby said, and
opened her letter. "Oh!" she exclaimed in disgust as she
read. As if she needed any further reminders of her grandmother's nudity!

"I believe mine holds the key," Jared said. "What does
yours say, Abby?"

Silently, she handed it to him. "Yes, yours is the transi-
tion, mine the key," he said, his tone carefully neutral.

"Read it!" Myles demanded.

The earl juggled the two pieces of paper, then read
aloud:

> *Pink silk, pink flesh*
> *Secret no more*
> *Pink marble indeed*
> *Holds the key to more.*

"Shakespeare has no cause to worry," Myles quipped.

"I believe we can all agree," the earl returned mildly, "that Clarissa's talent did not lie in poetry."

Abby held her head in her hands, thinking dire thoughts about the grandmother who had brought her to the point of holding court in her bedroom for an earl, a British army officer, her Boston neighbor, a butler and a housekeeper, all under the watchful eyes of London's most notorious courtesan, stark naked. If Abby had been gifted with magic powers, she would gladly have gone up in a puff of smoke, ignoring forever whatever wild-goose chase Clarissa Beaupré had devised.

"Has anyone any idea what this is all about?" Hannah Greaves inquired plaintively.

"What we are hunting?" Jared said, shaking his head. "I doubt it. I think the old girl is playing with us."

"A piece of jewelry?" Myles suggested.

"My father's birth records?" Abby ventured.

"Gold doubloons," Myles returned gleefully. "From some piratical ancestor."

"Confine your hopes to something small, brother," Jared told him. "Great expectations lead only to great disappointment."

"Unfair," the captain declared. "I don't doubt Clarissa wanted us to have a bit of fun, so let us enjoy it." He caught Abby's glare and grinned. "Smile, dear girl, no need to look so glum. No doubt the hunt is where the fun lies, with some bauble to dazzle us at the end."

"A diamond necklace," Hannah suggested, joining into the spirit of the game.

Not all the jewels in the world would buy what she most desired, Abby thought. Some miracle to smooth the way for Jared and herself. If that were the treasure they were seek-

ing—and Clarissa had chosen to make a May game of it—
then this hunt was well worth the effort.

There was, however, no need to reveal that her pique was
rapidly transforming into eagerness. "Very well," Abby announced with a display of cool efficiency. "Let us get on
with it."

"*Pink marble* is much too easy," Myles declared. "Here
are two fireplaces of it, staring us in the face."

The earl turned to the Deerings. "Is there pink marble
elsewhere in the house?" he asked. The butler and housekeeper immediately denied it. The two fireplaces in
Clarissa's bedroom were the only pink marble in Arbor Cottage.

"You take one, I'll take the other," Jared told his brother.
While Abby, with a carefully indifferent face, marveled over
the eagerness with which the Verney brothers attacked the
fireplace, an inner voice jeered: *Face it, Abby, you want to
be right in there with them.* Fearing her indifferent facade
would crumble, Abby hastily turned her attention to the
Deerings. They had to have known about the letters behind
the portrait. They also had to know about the hiding place in
the pink marble, for Clarissa could not have managed the
business by herself. But their countenances were as impas-
sive as her own, the blank stares of the perfect butler and
housekeeper. If Jared and Myles failed, would they take
Clarissa's secret to their graves?

"Here!" Jared cried. The earl, who had put aside the fire-
dogs and was on his knees inside the large fireplace, pried at
a loose brick in the chimney. Abby and Hannah moved forward. Myles dashed back from his fruitless search of the
other fireplace. The Deerings continued to hover. All eyes
focused on the hole where the brick had been. Jared thrust
in his hand, drew out a sooty letter that he waved at Abby.
She stepped forward and grabbed it. Another reach into the
hole, and a second letter was revealed. Jared felt around the
cavity, shook his head, and scrambled out, looking down
ruefully at what had once been a fine pair of slim and fashionable trousers.

"No one expects a fireplace to be pristine," he said over

Mrs. Deering's apologies, "no matter how many times it's scrubbed. Pray do not be distressed. I do believe I can afford another pair."

He turned his attention to Abby. "I suspect Clarissa is playing 'Ladies first,'" he told her. "So let us hear what she has written to you."

"Oh." Abby looked at the letter in her hand. "I seem to have yours," she told him. They quickly made the exchange. This time her grandmother's words were something she could read aloud.

> *Above your head*
> *You will find*

Jared added:

> *A branch with clue*
> *All entwined.*

The treasure hunters frowned, only the Deerings remaining phlegmatic. Four pairs of eyes moved upward, examining the plasterwork ceiling. Not a sign of a clue or anything other than the original design.

"The tester!" Myles exclaimed. "There are branches in the embroidery along the border."

"Excellent," Jared nodded, "so there are. Is there a ladder nearby, Deering?"

"No need," the captain declared. "If I can just get my boots off, this chair . . ."

"Spare the furniture," the earl instructed dryly. "We're both tall enough. A stool will be sufficient, I believe. There must be one about."

Deering waved his hand toward the veritable crowd of footmen and maids who had somehow materialized just outside the door. The wait was short. Since Jared had made the fireplace discovery, he allowed Myles to examine the top of the wooden tester with its elaborate border of crewelwork. A softly muttered profanity drifted down from above. "Nothing but a bit of dust," the captain pronounced with disgust.

They all restrained smiles at Mrs. Deering's gasp of horror. Some housemaid's head would roll.

Naturally, the earl had to take his brother's place and see for himself. "Perhaps beneath the embroidery?" Hannah Greaves suggested. With Deering insisting on moving the stool, his thin shoulders bobbing up and down with surprising agility, Jared circumnavigated the huge bed. There was no sign of another letter.

Encased in gloom, they all trooped back to the Wicker Room. "Do you wish us to remain, miss?" Deering inquired of Abby.

"Yes," the earl snapped before his hostess could answer. "We are well aware you aided Clarissa in this nonsense, Deering. So, yes, you may bear witness to our suffering. With any more clues like this, we may need to wring the truth out of you." Mrs. Deering paled, looking almost as if she were on the verge of tears.

Ignoring the angry looks Abby was directing at him, Jared plucked her letter from her hand before they all found seats on the cheerful chintz upholstery. He repeated the verses found in the fireplace.

> *Above your head*
> *You will find*
> *A branch with clue*
> *All entwined.*

"A real branch?" Abby suggested into the puzzled silence. "Outside?"

"Outside!" Myles jeered. "Among the thousand million branches above our heads?"

They all sighed. "Perhaps some luncheon?" Mrs. Greaves interjected. "I believe we could all benefit from a bit of food."

"Yes, please," Abby quickly concurred. At a wave of her hand, the Deerings scurried from the room, obviously relieved at their escape.

The earl, ignoring the byplay, was still staring at the letters. "It has to be a particular branch," he mused. "Something we could pick out, identify because it has significance."

"In the rafters?" Hannah asked.

"No," Jared shook his head, "I believe Abby may be right. Our branch is outside. That's why it must have significance for, as Myles says, the world outside is filled with branches."

"The arbor!" Abby exclaimed. "It has to be in the arbor."

The captain leapt to his feet. "Come on," he demanded. "What are we waiting for?"

"Lunch," said his brother, crossing his legs in front of him as if he had all the time in world. "Whatever it is, it's been there for months. It will wait while we increase our thought processes with a little food."

Grumbling, Myles sank back in his chair. "I suppose it's all a hum," he muttered. "Not worth the hunt. The old girl's up there laughing at us. Thinks it mighty amusing to send the Earl of Langley chasing from pillar to post and back again."

"Not to mention a captain in His Majesty's service," his brother teased.

"Or two ladies from Boston," Abby added tartly. "I cannot help but agree with you, Myles," she added more thoughtfully. "I believe Clarissa heartily enjoyed the planning of this particular challenge. And I must admit, I am beginning to enjoy it myself. A treasure hunt is most intriguing."

"Do not expect a pot of gold at the end of the rainbow," the earl warned.

"Did you not say the estate was not as large as it should have been?" Myles countered.

"Clarissa Beaupré was an expensive woman," Jared told him. "And she lived a good ten years after our grandfather's death. During that time she had to live on her assets, for I know for a fact that neither father nor I added to her coffers."

Myles shrugged. "Oh, very well, but a pot of gold has a nice ring to it. Inspiration for an afternoon's search, don't you think?"

For the first time since Clarissa's portrait was revealed to all, Abby smiled. "By all means, Captain, let us exaggerate the treasure as much as we like. So long as we all promise not to be disappointed if it turns out to be nothing more than a secret document or a single ring."

"A wedding ring?" Hannah gasped. "Do you suppose he actually married her?"

Three pairs of eyes turned to her in shock. "Impossible!" Myles exclaimed, then quickly subsided under his brother's basilisk stare. "My apologies," the captain murmured, momentarily embarrassed enough to wish himself elsewhere.

"Knowing my grandfather as well as I did," the earl said, "I believe we may safely assume we will not find a wedding ring."

Abby abruptly got up, stalking across the room to pause in the open doorway, her eyes fixed on the fountain in the courtyard. Behind her, Hannah Greaves held her hands over her mouth, eyes squeezed tight at the enormity of her faux pas. Jared followed on Abby's heels. "I'm sorry, Abby, truly I am. But I make no excuses for my grandfather. He lived by the rules of his times."

"As *you* must," she tossed over her shoulder without turning her head.

"*You* are not Clarissa Beaupré."

"I might as well be," she murmured just loud enough for Jared to hear her over the tinkling notes of the fountain.

"Luncheon is served," Deering intoned behind them.

Jared tucked Abby's hand through his arm, and the two of them led the way to an informal dining area in one corner of the Wicker Room. Their repast of fresh-baked bread, cold meats, cheese and home-brewed ale was consumed in near silence. The easy camaraderie that had formed among them over the past few weeks had once again turned awkward. The Verney brothers were the British aristocracy; the Americans were independent women from rebellious colonies. Representatives of the scorned middle class. Or so it seemed to Abby. The Earl of Langley had loved Clarissa Beaupré for forty years, but he had not married her. The present earl seemed ready to rectify that error, yet somehow it was not believable. Jared Verney must be mistaken in his sentiments. Or, if not, he was making the worst mistake of his life. Marriage to Abigail Todd would ruin him.

The moment when all were finished eating and Abby could signal the end of the meal came as a relief from the turmoil of her thoughts.

Jared stood back, allowing Abby to lead the way to the arbor. He had trod on her feelings more than enough for one day. Even abject groveling might not be enough to soothe her. Presuming that he *could* grovel. Truthfully, his experience was limited, almost nil. Oh, he had mastered charming apologies, but groveling was another matter entirely. As he watched Abby disappear into the arbor, the earl heaved a sigh. Perhaps, if he could find whatever Clarissa had hidden in such a whimsical fashion, he might be able to redeem himself.

"Above your head, You will find A branch with clue All entwined," the earl repeated, eyeing, with no little misgiving, the myriad twisted branches that formed the roof of the bower. Even if they had chosen the right spot, the task seemed impossible. In front of him, Abby and Hannah walked the length of the arbor, eyes raised to the solid green and brown canopy above. They did not appear to be having any success. "Get a couple of stout branches from that oak," Jared said to Myles, nodding at a massive tree in the far corner of the garden.

By the time the ladies returned, shaking their heads, the Verney brothers were armed with two three-foot long sticks. They started at opposite ends of the arbor, poking, prodding, lifting up broad grape leaves, their expressions turning more sour by the moment. "There's nothing here!" the captain exclaimed in disgust.

"Wait!" Jared maneuvered his stick up under a large green leaf, poking into a crevice between two serpentine grape branches. "Something feels different," he added. "I think—yes!" He twisted his stick, pulled. Something gave, moving slowly toward him. He twisted and pulled some more. Shoving aside the large grape leaf with his other hand, he spied the edge of a thin packet wrapped in dark oilskin.

"I have it!" he cried, then flushed as he realized he sounded more like an excited boy in nankeens than an earl of the realm. He ripped the packet open, handed Abby her letter with a sweeping cavalier bow.

Their eyes met and he knew he was forgiven. Even if he had not found the packet, he realized he would have been forgiven. That's what love was. And, suddenly—there in the very center of Clarissa Beaupré's bower—Jared had no doubt that his love was returned.

"Only one line," Abby moaned. "*A red rose seek.* What does yours say?"

Jared opened his letter and read: "*A key rests at its feet.*"

"That sounds easy enough," Myles approved.

"If the roses were blooming," Hannah Greaves pointed out.

Abby frowned. "When we arrived, many of the roses were still blooming, but somehow I can't recall a red one."

"Send for the gardener," the earl declared.

Abby shot him an approving glance. "Of course," she murmured.

"I'll go," the captain said. "Sit here and be comfortable. Woodruff must be about somewhere."

"A red rose?" the elderly gardener repeated when he arrived. Frowning in thought, he scratched his straggly gray head. "Fine bush it was, yes, indeed. Blood red, big as a house, them blooms. A shame it was. A great shame."

"What was?" Abby asked.

"Died, it did. Dead as a doornail. Never replaced it, seein' as there was no one here to say yay or nay."

"Where did it grow?" Abby prodded.

"Nothin' there now," Woodruff said mournfully.

"Nonetheless," Abby declared, "we would like to see where it once was."

The gardener turned and shuffled off. They followed him down one of the pebbled paths into the rose garden. "There," he said, pointing to a blank spot in the rose bed where there was nothing more than a layer of mulch covering the earth. "There be the place."

"A spade, if you please," the earl said.

The elderly gardener ambled off at a pace that caused Myles to grind his teeth. "We'll be at this a week," he muttered.

"Heaven forfend," declared Mrs. Greaves. "Clarissa certainly seems to delight in making things difficult."

When Woodruff reappeared, the earl grabbed the spade, declaring that since he had already ruined his clothes and the shine on his boots, he might as well have the honor of digging. The roots of the old rose were still in place, however, ruthlessly resisting the puny edge of the spade. Grumbling, Jared moved his digging farther out, wondering why Woodruff had left the old roots in the ground. Getting along in years, the old man was. Probably working as little as possible now that Clarissa was gone.

The spade clanged against metal. Startled, Jared moved more slowly, shoveling earth aside, uncovering a small metal box, not more than six inches long and three inches wide.

"Big treasure," Myles mocked, looking over his shoulder.

"Big enough for a key," Abby reminded him.

Jared eased the box from the ground. Myles offered a penknife. Together, the brothers pried open the lid. Inside, wrapped in oil paper, was a heavy key that looked remarkably like something which might open a pirate's treasure chest. With it were two small pieces of folded paper. Eyebrows arched, Jared weighed the key in his hand while Abby plucked the letters from the box.

Woodruff picked up the spade the earl had cast aside. "'Twas the metal what killed it," he intoned sadly. "Sartin' sure." With doleful step, he returned to whatever he had been doing. The four treasure hunters stared after him, suddenly realizing that the old gardener had known all along where the key lay, as he must have buried it himself.

"Let us sit for a while in the courtyard," the earl suggested. "In spite of the key, I have an odd feeling we are not yet near the end of this quest."

"The old girl is having too much fun with us," Myles concurred. Abby and Hannah found the idea of a break pleasing. So, scattering peacocks right and left, they seated

themselves on the white marble benches that ringed the
fountain, taking a few moments to enjoy the cool air stirred
up by the falling water.

Abby, quietly unfolding her note, found the other three
watching her. "Oh, dear," she murmured, "the mystery
grows thicker."

> *Safe in our coffins,*
> *Do we lie*

"*Our* coffins?" Jared questioned. "More than one?" He
quickly opened his own note, not bothering to hide his disgust when he read it.

> *In a place of peace,*
> *A place of rest.*

"An impasse, by God!" he exclaimed. "Makes no sense
at all."

Chapter Nineteen

*C*aptain Verney's chuckle was dark. "Are we to dig up her grave then?" he asked.

"Coffins, Myles. Plural," his brother corrected. "I doubt we must trudge off to the graveyard."

"A dead end," Abby sighed. "The whole garden is *a place of peace, a place of rest*. Even Arbor Cottage itself."

"The arbor then?" Hannah asked.

"We've had a clue there," Myles told her.

Four sighs filled the courtyard. Suddenly, Jared strode off toward the house, good manners forgotten as he bawled out Deering's name. The butler, obviously hovering close by, strolled into the courtyard, dignity intact. "Yes, my lord?" His eyes gleamed with bland innocence.

"We all know," the earl declared, "that Clarissa had to have help in hiding the clues to her treasure hunt. Do you possibly have instructions of what to do if we find one of her notes too obscure?"

The butler stared straight ahead. "She was afraid that might be the case, sir. So, yes, I am allowed to offer further hints at my discretion."

"Why, you old devil," the captain declared. "You've known where the treasure is all along."

"No, indeed, sir. I was not Miss Clarissa's only helper."

"Undoubtedly, she shot whomever it was and buried the poor man in the garden," Abby declared in acidic tones. "What then may you tell us, Deering? We would be most grateful for your help."

The butler delved into his inside jacket pocket, handing over two more folded notes, one to Abby, one to Jared. When matched together, they read:

> *Within the arbor*
> *You will find*
> *Each clue needed*
> *For peace of mind.*

"We've done that!" Myles protested.

"It doesn't say *Above your head*," Abby told him.

With a collective groan, the treasure hunters rose and trooped back to the arbor. "I am beginning to be annoyed," the earl declared. "Check under the benches, Myles. Perhaps Clarissa is ready to take pity on us."

When the very first bench turned up a clue, fastened securely to its bottom, the scramble was on, with even Hannah down on her hands and knees, oblivious of the dirt, reaching under one of the six wooden seats to reveal yet another oil-skin packet.

"Back to the house," the earl commanded. "Six separate messages, and no idea of how they go together. Best take them inside and be comfortable while we wrestle with the problem. Some ale, Deering," the earl ordered as they entered the Wicker Room. He looked up to encounter Abby's baleful eye. Once again, he had forgotten who gave the orders in this house. A problem, a veritable problem. The only solution he could see was removing the lady to his own house. Then, by God, there would be no doubt about who gave the orders.

And he'd undoubtedly be dead in a week.

"Hannah and I will have ale as well," Abby informed her butler firmly. The look she turned on the Verney brothers was cool. "Let us sit at the dining table," she said. "That way we can pass our letters around more easily." While they waited for their refreshments, the treasure hunters opened the six packets.

"*A few more inches, their course is run.* That could be a last line," Myles offered.

"Flowers, birds, trees, and sky," Abby read. "That seems to indicate the garden again."

"We lie in wait to bring joy and mirth. And once more, plural," Jared said. "What else?"

"Knight and maiden share the sun," Hannah read. "Is there a statue?" she asked, "Or does Clarissa mean Jared and Abby?"

Abby opened a second packet. *"All may be seen from where we lie.* That sounds more promising."

Jared read: *"Beneath verdant green inside dark earth.* It's buried, by God. Like the key."

Myles counted the pieces of paper. "That's all six. Now we've only to put them together so they make sense."

The ale arrived, with more bread and cheese. Abby produced paper and pens so they each might copy the six lines and work on the problem of turning them into an intelligible clue. Some ten minutes and a full pint later, the earl tapped his pen thoughtfully on his page, then nodded briskly. "I believe I have it," he announced. "See if this makes sense."

> *Flowers, birds, trees, and sky*
> *All may be seen from where we lie.*
> *Knight and maiden share the sun,*
> *A few more inches, their course is run.*
> *Beneath verdant green inside dark earth,*
> *We lie in wait to bring joy and mirth.*

"Excellent!" Abby cried, then subsided into a frown. "I fear it is still quite obscure."

"A place of peace, a place of rest," Myles reminded them.

"We found the notes under the arbor seats," Abby pointed out. "That fits."

"Yes, but what other places of rest are in the garden?" Jared asked.

"The marble benches around the fountain?" Hannah contributed.

"Too damp for letters," Jared mused. "And the ground is solid brick, not verdant green. Are there other seats, other places of rest?"

"The turf benches!" Abby exclaimed.

"Verdant green!" the captain shouted.

"Deering," Abby declared, managing to give an order before the earl opened his mouth, "I believe we may need the spade again. Please have Woodruff attend us at the grass benches."

"Miss Todd," said Captain Verney as he swept her a bow, "until I met you, I had not realized how infinitely boring my life had become since I sold out. Your adventures have put new spring in my step. 'Tis plain I am going to have to find something more to do with my life. Being a lazy, good-for-nothing younger son has lost its appeal."

"You are a rogue, Myles," Abby told him. "You are the enemy and I should hate you but, alas, I find I like you. You have been a fine addition to our adventures."

As the Verney brothers followed the ladies out the door, the earl offered an approving nod to his younger brother.

When the gardener once again joined them, carrying his spade, the earl fixed him with a stern eye. "Woodruff, if I were to say I wished to dig up your fine medieval seats, how would you feel about it?"

The gardener tucked the handle of the spade beneath one arm, rubbed his nose, leaving a thin streak of dirt. "Reckon if Miss Abigail agrees, you kin dig anywhere you like, my lord."

"You would not plead they are old and precious?" Jared persisted.

"Well, now," Woodruff admitted, "if you was careful like with the sod, my lord, I reckon 'twould be a lot easier to fix 'em back again."

"But you're not going to stand and defend them to the death," Myles prodded.

"Cap'n!" the old man protested, much shocked. "As if I ever would." Myles grinned. At that point even Hannah Greaves would have been willing to wager that the elderly gardener knew exactly what was buried in one of these seats.

"My turn," Myles told his brother, reaching for the spade.

"The sod, Myles. Be careful of the sod!"

Caught in the midst of a hefty swing, the captain groaned. As much as he had come to like her, there were times Abigail Todd could be most annoying. Taking a grip halfway down the handle, Myles carefully cut the grass on the top of the seat, dividing it into three sections, which he then pried up, stacking the resulting squares on the ground to the side of the bench. As he did the same for the front of the bench, the earl held his breath, expecting an explosion of profanity at any minute. Abby and Hannah stifled smiles behind their hands.

"There," Myles declared at last. "Your precious sod is saved." He eyed the resulting rectangle of dark earth. "May I?" he inquired, altogether too mildly.

"Get on with it," Jared laughed. "We've teased you long enough." The captain swung the spade in a mighty arc, intending to delve deep within the earth. His whole body quivered as the spade struck a barrier, the resulting thud widening all eyes. "By God, there *is* something in there!" Jared exclaimed. The captain shook himself and attacked the dark earth with more care. In less than a minute heavy wood was revealed. More careful spade work revealed a large wooden chest bound with metal strips. Woodruff, obviously well prepared, stepped forward with a thick cotton cloth to wipe the chest clean.

Vaguely, Abby noted that a crowd had gathered. Not just the Deerings, but every servant at Arbor Cottage hovered nearby. "Abby," Jared said, "I believe you have the key."

"I see why the key is so large," she murmured as she took it out of her pocket. "That's a very large chest."

"Indeed," Hannah agreed. "I can scarce believe it. 'Tis like a fairy tale."

It was certainly more than she had ever hoped for, Abby thought. This appeared to be a genuine treasure indeed. She stepped forward, fitted the key in the lock, finding it necessary to enlist Jared's help in turning it, for dirt still clung inside the lock. A blush swept over her as he fitted his hands over hers. The key scraped, groaned, and finally turned. Together, Abby and Jared lifted the lid, revealing a solid covering of black velvet. With a note on top. With shaking hands, Abby unfolded the note and read aloud:

> *Gems for Gemini*
> *Twin caskets wait*
> *Equal shares*
> *To Todd and Verney*
> *Then God grant love*
> *'Tis worth far more than money.*

"Oh, my," Abby murmured, her heart racing over the sentiment, even as her mind whirled with the thought of what they might find. Gently, almost hesitantly, she lifted the cloth.

A hush fell over the treasure hunters. There was a soft rustle as the servants crept forward for a better look. Abby reached out a tentative finger, touched one of the stones winking in the afternoon sun. Necklaces, bracelets, rings, brooches, and tiaras of every shape and description. Diamonds, rubies, sapphires, emeralds, amethysts, amber, opal, lapis lazuli, all in settings of gold and silver. Ropes of pearls, glowing white, warm pink, and the deep black of a moonless night. "Surely enough to buy Lily a younger son," Abby breathed.

"Not this son," the captain snapped, then swiftly apologized, his eyes still fixed on the sparkling contents of the chest.

"A single parure would be enough," Jared assured her. "This is a true treasure. The finest collection of gems I have ever seen."

"Fancy that!" Hannah whispered, shaking her head. "An honest-to-goodness treasure."

"There's more," Abby declared, rereading Clarissa's note.

"Impossible!" Jared snapped. "This is where my grandfather's fortune went. There can't be more."

"Gems for Gemini," Abby read. *"Twin caskets wait."*

They all swung around and eyed the other grass seat.

"Woodruff, may we destroy your other bench?" the earl asked.

This time the old man allowed himself a lopsided smile. "I reckon it might be worth your while, your lordship," he conceded. "And don't make no never mind 'bout the sod. I kin piece it back together. Wouldn't want the captain to bust his britches."

But it was Jared Verney who took up the spade, attacking the other grass bench with all the pent-up emotion of the last few hours. The second chest was as large as the first. The key, fitting this chest as sluggishly, finally clicked open. The black velvet, the note was nearly the same. Jared read aloud:

> *Gold for Gemini*
> *Twin caskets wait.*
> *Equal shares*
> *to Todd and Verney*
> *Then God grant love*
> *'Tis worth far more than money.*

"Twin caskets, twin souls," Jared murmured. Abby looked up, saw so much warmth and love in his eyes that she felt his gaze all the way to her toes. It didn't matter what was in this chest. They had found the most important treasure. Though a happy outcome of their love might prove more difficult than the deciphering of Clarissa's clues.

Abby nodded, indicating that this time Jared should lift the black velvet covering. Gold gleamed up at them. A sea of coins, solid all the way to the bottom, a full foot and a half down and nearly two feet across.

"I daresay she never heard of investments," came the captain's dry comment.

"Abigail," the Earl of Langley said in strangled tones, "will you trust me to lock these chests away in my strong room, for 'tis plain there's no such place at Arbor Cottage?" Abby, as close to speechless as she'd ever been in her life, nodded her assent. "Wheelbarrow, Woodruff?" the earl commanded.

"At once, my lord," the gardener said, and loped off at a surprising pace for a man his age.

"You may all step forward for a look," Abby told their audience. "And you may be certain I shall not fail to share this good fortune with those who served my grandmother so long and so well."

After allowing the servants their heartfelt murmurs of appreciation, Deering and his wife shooed them back into the house, leaving two stout footmen to assist the earl and his brother with the heavy chests. Abby staggered to one of the marble benches by the fountain and sat down abruptly. It was wealth beyond her wildest dreams. She could not begin to imagine what to do with it all. Settle Lily's affairs, certainly. Blatantly buy the chit's way into the *ton*. Jared could have Arbor Cottage as a gift. *Jared.* Her friend Jared, who had grown so dear she could not imagine life without him. He would be able to refurbish Langley Park, provide Myles with a stake toward whatever he wished to do with his life. But as for herself?

She could fund any number of charities. She could . . . Was it possible the marvel of finding a treasure could mitigate the scandal of the Earl of Langley marrying Clarissa Beaupré's granddaughter? Abby was not naive. Many a person had been forgiven less-than-illustrious ancestors because their pockets were well inlaid with gold. But was it enough? Could they chance it?

Did she *want* to chance it? Truthfully, a good deal of soul-searching since her conversation with Jared in London had brought Abby to the realization that without him her life was meaningless. Yet she loved him too much to ruin him. Perhaps, after all, *carte-blanche* was the solution.

For Abigail Todd of Miss Todd's Academy for Young Ladies in the staunchly Puritan state of Massachusetts?

Never!

There was one commission left. Could it possibly be the answer? Would Clarissa find a way? Or was Abby destined to live in misery, indifferent to whatever fortune she might own?

*   *   *

"Are the ladies still up?" Jared asked as Deering opened the door to him at nine o'clock that night.

"Indeed, my lord. They are taking tea in the drawing room."

"I'll announce myself," the earl told him. Deering allowed himself a satisfied smile as he watched the earl stride across the foyer. There was a match there, he and the missus were certain of it. Though they also agreed Miss Abby seemed yet to be convinced.

"Jared!" Abby cried, crossing to meet him, hands outstretched. Suddenly, she paused, conscious of all the unspoken thoughts that had passed between them during the course of a most unusual day. "You are very welcome, my lord," she murmured, withdrawing her hands and summoning Miss Abigail Todd, spinster, of Boston. "It is kind of you to return to us so late. We have been anxious to learn that all was well."

The cavalcade that had finally set off for Langley Park had consisted of Moorhead and Daniel, fully armed, aboard the coach with the treasure chests, with Jared, Myles, and two footmen riding alongside, also armed with shotguns as well as pistols. An impressive sight, but not one designed to inspire peace of mind in the ladies from Massachusetts.

Hannah Greaves, however, was far less worried about the fate of the treasure than by her concern for Abby. She put down her teacup and began to pack up her embroidery. "My curiosity will keep until tomorrow," she declared. "You two are best left alone, I think. With the pair of you long past your majority, I see no need to play gooseberry. I will be off." She paused, summoning a mighty glare. "However," she added, "do not, I beg of you, take my liberality as an invitation to excess." So saying, Mrs. Greaves swept from the room, leaving Abby with a serious case of the giggles.

She wiped her eyes. "I am so sorry," she burbled, "but I do believe Hannah has given up on me."

"Or else she is quite determined you should be so badly compromised that our marriage is assured."

"Not even compromise would do it, my lord," Abby told him roundly.

Jared heaved a sigh, even as he maneuvered his love to a seat beside him on the sofa. "It is not every day," he confided judiciously, "that a man may remain friends with a woman who has rejected his suit."

"I had thought our friendship above such—" Abby stopped abruptly.

"Above such petty squabbles?" the earl supplied.

Abby sniffed. "I am well aware of the honor done me, my lord," she informed him. "I was *not* going to call our disagreement a petty squabble."

"How reassuring," Jared purred. Abby shot him a look that should have stabbed to his very soul. Instead, he merely changed the subject. "The chests are locked up tight," he told her. "With two footmen standing guard, shotguns at the ready. I have sent for Smallwood to handle the inventory." Grim-lipped, the earl studied Abby's face. "It is awkward that we are served by the same solicitor," he said. "If you wish me to retain someone from a different firm—"

"Not at all," Abby demurred. "Surely you must be aware that I trust you implicitly."

"It's a great deal of money, Abigail. Even more than most royal dukes have seen in a lifetime."

With a sudden smile, Abby peeped up at him. "I think we must never let Lily know the whole of it. She will accuse us of cheating her of a duke or a marquess at the least. I fear she will never be satisfied with a mere 'Honorable.'"

"Lord, yes," Jared chuckled. "She would consider it proof that life in the *demimonde* is more profitable than marriage."

"On rare occasions," Abby amended with a considerable severity.

"Clarissa was one of a kind," Jared agreed. "Quite unique."

Reminiscence soon slipped back to practicality. "I will send a message when Smallwood arrives," he told her, "so you may be present for the inventory. No matter how much you believe you should trust me, this is merely good business practice. You have taught me a thing or two this summer, my dear Miss Todd. I have come to accept you as a highly intelligent independent woman capable of handling your own affairs. You have a right to be present at a moment which will define the rest of your life."

Abby closed her eyes, drawing in a very deep breath. "How absolutely wonderful," she said at last, "that you finally understand. Just as I had convinced myself to play the meek obedient female and allow you to handle the matter, you deign to grant me the freedom to be an enlightened woman, capable of deciding my own destiny."

"Not deign," Jared protested. "You wrested this admittance from me by the sheer power of your will." He ran an appreciative eye over her, his lips curling into a wry smile. "And perhaps, just a wee bit, by the power of your exceptional beauty," he added softly.

Abby cupped a hand along the side of his face, brushed her thumb over his full lips. "Dear Jared, I thank you. For both compliments."

Clasping her hand, he pressed his lips into her palm. For the briefest of moments he contemplated pressing his suit as well. But the suggestion of uniting their fortunes would be a misstep. He knew it, even as he was tempted to take shameless advantage of the moment. Instead, he took her other hand, raising both to his lips while regarding her, soulfully, from the depths of his silver-gray eyes.

A dangerous man, the Earl of Langley, Abby decided, although she would not tell him so. How could she have had the courage to refuse his suit? Would he, in fact, wear her down before she left?

"Fortunately, we have plenty of time left before the end of the month." The earl turned to practical matters even as his eyes spoke to her of love. With her hands still clasped in his, his body hovering within inches of her own, Abby had to force herself to pay attention to his words. "We have time to settle the matter of dividing the treasure and seeing to its safe transportation to the bank in London."

Abby thought perhaps he had said something that required her answer. She settled for a nod. And then she was hard against his chest, being thoroughly kissed, every one of her doubts and reservations flown from her head.

Fortunately, even after Deering, eyes alight with pleasure, firmly closed the drawing room door, the Earl of Langley did not forget Mrs. Greaves's exhortation about not taking her liberality as an invitation to excess. Abigail Todd was the woman he loved. He could wait. Though he could not deny a few breathless minutes on Clarissa's silk brocade couch had hardened his resolution to steel.

Chapter Twenty

Mr. Hector Smallwood brought with him an expert from Rundell & Bridges. While the solicitor counted gold coins, the jeweler examined each exquisite piece from the gem chest, frequently murmuring his appreciation of the stones or the craftsmanship. If he recognized many of the items as works commissioned by the old earl or other noble clients of the famed Rundell & Bridges, he was much too discreet to say so. When all the gold had been counted and every gem evaluated down to the last shilling, Captain Verney led a small army of outriders to escort the chests to the bank in London. The contents were now sorted in a different fashion, half the gold and half the gems in each.

Abby rode over from Arbor Cottage to watch their new-found fortunes begin their journey to the Bank of England. As the cavalcade set off, the earl was insisting, for what must have been the fourth or fifth time, on sharing half the burden of Lily's dowry. Abby, once again, refused. Langley Park had far more need of the money, she told him. She scarce knew what to do with hers. And, once again, the earl refrained—heroically, he thought—from suggesting the obvious: the re-combination of Clarissa's wealth through marriage. Until Abby finished her last commission, he conceded, there would be no reasoning with her. Yet she was wavering in her rejection of his suit, of that he was almost certain. It needed only . . . what? Abby had never been comfortable, he knew, with the thought they might share a common grandfather. If she discovered they were truly unrelated

by blood, would that be the straw that tumbled her decision
to his side? Ah, fool that he was. He was a victim of the Verney curse. If he could not have Abigail Todd, then it was
Myles who must produce the next heir to the title.

Their days together were growing short, each sunset
moving them inexorably closer to the third of September. As
the last dust of the well-armed cavalcade faded in the distance, gloom settled over them, at strong odds to the joy expected from two whose fortunes had been so gloriously
expanded.

Patience, Jared cautioned himself. There still bloomed a
small niggling of hope. With no need to voice their purpose,
they turned and rode, side by side, toward Arbor Cottage. It
was time to open the final letter.

The letter, like the treasure notes, turned out to be twins.
One for Abby, one for Jared. Each marked, *Private.* Abby
bent her head to hers.

> *My dearest grandchild,*
>   *Well-done, my dear! Your tasks are nearly*
> *complete. By now you have probably guessed that I*
> *hope for a match between you and Jared. For not all*
> *the treasure in the world can substitute for the love*
> *of a good man. If you have not already found love*
> *with my dear Jared's grandson, then I urge you to*
> *consider it most strongly.*
>   *If, however, you have discovered you cannot suit,*
> *then I wish you joy of your life, my child. At least I*
> *know you have learned about your English relatives*
> *and will have enough wealth that you may do*
> *whatever you choose with your life.*
>   *And now I have saved the best for last. At least I*
> *hope you will think it so. His name is Justin Westcott,*
> *Marquess of Stafford. Next to my beloved Jared, the*
> *finest man I have ever known. May you find him as*
> *fascinating as I did. There is no letter, my dear. If all*
> *has gone as I hoped, Deering has informed him that*

*you are at Arbor Cottage. Justin will be expecting
you.*
My love will be with you and yours forever.
Your grandmother,
Clarissa Bivens Beaupré

Abby looked up to find Jared watching her closely. "I
suppose her note to you is similar to mine," she sighed.

"Matchmaking, yes," Jared nodded, "but she says nothing of our last commission. . . . Stafford, by God!" the earl
exclaimed when Abby told him. "May I know exactly what
she said of him?" Abby handed him the letter. It was far too
late for secrets between them.

"A powerful man," Jared said, laying the letter aside. "A
strong figure in the Tory government for more years than I
can remember. Retired to his country house in Surrey after
his wife died. Only four or five years ago, as I recall."

Abby's green eyes held a plea. "Do you think? . . ."

"I think nothing," Jared told her. "It's better that way,
Abby. Foolish to get your hopes up over what is probably
another sentimental bit of nonsense."

"Sentiment is not nonsense!"

"Ah!" the earl exclaimed. "I believe I have caught you
out. Miss Abigail Todd of Boston came here without an
ounce of sentiment."

"Untrue!"

"Abigail Todd of Miss Todd's Academy for Young
Ladies was a stiff-necked Puritan who scorned every Englishman she laid eyes on."

"I could hardly wait to get here," Abby retorted, though
she could scarce deny the charge. "I was so ripe for adventure I practically fell into your arms. The more the fool, I."

"Love makes fools of us all, from kitchen maid to king."
Jared said softly. Then, embarrassed to find himself quoting
this age-old bit of wisdom, he bit his tongue over a startling
surge of further sentimental nonsense. Ruthlessly, the Earl
of Langley forced himself back to the task at hand. "We can
leave for Surrey as soon as the coach arrives back from London," he told her.

"Poor Moorhead," Abby sighed. "He will quit your service, I fear."

"He has loved every minute of it," Jared assured her. "Incredible as it may seem, I lived a dull life before you came along. And, besides, he will be able to retire with all the bonuses he has been getting for his recent efforts. And, no, I have not forgotten Daniel, either."

"You are very good," Abby murmured, looking down to hide a rush of tears. "By the time we return from Surrey—"

"There will be almost no time left," Jared finished. His voice firmed as he rejected the cautions that had been governing his actions lately. The silver eyes deepened to opaque gray. "Abby, you know how I feel, how much I wish you to stay. You have fulfilled all the terms of Clarissa's will. Why can you not accede to her last, her greatest, wish and—"

Abby's gloved fingers touched his lips. "No! Not yet, not now. I still hope . . . Allow me this last quest, Jared," she begged. "Silly chit that I am, I cannot believe Clarissa would leave me dangling like this. She would have *known* the scandal a marriage between us would incite."

"Wealth smooths a remarkable number of wrinkles."

"Go away, Jared," Abby whispered. "I find myself too cowardly to listen to your good sense."

"I will return this evening with a plan of our journey into Surrey. Smile, Abby, and know that, no matter what, I love you."

As she turned away, walking swiftly toward the cottage, he heard what sounded suspiciously like a sob.

Stafford Palace, the primary seat of Justin Westcott, Marquess of Stafford, was an imposing edifice of gray-pink sandstone. Its magnificence was so great, Abby nearly begged Jared to have Moorhead turn back to Arbor Cottage. A rebel maiden from Boston could not be on visiting terms with such ostentatious splendor.

"I've lost my last chance to impress you," the earl announced dejectedly, noting her pallor. "Langley Park will seem as nothing to you now." This sally brought a chuckle from Hannah Greaves and a tiny smile from Abby. Captain

Verney was not inside the coach, having chosen to remain in his role as an armed outrider, informing them that now they were so shockingly wealthy, they were both candidates for kidnapping. He had, indeed, kept on four of the men who had comprised the guard on the treasure's journey to London. Both Abby and Jared considered his fears exaggerated, but had decided to humor him.

All the way up the long drive, while the coach steps were being lowered, and, as Abby allowed Jared to take her arm while they ascended the many shallow steps up to the impressive symmetry of the great house, her heart pounded as if determined to burst from her body. How could she bear the disappointment if this was merely another sentimental visit to one of Clarissa's favorites?

"I am Langley," Jared told the butler, handing him his calling card. "This is Miss Abigail Todd of America. We would appreciate a few moments of Lord Stafford's time."

The butler, whose job it was to know quality when he saw it, immediately indicated that they should follow him into the drawing room. But Abby did not move. She stood, stock-still, staring at a portrait occupying a place of honor in the huge entrance hall.

"Abby?" Tears were running down her face, dripping off her chin. Jared thrust a handkerchief into her hand. "Abby, what is it? What's wrong?"

"It's my father to the life," she whispered. "I don't even have to see Lord Stafford. There can be no doubt."

The butler, discovering the guests were no longer with him, had returned to the foyer. "'Tis his lordship himself, miss," he told her. "Painted forty or more years ago by Sir Joshua Reynolds," he added proudly.

"My father is older now, of course," Abby said, almost to herself, "but the likeness is remarkable, as close as Clarissa and myself."

"My dear Abigail," said a voice from behind them, "I am delighted you have come at last."

He was older, so much older than the portrait, but Abby would have known him anywhere. In a quarter century her father would undoubtedly look the same. "You know about me then?" Abby asked as she rose from a deep curtsy to the Marquess of Stafford.

"Yes, indeed, my dear," declared the white-haired, but still tall and stately, marquess. "Clarissa promised she would send you to me. Langley." He offered the earl a friendly nod. "Come into the drawing room, both of you, and we shall talk."

Numbly, Abby and Jared followed the elderly gentleman, who, it appeared, must surely be her father's father.

"I was married when I met Clarissa," the marquess told them when they were seated. "I was completely dazzled. Could not believe my good fortune in winning her favor. And, yes, child, I can see you are offended, but that, I fear, is the way of the world. My wife had turned querulous with a third child on the way and turned me out of her bed. I make no excuses. I did as my friends did, and found consolation elsewhere. Except in my case, I was more fortunate than most. I was successful in acquiring the attention of Clarissa Beaupré.

"Alas," Lord Stafford added, unable to meet Abby's eyes, "our union was successful in a way we had not anticipated. I—" The marquess paused for a sigh. "I told Clarissa I would support the child, see that it was well situated in life, but she wished the babe to be raised totally without the stigma of illegitimacy. We decided emigration was the only answer. The Todds were tenants here on my estate, the very best parents we could find. As soon as the babe was old enough, I sent them all off to America with enough to es-tablish themselves well and provide a good education for the boy. Clarissa was always kind enough to keep me informed of his welfare. Of his marriage and of your birth and progress, my child. As for me"—once again, the elderly nobleman sighed—"if Clarissa had not fallen quite madly in love with Langley, I am not sure what I might have done. As it was, I returned to my wife's bed. Four children in all, twelve grandchildren. All of them your cousins, Abigail. I trust you will have an opportunity to meet them before you return—"

The marquess paused, chuckling with only himself to hear.

For the look that had passed between his granddaughter and the Earl of Langley left no doubt about how matters stood. Abigail Todd would not be returning to Boston. Life had come full circle. He did not doubt Clarissa was spying on them, shedding a tear or two herself.

"Clarissa and I corresponded during these last few years," the marquess said. "I agreed that if the two of you should make a match of it as she desired, I would acknowledge Abigail and put the full weight of my considerable power behind seeing her properly launched into the *ton*." Justin Westcott's eyes twinkled as he regarded the two young people before him, their faces aglow with burgeoning hope. "That meets with your approval, I trust?" He raised one elegant white brow.

Abby darted across the room, fell to her knees beside his chair. "My lord . . . grandfather . . . I don't know how to thank you."

The marquess placed one hand on Abigail's head, held the other out to Jared, who had risen to stand just behind her. "Great-grandchildren would be suitable, I believe," he told Abby. And gave Jared a solemn wink.

Epilogue

$\mathcal{J}$ustin Westcott, Marquess of Stafford, was as good as his
word, even to the point of making sure that his children,
their spouses, his grandchildren and great-grandchildren
were present for the wedding of Miss Abigail Todd to Jared
Verney, Earl of Langley. Lady Langley cried, but no one
could say her tears were anything other than the waterworks
traditional at weddings. Lady Mablethorpe and Lady
Christabelle took prominent positions in St. George's, each
planning a second wedding in the not-too-distant future,
now that Captain Myles Verney's fortunes had taken such a
marked turn for the better.

Quentin and Margaret Farleigh were present, heads high,
faces expressionless, as if they had never heard of their infamous relative Clarissa Beaupré. Eleanore Jerome's eyes
shone through the entire service and the wedding breakfast
to follow. Her dear cousin Abigail had offered her a modest
cottage in Vernhampton, close to Langley Park. She planned
to move the very next week.

Betty Mapes, in spite of her husband's burly form beside her, was smiling almost as widely as Eleanore Jerome.
For her darling Lily was the bride's sole attendant. Her
wondrous gem of a child was pacing the full length of the
aisle at St. George's, Hanover Square, dressed in the height
of good taste in a filmy gown of rose silk, the bodice embroidered in iridescent seed pearls. On her head was a
crown of virginal white rosebuds. No young woman could
have asked for a more spectacular launch into society. For

a few moments she was the cynosure of all eyes. If some had the bad taste to wonder if she might be a worthy successor to La Grande Clarisse, they kept their thoughts to themselves.

As for Dr. Lucian Todd, he glowed with pride as he gave his daughter his arm and they began their journey toward the altar. His initial meeting with his father had been as stiff-necked and tight-lipped as one might expect. But, in the end, they were too much alike, the American doctor and the British marquess. By the day of the wedding Lucian Todd had the satisfaction of knowing he'd been able to give his daughter the best of both worlds. A loving home and loving grandparents, even if the blood of the Todds was not the same as his own. And, now, a relationship to the highest circles of power in Britain. Though it had taken a considerable struggle with his sturdy American conscience to admit the advantage of his daughter being able to claim a marquess as her grandfather.

Dr. Todd was not, however, reconciled to Clarissa Beaupré. Both before and after the wedding, he refused to look at her portrait.

Abby, who had always thought herself in control—of her life, of her students, of herself—was well aware she would still be standing in the vestibule, waiting, if her father had not started them both moving inexorably down the aisle when the organ began to roar something by Purcell that sounded more like the harbinger to a full cavalry charge than the entrance of the bride at a *ton* wedding.

They were halfway to the altar when she focused her eyes, peering through the fine silk of her veil. He was there! Standing tall, straight and solemn. Looking neither bored nor as if he wanted to run. Jared was looking straight at her. And surely it wasn't the veil or her lively imagination which saw love in his eyes.

Myles. Dear Myles. At last she could take in her soon-to-be brother-in-law. Standing stiffly at Jared's side, he looked as if he would rather be facing General Jackson's troops at New Orleans. Poor Christabelle, Abby sighed.

Perhaps there wouldn't be a wedding there for some time to come.

Even hidden under a film of fine silk, she was the most beautiful sight Jared Verney, Earl of Langley, had ever seen. Her cinnamon-red hair easily penetrated the gossamer covering, glowing with the life and warmth of the woman coming to take her place at his side. Her perfectly plain gown of soft cream silk could not be faulted, even by her Puritan ancestors. Abby's only ornament was her glorious hair and a bouquet of rosebuds of a nearly matching shade, some trailing on the ends of long cream ribbons which fell in an irregular cascade from her waist to her knees.

Jared stepped forward to greet his bride. Never had he done anything with a more ready will. Shoulder to shoulder, they faced the Anglican priest.

A soft rustle as the congregation was seated. Hushed expectancy as the familiar words of the service began. *Dearly beloved . . .*

September, 1818

Abby juggled her baby girl in her arms, smiling down at the wisps of blond hair that were beginning to show a distinctive hint of cinnamon red. "Are you ready?" she asked her father, who was standing next to the pink silk draperies covering her grandmother's infamous portrait.

Dr. Lucian Todd did not respond. He reached up and pulled the silken cord.

A rather startling profanity echoed through the room. Recalling her own embarrassment on the several occasions she had viewed Clarissa's portrait, Abby could only grin. It wasn't every man who was treated to a view of a full-sized portrait of his mother exposed for all the world to see. Even a doctor might have cause to blush. Jared, who was standing behind them, turned his back, shoulders heaving with mirth.

Abby lifted the baby high. "See?" she said. "That's Great-Gramma. You might as well get used to it now, so you will not be shocked by it, as I once was."

Jared reached around from behind, lowering the baby down to her mother's breast, enfolding them both in his arms. His father-in-law might still be absorbed in the painting, but he no longer needed to look. He had his very own Abigail, warm flesh and blood. Neither of them would ever look elsewhere. Love, family, children, home, and hearth. For the Earl and Countess of Langley, the days of the courtesan were long past.

About the Author

With ancestors from England, Wales, Scotland, Ireland, and France, **Blair Bancroft** feels right at home in nineteenth-century Britain. But it was only after a variety of other careers that she turned to writing about the Regency era. Blair has been a music teacher, professional singer, nonfiction editor, costume designer, and real estate agent, and she has still managed to travel extensively. The mother of three grown children, Blair lives in Florida. Her Web site is www.blairbancroft.com. She can be contacted at blairbancroft@aol.com.

Signet Regency Romances
from

BARBARA METZGER

"Barbara Metzger deliciously mixes love
and laughter." —*Romantic Times*

MISS WESTLAKE'S WINDFALL
0-451-20279-1

Miss Ada Westlake has two treasures at her fingertips.
One is a cache of coins she discovered in her orchard,
and the other is her friend (and sometime suitor),
Viscount Ashmead. She has been advised to keep a
tight hold on both. But Ada must discover for herself
that the greatest gift of all is true love...

THE PAINTED LADY
0-451-20368-2

Stunned when the lovely lady he is painting suddenly
comes to life on the canvas and talks to him, the Duke
of Caswell can only conclude that his mind has finally
snapped. But when his search for help sends him to Sir
Osgood Bannister, the noted brain fever expert and
doctor to the king, he ends up in the care of the
charming, naive Miss Lilyanne Bannister, and his life
suddenly takes on a whole new dimension...

To order call: 1-800-788-6262

S435/Metzger